MAZE OF DEADLY DECEPTION

MAZE OF DEADLY DECEPTION

A Darla Kelly Mystery

M.A. KOONTZ

Cover photo by Tom Koontz

Published by M.A. Koontz

Print ISBN: 979-8-218-28626-2
eBook ISBN: 979-8-218-28627-9

Copyright © 2023 by M.A. Koontz

This book is a work of fiction. Names, characters, places, and incidents are the product of the author's imagination or are used fictitiously. Any resemblance to actual events, locales, or persons, living or dead, is coincidental.

All rights reserved. No part of this publication may be reproduced, distributed, or transmitted in any form or by any means, including photocopying, recording, or other electronic or mechanical methods, without the prior written permission of the publisher, except in the case of brief quotations embodied in critical reviews and certain other noncommercial uses permitted by copyright law. For permission requests, please contact the publisher through the website www.makoontz.com

Printed in the United States of America

Other Books in the Darla Kelly Series

SHARDS OF TRUST

THE CRY BEYOND THE DOOR

To readers and writers alike,

for one cannot exist without the other.

CHAPTER ONE

Darla Kelly read the cryptic text and frowned. Squinting, she read it again, hoping to make sense of the words this time, but instead she only became more confused. Warning bells rang in her mind, and she tried to tamp them down, telling herself she was making something out of nothing.

Tilting her head forward to examine the text message again for clues, errant strands of auburn hair fell across her vision. She shoved them behind one ear. As she did so, she felt goosebumps creep along her arms.

Unnerved by the trauma of recent years, Dar found she'd become overly accustomed to leaping to worst-case scenarios. In the past, those scenarios had all too often morphed into an ugly reality she had fought hard to forget. But despite her struggle for control, flashbacks of her biological father trying to kill her sliced through her concentration, causing her breathing to become rapid and her heart to race. Like she'd done so many times before, she forced herself to remember that Wesley Shade was securely locked away in prison for murder, assault, and drug charges. He couldn't harm her or anyone else. She was safe.

She shook off the haunted memories, allowing them to be scooped up by the cool breeze whisking across her back porch. It carried them off in a flourish, but like the breeze, she knew they'd return.

Once again, she stared at her phone. She needed to concentrate on the facts, beginning with anything in the text that stood out from Shawn's other texts. Now that she had a plan, she could feel her breathing growing steadier and her heart rate return to normal. It was then that she pinpointed the reasons behind her initial concern.

For one thing, Shawn had used her full name, "Darla" rather than "Dar." He always used the shortened version, so why had he chosen to be so formal? Maybe he was trying to convey the importance of his message covertly, knowing she'd pick up on it. But Dar couldn't imagine why.

Also, it wasn't so much what he'd said in his text, but rather what he *hadn't*. There were none of his usual silly emojis, including the heart that punctuated the end of every message he sent her.

She noticed additional voids now as well—holes where pieces of his personality were typically inserted. Their absence gaped back at her from the phone's screen. One such void was the absence of Shawn's random daily joke, compliments of one of his young cardiac patients. He sent them to brighten the start of her day. And it did, because even the jokes that made no sense whatsoever—ones that were so bad they made her groan—also made her smile.

She tried his cell phone again. Straight to voicemail.

Before her mind could complete a worst-case-scenario, she felt Merlin bump up against her as he raced past, causing her phone to fly into the air. She juggled it above her head, nearly dropping it twice before finally catching it. But Merlin paid no attention to the mishap he'd caused. Instead, he leapt down the steps and ran straight for the back fence, where his nose had detected a collection of new scents.

Dar covered the short distance across her backyard and caught up to Merlin, where he'd come to an abrupt halt in the warm sun. He had already sniffed the yellow daffodils and had moved on to the pink buds hanging heavy on the branches of the crabapple tree. When he began barking at an object in the tree, she followed his focus to a chrysalis that had formed there last fall. Despite having had one of the harshest Indiana winters, the chrysalis remained firmly attached to the branch. *A kindred survivor*, Dar thought.

"Merlin, let's go!" she ordered as she headed for her car. Spring in all its glory had distracted both of them, costing her time. She hoped she could still beat the downtown morning traffic near Currie Children's Center, or CCC as the locals called it.

CCC was where she'd first met Shawn. He'd been doing a fellowship under the guidance of her adoptive father, Dr. James Kelly, who was then the head of pediatric cardiology. She smiled at the thought, but the fond memory soon turned sour, and she tried to shake off the bitter reminder of her dad's murder.

Shawn had followed in her father's large footsteps, eventually becoming one of the hospital's most beloved pediatric cardiologists. She counted herself among the many who loved and admired him, though hers was a love that ran much deeper.

But it came with consequences. Her concern for Shawn caused her mind to whirl with questions. What could be so urgent that he'd insisted on speaking with her in person, and why didn't he want her to hear about it from someone else? Why hadn't he just called or told her in his text? Why so mysterious?

Dar sighed. Attuned to her anxiety, Merlin rushed to her side and settled on his haunches at her feet. She looked into his comforting dark eyes. She never would have guessed that the dog she had once rescued from the shelter where she'd volunteered would one day become her best friend. And naming him Merlin had been an easy choice after she'd discovered his penchant for stealing her shoes and making them disappear. Now, the only thing he stole was her heart.

She squatted down, allowing Merlin to nuzzle closer so she could wrap her arms around him. She felt the soothing rhythm of his heartbeat.

"Thanks, Merlin. I needed that. Everything's going to be fine. It has to be."

Standing, she swung the door to her Kia open, and Merlin jumped in, his black fur with its streak of white shining in the early morning sun. She'd brushed it that morning until it was shiny and smooth, then tied a red bandana around his neck. Merlin's tail drummed a rapid beat on the car seat in anticipation of visiting the sick kids at CCC and Reed Memorial Hospital, something they did every Saturday morning. Dar hoped he'd be equally as excited about their change of plans to see Shawn first.

"Good boy!" she said as Merlin settled into the back of the car.

She climbed into the driver's side, and as she started the car, a steel-gray cloud drifted in front of the sun, hiding its spring warmth behind a gloomy cover. Though she adjusted the car's heat, the chill remained, causing her to shiver. Feeling a new sense of urgency, she sped toward CCC, hoping whatever Shawn had to tell her would put her fears to rest.

CHAPTER TWO

Dar's intentions of beating rush-hour traffic in downtown Reed were nearly thwarted. She had not expected the car accident blocking one lane, nor the new road construction with flag men directing cars. Yet, somehow, she still arrived at CCC's visitor parking lot before it began to fill up. She parked the car, then quickly texted the volunteer coordinators from both hospitals to let them know that she would be late, but promised to do her best to bring Merlin later to see the kids.

Exiting the car, Dar attached an official volunteer tag to her sweater. She didn't want to waste any time getting stopped by a security guard this morning. But when she attempted to place Merlin's volunteer sticker on his bandana, it fell off with each try. Finally, she stuffed the useless sticker into her jeans pocket instead.

Only yesterday she'd stopped at CCC to see Mr. Reece, the hospital's CFO, about the issue with the stickers for the canine therapy dogs. She'd wanted to make sure he'd placed the order for the new bandanas with the hospital logo, but instead, he'd shown her the order form in his to-do pile as proof it would be taken care of the following day. It was only later that she realized "the following day" was today, Saturday. The soonest he was apt to place the order now was on Monday. She sighed. It would just have to wait until next week. Right now, she had more pressing concerns on her mind.

Dar guided Merlin through the side entrance, then down the hall toward the bank of elevators. Except for the background hum of fluorescent ceiling lights and a few nurses starting their shifts, it was quiet. But she knew it wouldn't be long before the hospital would be filled with doctors, nurses, and visitors, and the numerous orders, exchanges, and conversations between them.

Dar jumped at the sudden bold ding of the elevator. As its heavy door slid open, she stepped onto the lift, relieved to find it vacant. For once, she wouldn't have to field a barrage of questions from others about Merlin. Even though most days she was proud to do so, today she wasn't in the mood.

When the elevator reached the second floor, Dar stepped out, coaxing Merlin to the left toward Shawn's office. He whined at the change in his hospital routine. "Sorry, boy," Dar said. "We'll see the kids later. First, we're going to see your buddy, Shawn."

At the sound of Shawn's name, Merlin's ears perked up. Merlin loved Shawn, but Dar knew that part of his excitement was also because Shawn always had a treat for him. Merlin drooled in anticipation.

Dar shook her head at Merlin. "You're shameless."

The sudden sound of a door opening farther down the hall startled her, causing her to look up. Shawn came rushing out of an office, his white lab coat, covered in stickers, swirling out from his trim figure. He hurried toward her, plowing his fingers through his curly brown hair, giving him a slightly disheveled look.

"Shawn, what's wrong?" Dar asked. "What's going on?"

"Not here." Shawn scanned the hall. "Let's go into my office."

Grabbing her hand, Shawn rushed her and Merlin down the hall and into his office, where he began to pace, mussing his hair even more. Dar's patience wore thin, until she finally spun him around to face her. She was surprised to see the typical twinkle in his blue eyes had been replaced with a seriousness he normally reserved for his sickest patients and their parents. But there was a flash of something else there that she'd seen too many times in her own reflection. Fear.

"Shawn, you're scaring me," Dar said. "Please sit down and talk to me."

She wheeled Shawn's office chair behind him, and he collapsed onto it. Pulling up another chair in front of him, she sat facing him, their knees touching as Merlin nudged closer.

"Sorry, Dar . . . I . . ." Shawn started. He took a deep breath and continued. "You knew Mr. Reece, our CFO, right?"

"Sure," Dar said with a shrug. "I talked to him yesterday." She paused, furrowing her brow. "What do you mean, *'knew'* him?"

Shawn stood, shoving a hand through his hair again. "I came in early this morning," he said. "I thought maybe I could catch Mr. Reece to ask about funding for more medical equipment. I could've sworn we ordered enough, but our supply ran out faster than expected. Anyway, his office light was on, so I knocked. I heard a noise in the background, like a motor or something running, and I thought maybe he hadn't heard me knock. I tried knocking again, but when he didn't answer, I let myself in." Shawn hesitated for a second, but finally allowed the words to spill out. "Dar, when I opened the door, I saw Mr. Reece lying face down on the floor."

Dar gasped. "Was he okay?"

Shawn shook his head. "He was unconscious. His bathroom fan was running so loud that it was hard to check his vitals even with my stethoscope. I tried to turn it off, but the switch didn't work. None of it mattered. I felt for his pulse, but his body was already cold. Rigor mortis had already set in. He'd been dead for hours; there was nothing I could do for him. I called the police and Mr. Harrison, CCC's president, after that."

"Oh, Shawn, I'm so sorry. That's awful!" Dar said. "Do you think he had a heart attack?"

Shawn plopped back down in his chair, his face pale. He clenched his hands in his lap, focusing on them as though they held all the answers. "The coroner will have to determine cause of death."

Odd, Dar thought. It wasn't like Shawn to avoid his professional opinion, especially when it was just the two of them. Maybe an administrator had asked him not to say anything for fear of bad publicity for the hospital, or worse, a lawsuit.

Shrugging her thoughts away, Dar asked, "How did I miss seeing the squad cars?"

"They came through the employee entrance. It was still early, around quarter after seven, I think," he explained.

He bounced his knee up and down like a spring that had been tightly wound. Again, he started to run his fingers through his brown curls, but this time Dar stopped him, taking hold of his hands. The simple act seemed to calm him. Leaning forward, she touched his face, still smooth from his morning shave. But as she gazed into his blue eyes, there was a twitch, then another. Dar dropped her hands from his face and crossed her arms as she slid back on her chair.

"Okay, Shawn. Spill. What exactly aren't you telling me?"

CHAPTER THREE

"There's something fishy about Mr. Reece's death," Shawn said in a near whisper.

Dar could hear the thread of fear in his voice, and she sat back, trying to absorb what he'd said. "What do you mean by 'fishy'?" Shawn had enough experience with such matters that she trusted him, but she was still curious what could've spooked him.

"Some things were just off," Shawn said.

"Like what?"

"Like the fan that was running in his bathroom."

"Oookaay." Now she was beginning to worry about Shawn. He probably shared small talk with Mr. Reece daily; finding him dead was probably more of a shock to Shawn than she'd first realized. "That hardly seems suspicious." Deciding a change of subject might be best, she asked, "Have you eaten? Maybe I can get you a cup of coffee or a bite to eat."

"I'm fine," Shawn said, his tone dismissive.

"All right." Dar had never heard Shawn speak so gruffly, and it puzzled her to see him jump to such a conclusion, especially since she knew he preferred facts over theories. So, what caused him to do so now? She decided to tread lightly and opted for a different approach to learn more about his suspicions.

"You said 'some things were off,'" she said, trying to keep her voice calm. "What else didn't seem right?"

Shawn hesitated a moment before saying, "Yesterday, Mr. Reece and I left at the same time, around six o'clock. When I saw him lock his door, his light wasn't on." He ran a hand through his hair, but stopped when he caught Dar's frown. "Don't you see, if Mr. Reece died hours before I found him this morning, he would've had to return to his office in the middle of the night."

"But why would Mr. Reece return to his office so late?" Dar asked.

"That's what I'd like to know," Shawn said. "And this morning, something was different in his office, but I can't put my finger on it. I've been wracking my brain trying to remember ever since I found him." He sighed, leaning back against his chair dejectedly. "You must think I'm nuts," he said.

Dar had never seen Shawn look more helpless. "Hey, you'll figure it out. Maybe if you think about something else, it'll come to you."

"I hope so." He ran his palms back and forth along the length of his thighs. "I should get started on my rounds. I'm really sorry about the cryptic text message," he said, covering Dar's hand with his. "I just didn't want you to find out about Mr. Reece's death from the police, and I didn't want to tell you over text." He shook his head. "It's still possible his death was due to an illness, nothing more," he said, though his voice lacked conviction.

Dar frowned at his words. "What do you mean you didn't want me to hear about his death from the police? Why would the police want to talk to me?"

When he didn't say anything right away, she said, "Don't tell me there's more bad news."

"Define 'bad,'" Shawn said.

Dar shot him a "don't mess with me look" that caused him to cringe. Shawn reached for both of Dar's hands, placing them firmly between his own.

Normally, she loved this gesture and embraced his warmth, but this time it felt more like a warning, a protective caress before . . . what? She braced herself.

"The police want to speak to anyone who met with Reece or had been in his office for any reason yesterday," he said. "It's strictly a precaution, Dar."

She stiffened. "And standard procedure for a murder investigation," she added, her voice flat. "I was in his office yesterday, which means the police will want to interview me." She blinked, then stared at Shawn, trying to digest the information. "Do the police have reason to suspect that he was murdered? Am I a suspect?"

Now it was Shawn's turn to calm her. "They just want to talk to you because they found your name on Reece's appointment calendar under yesterday's date. Like I said, it's strictly a precaution in case they discover signs of foul play."

"Which you as much suggested, though I think 'fishy' was the word you used." Dar's mind whirled with thoughts of a possible murder investigation, before settling on thoughts of Mr. Reece. He had always been a nice, even-keeled guy. She couldn't imagine anyone wanting him dead.

"Maybe I spoke too soon," Shawn said, trying to backpedal. "Since I was the one to find Mr. Reece's body, an officer already took my statement, though I was told that a detective would have additional questions."

Dar's heart began to race. It was one thing to learn about poor Mr. Reece's death, but if it was murder . . . she wasn't sure she could handle another murderer on the loose. She didn't want to consider the possibility that once again a person she might have met in these halls, or worse yet, knew well, could be a killer. It brought back memories of nearly having been a victim herself. It'd taken months of hard work with Dr. Sanderson's psychiatric help to get the panic attacks and nightmares under control from the last two murderers she'd fallen prey to. She'd hoped, no prayed, she'd never repeat those experiences. She had narrowly escaped with her life each time. How could she survive it again?

Merlin's ears perked up, and within seconds, he nuzzled close to her.

Dar's breaths shortened, becoming quick bursts as an invisible vice squeezed tighter around her chest. Fighting to suck air into her lungs, she felt as though she were trapped beneath the murky waters of a frozen pond, desperately searching for the surface.

She sensed a gentle pressure on her arms. Shawn was leaning over her now, so close she could detect the scent of his cologne. She read his lips more than heard his words.

"Watch me and breathe with me," Shawn said. "Slow, deep breaths. Slower. Good. You've got this."

Dar sought reassurance in his eyes. As he moved his hands to her shoulders, she felt the gentle yet firm pressure grounding her. Her panic began to subside and air began to fill her lungs again, easing the pressure in her chest.

Once she'd regained her composure, Shawn gave her shoulders a comforting squeeze. "Better?" he asked.

She nodded, still concentrating on her breathing for fear of the panic attack returning. Once satisfied that it wouldn't, she relaxed enough to speak. "I thought I was over my panic attacks." She glanced down at Merlin, whose paw rested on her leg, and gave him a quick scratch behind an ear.

Shawn straightened, then strode to his desk and picked out a doggie treat. He tossed it to Merlin, who readily devoured it. "Thanks for your help, big guy," he said. Then, with a heavy sigh laced with guilt, he raked a hand through his hair and looked straight at her.

"This was all my fault," he said. "I never should have sent you that text or told you about Mr. Reece's death the way I did. I wasn't thinking. I'm so sorry."

"It's not all your fault, Shawn. When I got your text, I couldn't help but imagine the worst, and I was terrified that you might be in some kind of danger. I'm so glad you're safe." She paused, then added, "And I'm guessing it was my history of panic attacks that led to your decision to tell me in person."

Shawn nodded. "But I did a lousy job of it. I promise, I'll let you know the minute I hear any news—if that's what you want, of course."

As Dar stood, Shawn reached for her and gave her a gentle hug. She was about to return his affection with a kiss when a loud beep from his pager stopped her. But when the sound of "When Irish Eyes Are Smiling" began playing on her phone as well, they stepped apart and frowned.

"Now what," they said in unison.

CHAPTER FOUR

Dar read her caller I.D., and her shoulders slumped. The Reed Police Department hadn't wasted any time in contacting her. Clearing her throat, she hoped that her voice wouldn't come across as shaky as her hands.

"Hello?" she said.

A man's angry shouts, which seemed to be originating from somewhere down the hall, forced Dar to cover one ear while she strained to hear the person on the phone with the other. But her effort proved useless.

"I'll have to call you back," she yelled above the din. "I can't hear you." She ended the call abruptly, then turned to Shawn. "Who's doing all that shouting?"

"I've no idea, but please stay out of it," he begged, looking up from his pager. "I hate to leave you like this, but I've got to run. I've got a patient who just arrived in serious condition." He brushed Dar's lips with a kiss, then tipped his head toward the angry shouts. "I'll take the stairs and call security on my way. You sure you're okay?"

As Shawn searched her eyes, she put on a brave face and smiled. "I'm fine. Go," she said.

Satisfied, Shawn added, "Love you." Then he pointed a stern finger at Merlin. "I'm trusting you to keep an eye on her for me." Merlin barked.

Dar grinned at their exchange. Merlin would follow her orders over Shawn's any day, but in that moment Shawn had far more important things on his mind. She watched with relief as he headed in the opposite direction of the shouting.

Counting to five, she waited before peeking out into the hall. The exit door to the stairs slammed shut behind Shawn, and she edged farther out into the hallway, needing to see what was going on. But as she did so, Merlin was immediately at her side, nudging her back inside the office.

"Not this time, Merlin," she said. "Stay here. I'll be right back." Merlin obeyed but whined his disapproval.

Slipping into the hall, Dar followed the sound of the gruff voice coming from the opposite direction of the stairs, toward the nurses' station. As she neared, she spotted a petite nurse cowering beneath a broad muscular man. Dar recognized the nurse as Spike, whose nickname had been affectionately given to her because of her short-cropped dark hair that stood ramrod straight.

But Dar had never seen the man before. He stood inches from Spike, making ugly accusations and threats, each punctuated with the stab of a thick finger that grazed the tip of Spike's nose.

Spike attempted to shrink away from him, but had instead backed herself into the counter of the nurses' station. Trapped, she cringed and threw her hands up for protection as the scowling brute raised a massive tatted arm above his head.

A surge of adrenaline pumped through Dar's body as she shouted, "Stop!" Trying to muster the sound of authority, she dropped her voice an octave and ordered, "Back away from her and lower your voice. There are sick kids here."

Not a single muscle on the guy's body twitched. Dar gulped. She hadn't exactly thought this through and realized too late that she'd probably provoked the brute into crushing her. Without taking his eyes from Spike, he pointed a finger directly at Dar. Before she could figure out a plan B, he spit out two words: "Get. Lost."

Dar's nostrils flared. She hated bullies. Though there was no way she could punch this guy in the nose without dire consequences, she had to do something.

Taking a deep breath, she prayed that what she was about to do wouldn't set off another panic attack. On the other hand, maybe feeling in control was exactly what she needed. Maybe by taking action, she wouldn't feel so helpless like she had at the onset of past panic attacks. She squared her shoulders.

"I don't know what your problem is," Dar said with more confidence than she felt, "but you need to leave now. Security is on their way, so you can either leave on your own or have security escort you out. Your choice."

The pounding of her heart reverberated in her ears as the brute tore his eyes from Spike to turn them onto Dar. Pure hatred reflected in his gaze, but she forced herself to stand her ground for Spike. A loud ding came from somewhere nearby, and she imagined she'd been summoned from the safe corner of a boxing ring to its center, where she'd be forced into a pulverizing face-off with a well-seasoned boxer.

An elevator door opened, and she gave a sigh of relief as a security guard in his mid-forties stepped out. He tugged at his belt while sucking in his excess girth, but otherwise showed no hesitation before striding over to the man with the wide neck and tapping him on the shoulder.

"Sir, I'm going to have to ask you to leave," he said.

Dar could feel the tension in the air as everyone waited to see who would make the next move. Then the bully's eyes hardened as he slowly turned to see who dared to touch him. When his dark eyes narrowed at the guard, Dar cringed, expecting him to land a blow on the guard's soft jowl.

But even as Spike's tormentor clenched first his jaw, then his fist, the guard didn't flinch. Instead, he remained unflappable, his face calm and his feet planted firmly in place. No one moved. No one breathed.

Finally, the bully took a step back. Dar was certain the confrontation had come to an end, until the guy, in one swift movement, again thrust a finger in Spike's face.

"You'll regret this," he hissed.

With surprising speed, the guard jumped between them, giving the thug a shove in the process. "Leave. Now," he commanded, showing far more authority than Dar had been able to muster.

With a smug grin, the guy turned and strode down the hall, every step landing decisively, like a prize fighter daring anyone to challenge him. Dragging out every last semblance of control, he passed the elevator bank and moved on toward the stairwell exit that Shawn had rushed down only moments earlier. Dar waited for the door to completely close before allowing herself to exhale. It was only then that she turned to Spike, who was still trembling.

"Are you okay?" she asked.

Instead of answering, the last remaining color drained from Spike's face, and her legs buckled beneath her.

CHAPTER FIVE

Dar jumped forward, catching Spike before she could hit the floor. The security guard was also quick to respond, grabbing a chair from behind the nurses' station. Together they eased Spike onto it just as another nurse appeared.

Dar glanced at the name card that dangled from the lanyard around her neck. It identified her as Ava Hicks, second floor head nurse. Dar stepped aside as Ava quickly assessed the situation, then gently helped Spike put her head between her knees. Soon tinges of pink replaced the ghostly white on Spike's cheeks, and she sat up. Ava handed her a bottled water and instructed Spike to take small sips.

Relieved to have someone take over, Dar took the time to calm her own nerves. It had felt good to defend Spike and stand up to a bully who took pleasure in exerting his power over someone smaller than himself. Still, she knew it wasn't bravery that had caused her to do so, but rather adrenaline bubbling up from a past experience.

It had been during her first year of junior high. A girl twice her size, for reasons unknown to Dar, had chosen to belittle, humiliate, and terrorize her every chance she got, all under the staff's radar. The girl had duped the teachers into believing she was a sweet, studious kid. Dar had tried everything from ignoring her to reasoning with her to no avail. She knew that reporting the girl to a teacher or administrator would've proven useless and would've only succeeded in provoking her further.

Then one day, when her tormentor had again been picking on her at her school locker, her best friend, LaVon, had appeared from around the corner. She'd overheard every vile word the girl spewed out. The girl never saw LaVon's fist coming, but Dar could never forget the sound of the crunch as it connected with the girl's nose.

The incident was never reported. Instead, the girl went to great lengths afterwards to avoid Dar, and especially LaVon. Though LaVon had to ice her hand for a week, she'd proudly told Dar, "It was so worth it!" Dar had been grateful to her friend, but secretly wished she'd had the guts to confront her bully herself.

It wasn't all it was cracked up to be.

Dar sensed the adrenaline rush she'd experienced while defending Spike was beginning to plummet, and the harsh reality of what could've happened replaced it. This was no junior high troublemaker. The guy could have killed her. Then she looked at Spike, still pale and shaking, and despite feeling the trembling in her own body, she knew she would do it all again.

The security guard, who introduced himself as Pete Hanson, straightened himself to his full five foot eight inches then asked, "Can someone tell me what happened before I got here?" He looked expectantly at Spike, but when she didn't answer, he turned his question to Dar.

Explaining that she hadn't seen everything, she told Pete what happened after she arrived and before Pete stepped off the elevator.

When she'd finished, the guard's stern look made her feel like a scolded child.

"Dr. O'Reilly warned me that you might try to intervene in the conflict when he called," he said. "He begged me to hurry, but I was in the middle of handling a situation in the ER."

At least he'd shown up, Dar thought. She was curious as to where Ava had been through all the shouting. As though reading her mind, the charge nurse spoke up.

"I'm sorry I wasn't here to help," Ava said. "I'd heard the commotion, but there was a complication with one of the patients, and I wasn't able to leave him until he was stabilized."

"Well, I'm grateful you both showed up when you did," Dar said. "I'm Dar, by the way. You're Ava, right?"

"Yes," Ava said before turning to Pete. "And this is one of my best nurses, Myra Evans, but she likes to be called Spike."

Pete acknowledged the three women before changing the subject back to the unwelcome visitor. "What can you tell me about this man, and why do you think he singled you out, Miss Spike?"

"His name is Bruno," Spike said, finding her voice. "Bruno Rossi. He's my ex-boyfriend." She stared at the bottle of water she held clenched between her hands. "I broke up with him when I realized his charming, sweet personality was an act, and he's not taking it well."

"That's one way to say it," Dar said. Dar knew something about betrayal. She didn't know which was worse; someone who pretended to like you before turning all their anger on you, or someone who didn't even bother to hide their dislike for you from their first encounter. Having experienced both, in each case she'd found herself to be merely an obstacle for the creep—one that required elimination. She hoped that wasn't the case for Spike.

Spike nodded, and Dar noticed her knuckles turned white from her grip. "He used to work here—on the custodial staff—but he was fired. I hadn't seen him in two months—until today. He's been making threats. I got a restraining order against him after he left bruises on my arm. I thought everything would be better after the restraining order, but I guess I was wrong."

Ava grabbed some tissues for Spike. "I had no idea you were dealing with all this," Ava said. "Is he the guy I saw months ago yelling at you in the parking lot? I think he saw me staring and took off. I'm sorry I never asked you about it."

"You saw that?" Spike sniffed. "He wanted me to drop the restraining order."

Spike's shoulders, which she'd held near her ears through all the tension, now dropped low as she slumped in the chair. "I thought this nightmare was over. I don't know what else to do. Bruno blames me for everything— our breakup, the restraining order, and his getting fired."

"Of course he does." Dar's sarcasm came out thick. "I'm sure that every sad, pathetic thing that happens in poor Bruno's life is all your fault. And I doubt he'll ever see it any other way." Dar squatted down to put herself at eye level with Spike. "But you know it's not your fault, right?"

Spike looked away.

Pete's gaze held a mix of sympathy and resolve. "Would you like me to report this? It's a definite violation of his restraining order."

"No . . . Maybe . . . I don't know," Spike said, shaking her head.

The guard looked puzzled, and a tad less sympathetic.

Dar patted Spike's hand. "You need to do this, Spike I know you probably don't want to do anything that might create more conflict with Bruno, but sometimes taking a stand against a bully is the only way to make him stop."

Spike stared at Dar as though she'd asked her to run into a burning building. "It could make things worse, a lot worse."

"It could also earn him jail time, or at least go on his record. Plus, it'll send him the message that you're not backing down." Dar patted Spike's hand again. "I'm sure it's not an easy decision, but it's your decision."

Dar wasn't sure Spike heard a word she'd said.

Finally, Spike spoke, her voice cracking. "I'm sorry. I can't."

She looked so forlorn. It broke Dar's heart.

"Sometimes the law can't protect you," Spike said.

Pete looked disappointed. "You're sure? I could make the call and say you knew nothing about it."

"Please don't," Spike said, her eyes widening in panic. "It wouldn't matter. He'd still blame me for not stopping you."

"Okay, then. But if you change your mind, you know where to reach me," Pete said before walking away.

Once he was gone, Spike seemed to fold in on herself. The strong competent nurse Dar had previously seen now seemed a mere shell of that person, totally drained and full of self-doubt.

Ava told Spike to take as much time as she needed before returning to work. She also offered to help the other nurses on the floor cover for her if she needed to go home, or at least until she felt ready to finish her shift.

"Come with me," Dar said. "There's someone I think you should meet."

"I'm really not in the mood to meet anyone," Spike sniffled.

"You may not know me well, but trust me on this."

With more than a little reluctance, Spike followed Dar down the hall. "Thank you for standing up to Bruno." It came out as a throaty whisper. "But you could've gotten hurt."

"I have to admit, I was plenty scared," Dar said, placing a hand over her heart. "But I hate bullies."

"Lucky for me." Spike touched Dar's arm. "I've lived in fear of what he might do next, but his showing up here . . ."

Dar stopped. "Has Bruno been here other times recently?"

"Other than the time he confronted me in the parking lot? I don't know for sure. There's only one coworker I've confided in about Bruno. She thought she saw him across the street from the hospital parking lot one time, but the guy she saw was half-hidden by a tree. She did see tattoos up and down an exposed arm, which Bruno has, but she couldn't be certain. Why do you ask?"

"Never mind," Dar said, not wanting to alarm the woman. Still, she couldn't help but wonder if Bruno had ever had a conflict with Mr. Reece as well.

She opened the door to Shawn's office. "Spike, I'd like you to meet Merlin." Dar knelt on one knee and immediately Merlin was all over her, licking her face and wagging his tail so hard, she feared he'd knock something over. She placed a dog treat in Spike's hand. "Give him this, and he'll be your friend for life."

Spike hesitated, then held out Merlin's treat, which he promptly gobbled up. Dar smiled. "Merlin's actually a therapy dog. We come in once a week for the kids, but sometimes our visits include staff. They can get stressed out too."

Merlin sat while Spike lavished him with scratches behind the ears first followed by full-on hugs. Dar debated who was benefiting the most, but decided it didn't matter. "Have you ever thought about getting a dog?"

"Sure. How about this one?" Spike grinned as she said it, wrapping both arms around Merlin's neck.

"Not a chance," Dar replied with a laugh. The sound of "When Irish Eyes Are Smiling" interrupted their banter, and Dar checked the caller I.D. on her phone, then smacked her forehead. Spike's eyebrow shot up.

"I'm so sorry," Dar said, "but I need to take this. I completely forgot that I was supposed to return a phone call earlier!"

"I think it was more my fault than yours," Spike said. She thanked Dar again and insisted that Merlin had magically made her feel better. They both laughed. But as Spike started to leave, Dar's forehead wrinkled.

"Don't worry, I'll be fine," Spike said.

But Dar heard no conviction in her words. She stepped into the hall with Spike, then watched her walk back to the nurse's station. She wanted to make sure Bruno hadn't returned. Along with Spike, she truly wished that everything would be fine, but Bruno had proven to be too relentless of a bully to give either of them much hope.

CHAPTER SIX

Dar stepped back into Shawn's office. "I'm so sorry I didn't call you back," she said after answering her phone. The familiar grumpy voice on the other end was oddly loud.

"I'm afraid that's not good enough," came a voice behind her.

Dar spun around. Mike Shafer, Reed's finest detective and her friend, stood in the doorway. He ended the call and stuffed his phone into an inside pocket of his jacket. Dar nearly dropped her own phone as she stared at the man who'd helped her out of more dangerous situations than she cared to remember. He'd gained an extra five or more mid-life pounds around the waist since she'd last seen him, but otherwise he looked the same.

"Mike, what are you doing here? I meant to call you, but things have been a little crazy around here this morning."

Mike raised an eyebrow at her. "Crazier than Shawn finding a dead body?"

"Well, when you put it that way, I guess not." Dar considered telling Mike about the incident between Spike and Bruno, but since Spike had refused to file a complaint or even allow the security guard to file it, she wasn't sure it was her place to mention it.

"I'm guessing you want to talk to me about Mr. Reece's death." Dar fidgeted with her Irish Claddagh ring, twirling it back and forth on her finger. It had been a gift from her father, Dr. James Kelly, and reminded her of how much she missed him, especially at times like these. She missed both of her parents, but she'd been so young when her mom died that memories of her were hazy. Her dad had been her rock after that, right up until the day he died. She tried to imagine him by her side now, giving her support as she faced Mike's questions.

"Shawn told me he gave an initial statement to the police when they arrived," she said.

"He did, but I have follow-up questions for him," Mike said. "I understand he's in the middle of an emergency surgery right now, so I guess I'll have to talk to him later." He shifted his weight from one foot to another. "Why is it that whenever there are dead bodies around, I find myself talking with you and Shawn?"

"Cursed, I guess." Dar tried to sound lighthearted, but she felt anything but. The thought that a staff member at CCC could be responsible for Mr. Reece's death made her nauseous.

Dar scowled at her chewed-up fingernails, exhibits of her bad habit worsened by anxiety. She could only hope that Mike had a report from the coroner that said cause of death was natural. Her nerves had been shot since Shawn had told her he suspected Mr. Reece's death was "fishy."

"I suppose it's too soon to have heard from the coroner regarding Mr. Reece's autopsy," she said.

Mike frowned but refused to be bated. "My notes state that your name was penciled in Mr. Reece's calendar. What time did you see him and why?"

"It was late yesterday afternoon," Dar said, disappointed that Mike wasn't sharing any information. She knew the Reed Police Department expected him to be a detective first, and a friend second, but she hoped he'd come around. All she could do at this point was answer his questions.

"I left The Contented Canine around four yesterday afternoon and called Mr. Reece on my way to CCC. He said he could only give me five minutes of his time, and asked if I could be at his office in fifteen minutes."

"Why did you have to see him in person?" Mike asked.

Dar wondered where this was going. "This feels like a lot of questions for a guy who supposedly had a heart attack." She crossed her arms and sat back.

"Relax," Mike said, a sympathetic look crossing his face briefly. "It's standard procedure. I'm just doing my job, talking to everyone who visited Mr. Reece yesterday."

That was exactly what Shawn had told her, which should have relieved her, but instead she said, "I'm not buying it. Since when do you go into investigative mode unless there's a good possibility there's been foul play?"

Mike tipped his head down, seeming to mull over some decision. Finally, he sighed, having reached a conclusion. "I guess you'll find out soon enough. This information did not come from my lips. Got it?"

She nodded, now regretting having asked. Chewing on a fingernail, she waited for whatever he was about to tell her.

Mike glanced at the doorway before focusing back on her. "A preliminary report from the coroner is indicating Mr. Reece may have been poisoned."

Her heart plummeted in her chest. It was happening again. "Poisoned? He was murdered?"

Mike did not respond.

Dar uncrossed her arms and spread her hands wide, palms up, and asked, "But why? Who could possibly want to kill Mr. Reece?"

Again, Mike didn't answer.

A familiar uneasy feeling began gnawing at her. She pressed her spine into the chair's back, but instead of feeling its support, she felt a wall instead, one that blocked her retreat and pinned her against it.

"You don't think I killed him, do you?" The pounding beats of her heart picked up their pace, echoing painfully in her head. Mr. Reece had been very much alive yesterday when she'd seen him, but now he was dead. Of course she was a suspect.

The sense of security she'd fought so hard to regain after she was the victim of not one but two killers, began to wane. She could feel the familiar shards of trust forming a vortex that clutched at her, pulling and spinning her downward toward its center. She didn't want to go through this again. She didn't want to wonder if the murderer was someone she knew.

When Mike cleared his throat, Dar once again became aware of his presence. Though he sat on the edge of his seat, tapping a pencil on his notepad, he was otherwise silent, exhibiting a patience that Dar knew did not come easily for him. She took a deep breath.

Finally, Mike spoke. "We can do this later if you need more time."

"No, I'm fine," Dar lied. She'd only feel better when she'd finished with Mike's questions. She started again with his previous question.

"You asked me why I went to see Mr. Reece in person," she said. "I went to his office to see if he'd ordered the new bandanas we designed together for the canine therapy program. He kept forgetting to do it even though I called several times to remind him, so I hoped I'd have better luck if I reminded him in person."

"Why in the world would a CFO handle a task like that himself?" Mike asked.

"Mr. Reece loved dogs; he had three of his own. I think that's why he'd taken such a personal interest in the hospital's canine therapy program. Anyway, when I got there, Mr. Reece apologized and explained that he hadn't had a chance yet to place the order. But he showed me the completed order form and promised me it was on the top of his to-do pile for the next day. Before I left, he gave Merlin a treat and ruffled his fur, and that was it. I was probably in his office less than five minutes."

"Did you notice anything unusual?" Mike asked. "Anything different about his mood?"

"No, he seemed fine when we spoke," Dar said. "And I didn't notice anything out of the ordinary." She paused, causing Mike's eyebrows to raise again. "Wait. There was a maintenance or construction guy coming out of Mr. Reece's office, but we only spoke briefly."

Mike leaned forward. "Did he mention his name? What did he say?"

"He must've done a repair in Reece's office," she said, "because I heard him tell Mr. Reece that if he ever needed anything fixed again, he knew how to reach him."

"Did this guy say anything to you?"

"He said 'hi,' then complimented Merlin. There was one strange thing, though," Dar said. "When he reached out an arm to pet Merlin, Merlin growled at him. He never growls at people. After I apologized, the man exited through the stairwell down the hall from Mr. Reece's office."

Dar stared at her nails again, chagrined at the damage she'd inflicted on them. But when Mike sat back in his chair and stared straight at her, she chewed on one again.

He jotted down a few notes. "That's helpful," he said in an even, professional tone.

If she were anyone else, she might think Mike was relaxed, just doing his job. But she knew better. His nostrils always flared—like they were doing now—whenever he was trying to hide his anger or impatience. She preferred his agitated self to this calm façade. At least then there was no fear of him exploding when he could no longer continue the charade.

More than that, she didn't want him to see her as a fragile child whom he needed to tread carefully around. After all, his probing questions had helped save her life more than once. She didn't want him to change his investigation tactics or temperament for her benefit, though she knew it was her own fault that he felt obliged to do so.

"Can you remember any details about this guy, maybe a description?" Mike asked. He sat forward again, pressing his questions rapidly now. "Was he short or tall, the color of his hair, identifying marks—anything?" All that bottled-up emotion was being released into his face, which now turned crimson. "Think, Dar. Think!"

She chewed on a nail, trying to remember. Merlin's reaction to the guy had taken her by surprise. She hadn't really looked at him, having been more concerned about getting Merlin to calm down. Wincing, she recalled her dad's advice: "You really need to pay more attention to your surroundings." Yet it had been her dad who hadn't heard the man close behind him about to strike a fatal blow.

Mike's patience crumbled, and he growled, "Don't make me pull the information out of you!"

The real Mike was back. Struggling, Dar tried to picture the man she'd seen yesterday coming out of Mr. Reece's office.

"He was carrying a bag that I assumed was his tool bag. He had on a plain gray cap, pulled low, so I didn't see his face or hair color. He was wearing work clothes, you know, like the ones all the other construction guys working on the remodel here wear. He must've been one of them."

"Are you sure he carried a tool bag rather than wearing a tool belt?" Mike asked.

"Positive," Dar said. "I remember because he switched the bag to his left hand so he could pet Merlin with his right, but Merlin wouldn't allow it. Guess he's right-handed. Oh, and when he reached his arm out to pet Merlin, I saw a tattoo on his right forearm. He pulled back too fast for me to catch what it was for certain, but I think it was a snake."

Mike scribbled some notes. "That helps some, but I'm guessing two-thirds of the construction guys here have tats, and in my experience, snake tattoos are fairly common. Did you happen to see a name tag on his shirt or a company logo?"

"No, although that does seem odd," she said. "I'd think the construction company and the hospital would both require it. I wondered, too, what type of repairs he'd been working on in Mr. Reece's office because his clothes didn't seem very dirty. All the other construction workers look a little messier than this guy did. Maybe Mr. Reece knew the guy personally. But that doesn't make sense either. Why would someone who didn't work directly for the hospital be doing repairs in Mr. Reece's office? Normally the hospital authorizes jobs like that."

"Had you seen him around here before?" Mike asked.

"I don't think so, but there always seem to be construction workers coming and going. Usually, I don't see any of them on the elevator since they tend to use the back entrance and the stairs."

"Did you actually see him open the stairwell door?" Mike asked.

"No, sorry," Dar said. "Merlin was tugging on his leash and growling. It took some effort to calm him down, and by the time I looked down the hall again, the man was gone."

"So you went into Mr. Reece's office then," Mike stated. "How did he seem to you?"

Dar frowned, thinking back. "Actually, before he noticed me standing in his doorway, his face was flushed, and he was clenching his jaw muscles. I knocked, but he just sat there, staring at the wall. It wasn't until I cleared my throat and spoke his name that he saw me."

Dar focused on Shawn's desk, trying to picture Mr. Reece sitting behind his desk that day. "As soon as he noticed me, he composed himself, and then flashed a big smile and gestured for me to come in. It was as though he'd shoved whatever was bothering him into a desk drawer and slammed it shut. We spoke briefly, and in four, five minutes tops, I was out of there."

Dar couldn't believe she'd missed so many details until now and wondered what else she'd missed. "I'm sorry, Mike, but I was so focused on how I planned to appeal to Mr. Reece that day, nothing had registered as concerning until now."

Mike handed her his business card. "If you remember anything else, call me."

Dar accepted the white card with the words "Detective Mike Shafer, Reed Police Department," printed in bold font above two phone numbers, one office and one cell. "You know I have your number on speed dial," she said.

"You should," Mike said. "I don't know if trouble finds you or you find it, but either way, it always involves someone getting murdered."

She wanted to protest, but trouble did seem to find her. No matter how much she wished it wouldn't.

Mike pointed to the card he'd handed her. "That first number is for my department at RPD in case you can't reach me on my cell. They'll know how to contact me. Don't lose it."

"Excuse me?"

Mike looked at her incredulously. "If I recall, the last time you lost your phone, it nearly cost you your life."

Of course, she remembered all too well. "So, am I still a suspect?" she asked, changing the subject.

Mike rubbed his balding head, refusing to commit to an answer. Instead, he replied, "No trips. You can go between Reed and Fort Wayne, but that's it. I need you available for questions."

And to keep tabs on your suspect, Dar thought.

CHAPTER SEVEN

It wasn't difficult for Dar to see why Merlin loved their Saturday morning ritual of visiting the sick children at both CCC and Reed Hospital. The kids' dull eyes often lit up at the sight of Merlin with his thick coat of fur, a welcome contrast to their sterile environment, full of tubes and beeping machines. Even those who were timid around dogs eventually ended up petting his soft, fluffy coat. When they looked into his brown eyes, they couldn't help but wrap their often-frail arms around his neck, causing Merlin's tail to wag in delight. In those moments, all the hours Dar had put into training Merlin to be a therapy dog had proven worthwhile. Not only could Merlin provide a bright moment for the children, but he also gave them a chance to forget their illnesses, at least for a short time.

Dar checked the time after emerging from the last patient's room at CCC. With all that had happened earlier in the morning, she'd forgotten about her lunch date with Shawn and her newfound twin brother, Daniel.

It had been Daniel's suggestion that they meet for lunch at least once a week to get to know each other better. Following the tragic ending of a biological family they'd known nothing about, Dar and Daniel had discovered they were not only siblings, but also twins, and had lived separate and very different lives for nearly thirty years. Through the reading of their biological mother's will, they were also surprised to learn that they'd inherited both the Montgomery Farm Estate and Black Knight Pharmaceuticals in Fort Wayne, Indiana.

Overwhelmed, they'd agreed that, for now, it would be easier if Daniel moved into the estate and sat on BK Pharmaceutical's board, where he could make use of his financial background to gain an understanding of the company. Dar had opted to stay in Reed where her new business, The Contented Canine, and Shawn were located.

Daniel had offered to meet her in Reed for lunch this week. She appreciated him driving the hour and a half from Fort Wayne since it gave her enough time to drop Merlin off at home first.

Within ten minutes, she arrived at her craftsman-style house. Though small, it was the perfect size for her and Merlin, and a short commute to Reed's two hospitals and The Contented Canine, which she co-owned with her best friend, LaVon.

She bounded up the back steps, Merlin at her heels. Once inside, she found his empty bowls and poured water in one and food in the other. Next, she located his favorite toys from beneath her bed and behind the couch, then set the TV to his favorite animal show, *Dogs at the Park*. She gave Merlin a scruff behind the ear and a hug. "Be back soon," she said, then hurried out to her car. Her phone began playing her dad's favorite tune. She frowned at the interruption but answered Mike's call anyway.

"Did you remember anything else?" he said abruptly.

"No, and hello to you, too," Dar replied. "Is there something specific you need to ask or tell me? I was just leaving to meet Shawn and Daniel for lunch."

"No, but I was hoping you remembered something new. Evidently not. By the way, where are you meeting? I'm always looking for a restaurant where I can take my niece, one where I can hear what she's saying."

"Twin Forks Restaurant in downtown Reed," Dar said. "They have a kid's menu, but it's nothing fancy. And you'd be happy to know that even you can carry on a conversation there."

"Careful," Mike said, then ended the call.

By the time she pulled into the restaurant parking lot, Daniel was already waiting for her next to his car. She parked her Kia, then walked over to him and gave him a quick hug.

"Thanks for meeting in Reed this time," she said.

Daniel beamed. "No problem, sis. Hey, there's Shawn. Why didn't you two love birds drive together?"

"Love birds? Really?" Dar laughed. "Shawn has a new patient who's still critical, so he drove his own car in case he got called back to the hospital."

Shawn joined them, and kissed Dar. "I always have dessert first," he teased, bringing a warm flush to her face. He greeted Daniel, the two guys shaking hands in a one-armed man-hug.

Daniel grinned at Dar and Shawn. "You don't know how good it feels to finally have family. The foster homes didn't come close, especially the last one."

Shawn rested his arm across Dar's shoulder and whispered in her ear, "Someday maybe I'll officially be part of the family, too."

Dar turned and saw tiny prisms dancing in his blue eyes. He bent and kissed her gently once again.

"Either get a room or let's eat," Daniel said. "I'm starved."

"If I weren't so hungry myself . . ." Shawn said. His eyebrows danced up and down.

A fresh spring breeze tousled Dar's long hair, and she laughed at his unspoken reference. In that moment, she could almost forget about Mr. Reece's murder and the questions swirling around in her head.

As the three of them entered the restaurant, an eager young hostess greeted them and led them to a booth, followed by a waitress who offered to take their orders. Famished, all three ordered immediately.

"I found out some information about Mr. Reece's murder from Mike," Dar said in a low tone. "I hate to bring it up here," she said. She glanced at the empty booths on either side of them, before adding the bombshell, "but you should know that he was poisoned."

"Who's Mr. Reece?" Daniel asked.

Shawn ignored his question. "Poisoned? I knew he didn't die of natural causes!"

Daniel sat forward, shaking his head. "Will someone please tell me what the hell is going on?"

"Dar is holding out on us, that's what's going on. It's a trait you'll soon learn your sister has in spades." Shawn gave her a sideways look.

"Uh-huh. Look who's talking," she retorted. "The guy who sends cryptic text messages."

"Touché," Shawn replied. His boyish grin returned.

"Who's Mr. Reece?" Daniel asked again. "And why was he poisoned? What cryptic text? Will you two please tell me what you're talking about?"

"Sorry," Dar said. "He's the CFO—was the CFO—at Currie Children's Center. Shawn found him lying dead on his office floor this morning."

Shawn and Dar brought Daniel up to speed on all that had happened earlier that morning, though to Dar it seemed like days ago. Daniel was quiet a moment, then started to ask a question when Mike sauntered over to their table.

Dar guessed it had been Mike's plan all along to catch them together, and she'd made it exceptionally easy for him. It wasn't that they didn't enjoy chatting with Mike, it's just that their lunches were sacred time. One look at Mike, and she sensed he was in detective mode. Why else would he be there without his niece?

Mike slid into their booth next to Daniel, across from her and Shawn. Glares from both Shawn and Daniel shot directly at her. She guessed she should have acted more surprised to see Mike.

"Relax," Mike said. "I tricked her into giving me the name of this place." The waitress arrived, and he ordered a coffee but no lunch. When she left, he added, "I can see by the look on Daniel's face that you told him all about Reece's murder."

"He's family," Dar said. "Besides, he might be able to help. Maybe he knew him. They're both CPAs, or were— Mr. Reece, that is." She brought her nail to her mouth again, unable to stop herself from nervously biting it.

"I know it's hard for you to remember, but last I checked, I'm the detective, not you, and it's my job to ask the questions." Then he turned to Shawn. "And you're a hard man to catch to do exactly that."

"Shoot," Shawn said, but when Mike scowled at him, he added, "Sorry, I mean, ask away."

"Just for that, I'll start with you, Dr. O'Reilly. Tell me again why you went to see Mr. Reece this morning."

"I went to see Mr. Reece about funding to purchase a new supply of ventricular assist devices. I could've sworn we ordered more, but we're running out of our supply faster than expected. I thought I could catch him early, before either of us got too busy."

"Oh yeah, I think my niece, Sarah, had one after her heart surgery. It's a temporary support for the heart, right?"

"That's one of its uses, yes."

"So you didn't have an appointment?" Mike questioned.

"No," Shawn said. "I noticed his light on." He repeated his story about finding Mr. Reece face-down on the floor.

"That must've been a shock," Daniel said. Shawn nodded.

"What time did you enter his office?" Mike asked.

"Around seven a.m., maybe a few minutes after. I thought I'd gotten lucky because he's usually not in until eight or so."

"Did you touch anything other than the victim?"

"No. Wait, yes—the doorknob. His door was closed, so I knocked first, and when he didn't answer, I opened the door. I think I told the police officer that, but I was a little shook at the time."

"Well, that explains why your fingerprints were on the doorknob, but can you explain how your fingerprints were also found on the fan switch in Mr. Reece's office?" Mike studied Shawn's reaction.

"The fan," Dar interrupted. "Remember, you told me it was running, and you had trouble listening for signs of breathing or a heartbeat."

"That's right," Shawn said. "I tried to turn it off so I could check Mr. Reece's vitals, but the switch was already in the 'off' position. Toggling it again didn't do anything. I guess I forgot to mention it to the police officer before we were interrupted by someone from forensics."

"But you're positive the fan was running when you got there?" Mike asked again.

Shawn's neck tinged with red. "Yes," he said. "I remember it making a rattling noise, like it wasn't working quite right."

"Interesting," Mike said. "Your fingerprints were the only prints in the bathroom."

"Shouldn't Mr. Reece's prints have been all over the room?" Dar asked.

"Yes, but it seems someone carefully wiped everything down."

"But why?" Dar asked. "His body wasn't found in the bathroom. It was on the floor, near his desk. And before you ask, I know because Shawn told me. Could Mr. Reece's body have been moved?" She noticed Mike still studying Shawn and shot him a look of disbelief. "Surely you don't suspect Shawn? It wouldn't make sense for him to wipe everything down, but forget something as obvious as a doorknob or a fan switch."

Mike raised an eyebrow. "Personally, do I think Shawn killed Mr. Reece? No. However, I do know that murderers make mistakes, even with the most careful planning. That's usually how we catch them." His eyes focused again on Shawn. "One more thing. Was Reece's office window closed or open when you found him?"

Shawn thought a moment. He ran his fingers through his hair before replying, "I'd forgotten about the window, but now that you mention it, it was open, maybe halfway. That's probably why it was cool in the room, but I never touched it."

"So why did Mr. Reece go back to his office so late at night?" Dar asked. "Did he do that often?"

"His wife says he didn't," Mike said. "She had no idea he'd gone back to his office that night because she was out of town at her sister's."

"Was there anything on his phones?" Dar asked.

Mike stared at her. "What do you mean, 'phones'? We found one cell phone in his pocket, and are still checking his contacts, texts, and everything else on it. What makes you think there's a second one?"

"The last time I saw him, I didn't see any phones, but the day we met to discuss the bandana design for the therapy dogs, there were two phones on his desk." She looked at Shawn. "Did you ever see two phones on his desk?"

"No," Shawn said. "Someone probably just forgot their phone when they stopped at his office. I wouldn't read too much into it. People forget their phones all the time."

"I'll have my men keep an eye out for a phone, just in case." Mike rubbed his temples, then turned his attention to Daniel. "I know you don't work at CCC, Daniel, but have you ever met Mr. Robert Reece before, like Dar suggested, possibly at a CPA conference of some kind?" He pulled out a photo of Reece and showed it to Daniel.

Daniel studied it, then said, "He looks familiar." He furrowed his brow and examined the photo again. Then his eyes lit up. "That's it! I remember now. He spoke at a conference that I attended in February, but I didn't make it to his presentation."

"That was just a couple months ago," Mike said.

Daniel nodded. "It was the ISA, the Indiana Society of Accountants conference. I'm sure he was one of the speakers."

"Did you actually meet him or have a chance to talk with him?" Dar asked, jumping into the conversation. But when Mike cleared his throat at her interruption, she acquiesced, sitting back and motioning for him to continue.

Daniel addressed his answer to both. "After the event, there was a small reception. I introduced myself to Mr. Reece, but he'd barely said hello before someone pulled him aside. He excused himself, and a short time later, he disappeared. Several people were asking where he went, Not even the event coordinator seemed to know."

"Someone interrupted the two of you?" Dar jumped in again.

"Kind of like someone else I know," Shawn said, rolling his eyes at her.

"Yeah," Daniel said. "She was hard to forget. The woman wore expensive clothes and jewelry. She reminded me of a celebrity. What's her name? You know, the one that sings, dances, and the media likes to splash her scandals in the news."

Mike sighed. "That could be a long list of possibilities."

Daniel continued. "Anyway, she was really hot. She kept touching Mr. Reece's arm and his tie with these red polished nails. She was flirting with him, which surprised me."

"Why's that?" Mike asked.

"Well, no offense to Mr. Reece, but she seemed way out of his league."

"And he's married," Shawn added.

"Could she have been a hooker?" Dar asked.

"I don't think so." Daniel closed his eyes a moment, then opened them. "She was wearing a name tag, but I couldn't see the name from where I stood. She had long, wavy blonde hair—it covered her name."

"So she had blonde hair; do you remember any other features?" Mike asked.

A bright shade of red began creeping up Daniel's neck to his face. "Did I mention she was, ahem, well blessed by Mother Nature?"

Mike laughed. "Are you trying to say in a very awkward way that this lady was stacked?"

Daniel tapped the side of his nose. "She was wearing a fitted red suit and a low-cut blouse that made it hard to miss, and she made sure no one missed it, especially not Mr. Reece. Anyway, she lured Mr. Reece to a quiet corner. It seemed odd to me. I mean, why would a lady that hot be hitting on a middle-aged guy like Mr. Reece? Maybe I was wrong; maybe she actually was a hooker."

"Since when do hookers get their own name tags?" Dar asked with a frown. "I can't even get a decent volunteer tag for Merlin at the hospital. If she did, then I swear there's no justice."

Mike shook his head at her comment, then asked Daniel, "Did you see Mr. Reece again?"

"No. I got into a conversation with another CPA," Daniel said, "and when I searched for Mr. Reece after that, he was gone. So was the lady in red. I never saw either of them again."

Everyone was digesting Daniel's story, when he added, "You know, I don't think I saw her at registration. She'd have been hard to miss. She must have arrived late.

Do you think she had something to do with Mr. Reece's murder?"

"I'm still gathering facts," Mike said. He thanked Daniel and Shawn, then stood and shook their hands before turning to Dar. "Any plans to move into the Montgomery estate, like your brother did?" Dar's face reddened, and Shawn bristled. "And that's my cue to leave," Mike said and started to leave.

Shawn's pager went off, and he checked the device. "I'm sorry, but I'll have to take a rain check on lunch. I'll walk out with you, Mike." He leaned over and brushed Dar's lips, then whispered in her ear, "We need to talk. Just the two of us." He locked eyes with her, then followed Mike out the door.

Dar watched them leave, wondering about Shawn's request and how that conversation might end. They had to consider future living arrangements, but that decision depended on how they fit their complicated careers and dreams into their relationship. And finding time to talk wasn't easy either, since they both seemed to be busier these days. Reece's murder had made it even harder. She sighed. She really missed their alone time.

Without realizing it, her focus drifted to a small group of people waiting near the bus stop across the street. The entire group moved closer to the curb as a city bus rounded the corner, except for a lone man in a camouflage hoodie. She noticed he was facing in the direction of Shawn and Mike when he pulled out a cell phone. As he conversed with someone, he nodded, his other hand remaining in his pocket. She strained to see his face, but his features were shaded beneath the hood of his camouflage jacket, along with the two dark circles of his sunglasses.

The bus pulled up and its passengers got on, leaving the man in the camouflage hoodie still standing on the sidewalk. After the bus pulled away, he turned and hurried down the block in the opposite direction of Shawn and Mike.

Before turning the corner, though, the guy looked over his shoulder, toward the parking lot. She could no longer see Shawn and Mike, but she guessed they were getting into their cars by now. Dar felt her entire body tense as the man then swiveled his head toward the restaurant. Even with his sunglasses on, she sensed him straining to see inside.

The goosebumps she'd had earlier that morning returned, the tiny hairs on her arms picking up new signs of danger. Was it real or imagined? She shivered as the man disappeared down a side street.

Her mind scrambled to sort through all the possible "what if's" and "maybes" of what she'd observed. It was possible she was being paranoid, jumping to conclusions based more on a gut reaction than any facts. Yet in the recesses of her mind loomed the feeling of déjà vu, refusing to reveal its source of origin. She found it odd, though, that the feeling hadn't appeared until she'd watched the stranger walk away.

CHAPTER EIGHT

Dar heard Daniel's voice before his words registered in her mind. She turned her attention back to him and found him leaning forward across the restaurant table with a frown on his face, waving a hand in front of her.

"What is so interesting out there that made you zone out on me?" Daniel asked. He swiveled around, placing an arm on the back of the booth, and looked out the diner's front window. He looked back at Dar. "Did you see someone you know?"

"Sorry," she said, shaking her head. "I thought I did, but I was wrong."

"Uh-huh," Daniel said, unconvinced.

Dar smiled at her brother's intuition. Even though they'd known each other for barely a year, he had the uncanny ability to sense her thoughts, even those she tried to keep from him. They'd also found they could still communicate with each other through a unique sign language they had once shared as toddlers. Despite having been separated at such a young age for nearly thirty years, their special bond had remained intact.

Thinking about the stranger again, Dar tried to recall what about him tugged at her memory. "I'm not sure if I knew the guy or not," she said. "He had on a camouflage hoodie and sunglasses, so it must have been something else besides his face that seemed familiar." But unable to pin it down, she moved on. "What do you think of Dr. Sanderson? Isn't she amazing?"

Daniel held both palms up. "Whoa, I can't keep up with your train of thought! Going back to your déjà vu, it's probably your brain trying to send you a message. It'll come back to you when you least expect it."

"That's weird," Dar said. "I told Shawn the exact same thing when he was struggling to figure out what had been different in Mr. Reece's office. Maybe, since you seem to be able to read my mind, you can pop in my head and find out what was familiar about that guy for me." She raised an eyebrow. "Or you can answer my question about Dr. Sanderson."

"Isn't that confidential?" Daniel insisted.

"Definitely not between twins. Now spill."

"For starters, she's much more patient than you," Daniel said with a grin.

Dar laughed. "I can't argue with that."

"Plus, she always nods in agreement when I talk about my crazy sister," Daniel teased. Dar kicked him under the table. "Ow! Case in point for my next therapy session.

Seriously, though, it's been a relief to talk about the whole adoption mix-up and foster home experiences. But almost getting killed might take the longest to work through."

Dar nodded. "Still working on it too," she said. "And being the new owners of the Montgomery Farm Estate and BK Pharmaceuticals has added a lot of pressure, especially for you since you're living at the estate and on BKP's board."

Both sat in silence, then Daniel asked, "Speaking of our inheritance, have you given any more thought about staying at the estate? I swear I rattle around in that big place. Rosie's there, but she retires to her own apartment in the north wing in the evening. Bring Shawn with you."

Dar sighed. She missed seeing her brother, and Rosie, too. Rosie was more than their live-in housekeeper/cook at the Montgomery Estate; she had basically raised their biological mom—a mom neither she nor Daniel had known. Dar felt a bond with Rosie, who had once saved her life with a frying pan.

"I want to be there," Dar said. "I want to learn more about our family's history and get to know you better. We have lifetimes to catch up on after being separated so long. It's a big part of why I try to stop by at least once a week, and why our weekly lunches are so important to me. Plus, there's the equine therapy program that I hope to start soon."

"But . . . ?" Daniel asked.

"But I have The Contented Canine in Reed. I've put my heart and soul into getting it started. How can I sell it, now that it's finally well-known in the community? And what about LaVon? I don't want to let her down. She's not only my business partner, she's my friend, too."

She fidgeted with her napkin. "Then there's Shawn. His work is in Reed, not Fort Wayne. I couldn't ask him to leave his practice, not to mention his grandmother. Ethel depends on him." She shook her head. "Did you see how he reacted when Mike asked when I was going to move into the estate? I don't know what to do."

Daniel patted her hand. "Slow down. No one's expecting you to decide today. Talk to Shawn and LaVon about it. It'll all work out."

"I wish I had your optimism," she said.

"Trust me, I have my own issues. Like knowing exactly where I fit in with BKP's operations. It hasn't been easy. I want to learn as much as I can about the company before I offer any suggestions for change."

"Sounds smart to me," Dar said. "Oh, and thank you for helping me purchase a fourth horse. I think Chestnut's going to be a natural for the equine therapy group. She seems gentle and already gets along with our other three horses. All four will be great with the kids in the program."

Daniel grinned. "You know, I have to agree with you about her being a good pick. Adding a pony for our smaller children might be beneficial, too. Let's keep an eye out for the right one," Daniel said. He paused a moment, his gaze turning serious. "You always go after your dreams, sis. Have I mentioned that I'm proud to have you for a sister?"

"No, this is the first." Dar screwed up her face. "Actually, part of me is beaming from the praise, but another part of me is gagging, because it's coming from my brother."

"Oh, so that's how it is," Daniel said, sitting back. "You'd prefer I hurl insults at you."

"That's not what I meant, and you know it. Feel free to keep the compliments coming." Dar swung her hands toward herself as though taking it all in. "By the way, how's Knuckles working out as a stable hand?" She admired her brother for giving Knuckles a chance with the job, despite their previous clashes at the homeless shelter where Daniel had volunteered. He'd even covered Knuckles's mental health care expenses after the shelter refused him admittance due to his temper. Her brother was one-of-a-kind, but she worried others might take advantage of his big heart.

"Let's just say Knuckles is a work in progress," Daniel said. "Yesterday he was mucking the stalls and caught the edge of the door as he was pushing a wheelbarrow full of manure out of the barn. The whole load got dumped. In true Knuckles fashion, he punched the side of the wheelbarrow. I can't believe he didn't break his hand."

Dar's eyebrows arched up. "Are you sure about him? We'll have kids starting the program soon, and their safety needs to be our number one priority."

"I'm sure," Daniel said. He sounded a lot more confident than she felt. "You should see him around the horses. He's a different person when he's with them. Yesterday, I saw him feed an apple to Chestnut that he'd saved from his own lunch."

"Still, let's keep him away from the kids for now," Dar said, unable to shake the worry she felt, "and make sure he's supervised during sessions."

"Okay," Daniel conceded, "but I know he can do this."

They finished their lunches, each preoccupied with their own thoughts. Following lunch, they both left, saying their goodbyes at the parking lot. Daniel climbed into his car and left as Dar walked toward her car farther back in the lot.

A tingle crept up her spine, and she spun around to scan the lot. Walking back to the sidewalk, she surveyed both sides of the street. The lunch crowd had dwindled; no one stood outside the restaurant any longer. She searched the entrances of the businesses across the street, but there was no sign of the man in the camouflage hoodie.

Dar stared at the deserted street. A tingle shot up her spine again. Even though she had no proof, her instincts were screaming, and she couldn't ignore them. She was being watched.

CHAPTER NINE

Dar popped two antacids into her mouth before driving back to CCC. Lunch had not gone as expected, and Shawn's reaction to Mike's question about her moving into the Montgomery Farm Estate had left her stomach churning. She knew that he wouldn't ask her to stay in Reed; it wasn't his style, especially if he thought for a second that doing so would stand in the way of her dreams. But if they were going to be a couple, the choice needed to be a team effort; they needed to talk about it. Hoping she could catch him in his office, she could at least make sure they were okay, and try to find a time to talk.

She had just stepped out of the elevator onto the second floor when she heard someone call her name, then noticed Ava waving at her from the nurses' station.

"If you're looking for Dr. O'Reilly," Ava said, "he's in a meeting with the parents of one of his patients. It might be a while."

Dar thanked her, then decided that while she was there, she might as well pay a quick visit to a patient. She started down the hall to her left, but hadn't gone far before she heard a child moaning and the rattle of an IV pole. The sounds seemed to be coming from the last room on the right—Sarah's room.

Fearing the worst, Dar rushed to the room to see how she could help. But when she arrived, she stopped at the sight in front of her and stifled a laugh.

Sarah lay in bed, tugging at her hospital gown, which had become twisted around her thin body. It seemed to pose an impossible task for the young girl as her IV tubing further hindered each attempt. At last, she smoothed out the final bunch in her gown, only to discover that her whole backside was exposed.

"Ugh!" Sarah pounded her fist into the bed.

"Having a bad day?" Dar asked, trying not to smile.

"The worst," Sarah said. She pursed her mouth into a pout. "I hate these gowns." Sarah tugged again at the flimsy cotton material and tried to close the gap.

Dar stepped aside when Nurse Spike came to Sarah's room as well. Her scrubs held scattered prints of Mickey and Minnie, partially hidden by a pink sweater, and topped off by a stethoscope that hung around her neck. Dar greeted her as she approached Sarah's bedside.

"Did I hear someone complaining?" Spike asked. "Maybe what you need is a cellmate."

"What's a cellmate?" Sarah asked.

Spike coughed. "Roommate. I meant roommate. Maybe then you could complain to them instead of the nurses." Spike laughed, then wiggled a finger at Sarah. "Is there a problem today?"

"Ye-e-e-e-s!" Sarah said. "I hate this hospital gown, and I hate this hospital. Not you guys, just the stupid gown, the food, and the tests they keep running. Why did I have to go through so many tests again, just because I got dizzy?" She tugged at her hospital gown again. "Plus, I'm so far from the nurses' station this time, I can't hear the nurses talking about their families or anything. And if I ask for an orange Popsicle, it takes for-e-ver. I really, really, really want to go home and play with my friends."

"Good," Dar said. "That means you passed CCC's most important test, designed especially for ten-year-old girls like you. Isn't that right, Spike?"

Curious, Sarah looked at Spike. "What test is that?" she asked.

The corner of Spike's eyes crinkled, and she followed Dar's lead. "Oh, it's the one where we torture kids with annoying IVs, funky hospital gowns, and food that you would never eat at home. Then, when we think the patients can't take it anymore, we tell them that their TVs don't work, so their only entertainment option is to listen to me sing. By then, they're usually begging to go home."

Sarah giggled. "What happens if they don't?"

Spike checked Sarah's IV flow before answering. "Well, if anyone doesn't, then we know we have a super sick kid on our hands who is right where they need to be."

Sarah's face lit up. "So, since I begged to go home, does that mean I passed the test and can go home, for real?"

As Spike placed a thermometer near Sarah's forehead, Dar winked at Sarah. "You know Spike can't make promises," she said.

On cue, Spike bent down and whispered in Sarah's ear, "But it's looking good."

Sarah's face lit up. "This afternoon?" She put her hands together and pleaded using her best puppy dog eyes.

Dar and Spike laughed at the amateur starlet. "Maybe, but it's more likely you'll go home tomorrow," Spike said. "Your doctor should be in later to do another exam first."

"He can skip the exam," Sarah said. "I feel great!"

Spike smiled back at her. "That's what we like to hear, but remember, I can't make any promises. It'll be up to your doctor."

Dar saw the gleam in Sarah's eyes, certain that Sarah had interpreted Spike's words to mean that it was a done deal. Dar could hardly blame her.

"I'm sure your Uncle Mike can't wait to see you go home, too," Dar said. "I'm beginning to think you're his favorite niece, the way he talks about you all the time."

"I'm his ONLY niece," Sarah giggled.

Dar laughed at the spunky girl who meant the world to Detective Mike Shafer. "I've got to run," she told Sarah and Spike. Good luck with going home soon, Sarah. And good luck dealing with her until then, Spike." She grinned and waved goodbye to both. "I'll leave you two to figure it out."

CHAPTER TEN

Spike continued to fuss over Sarah after Dar left, fluffing her hospital pillow, finding her an extra blanket, and retrieving an orange Popsicle from one of the nearby refrigerators.

"All right, Miss Sarah," she said with her nose in the air. "Unless you need anything else, there are other patients who require my attention."

"I bet you don't like them half as much as me," Sarah said with an impish smile. Then she lowered her head and looked up at Spike, her lower lip protruding. "I wish you could stay in my room all the time."

"Oh, you're so bad," Spike said. "Do you think that's the first time a kid has tried those puppy dog eyes on me? It won't work. I'll be back to check on you later."

Spike winked, then spun around to leave, but froze when she reached the hallway. Sarah watched her from her bed, wondering if Spike had changed her mind. The nurse stood there with her eyes wide and her mouth open. The smile on her face had disappeared, replaced by a frown.

Spike glanced back at her with furrowed brows. Sarah frowned as well. Maybe Spike had gotten some bad news from the doctor. But then Sarah couldn't think of a single one of her doctors who was afraid to give her updates, no matter how bad the news.

Spike raised a quivering chin, clenched her teeth, and whispered to someone in the hall out of Sarah's view. A man's muscular arm reached out. He gripped Spike's upper arm so hard she rose up onto her toes. She tried to pull away, but the man only intensified his grip, speaking in a low voice.

Even though Sarah could tell he didn't want anyone to hear him, she could still hear anger in the man's voice from her hospital bed. He sounded madder than the hornets had when her dad bumped their nest while trimming a tree in their yard. But how could anyone be mad at Spike? Sarah knew it couldn't be one of the doctors. They would never be so mean.

Sarah felt her sweaty hands slip on her IV pole as she struggled to move it to reach her call button. But the pole caught on a thick white cord connected to one of the machines near her bed. She yanked on it, but instead of untangling it, the cord came unplugged from the wall and the entire pole came crashing down toward her. Throwing her legs to one side, she managed to dodge the pole as it slammed onto the bed. Again, she stretched for her call button, but the button remained out of reach. She heard the low growl of the man's voice getting louder now—and angrier. She hoped he didn't come in to see what all the noise was. Closing her eyes, she wished her mom and dad were there to make the mean man go away.

Sarah heard the man's gruff voice and Spike's shrieks, and pressed her hands against her ears to block out the sounds. Her heart started racing, but the machines attached to her were unplugged and didn't beep in response. A scream stuck in her throat as she uncovered her ears for an unbearable second to scramble beneath her blanket. Pulling her knees to her chest, she rocked, listening to the wild thumping of her heart, its pulse echoing in her ears. She wondered if her heart, the one she'd insisted was fine, would survive—if she would survive.

Huddling tighter into herself, Sarah pressed her hands even harder against her ears. She had no concept of time passing, only an intense desire to be safe, to have her mom and dad by her side. But as more time passed, she began to wonder if Nurse Spike was okay. She tried to move so she could check on her, but her body refused, curling up like one of the roly-poly bugs she'd once found under a rock. Another minute passed, then another. Finally, she forced her hands from her ears and strained to hear the slightest sound, but the pounding of her heart was too loud in her ears. Sarah mustered every ounce of courage she possessed, then took a deep breath. Trembling from head to toe, she inched the covers up and peeked out.

CHAPTER ELEVEN

Dar couldn't believe she'd forgotten girls' night out, even though she'd been looking forward to it all week. After she'd returned to her home, she'd taken Merlin for a walk before tackling some long overdue cleaning and laundry. She kept mulling over the few details she knew about Mr. Reece's murder, but she'd been getting nowhere. That's when LaVon's text popped up, followed by Mo's, both saying, "See you tonight!"

She checked the time on her phone and sighed. Garnering a boost of caffeine from a soda, she showered in record time, threw on jeans and her favorite T-shirt, then collected Merlin, her jacket, and purse before rushing out to her car.

Ten minutes later, she pulled onto the lane leading to Shawn's farmhouse. The farmhouse sat adjacent to The Contented Canine, separated only by a field that contained remnants of corn stalks from last fall's harvest, waiting to be plowed under for the spring planting.

Dar glanced at the time. She hated being late. Shawn's grandmother, Ethel, had been kind enough to invite Merlin over for a play date with Buddy when she'd heard Dar mention a girl's night out, even volunteering to keep Merlin overnight. Shawn's dog and Merlin got along as though they'd known each other since pups, so she knew Merlin would not miss her at all for the evening.

Pulling up to the house, Dar saw Ethel standing at the door, ready to greet them. Dar hurried to her, and Ethel welcomed her with a warm hug, then bent to greet Merlin. Dar apologized for her tardiness, but Ethel waved it off, as though it were a dusting of flour on her kitchen counter. When Ethel insisted Dar take her time picking Merlin up in the morning, Dar thanked her and threw her arms around the sweet woman, who smelled of cookies and muffins. Her stomach rumbled with hunger, reminding her that she was still running late.

Dar left the farmhouse and sped downtown, finding a rare parking spot on the street. As she stood at the stoplight, she looked across the street at CCC's parking garage and was surprised to see neither LaVon nor Mo waiting for her on the sidewalk in front of it. But as she crossed the street, LaVon turned the corner and was walking toward her. Dar detected an extra spring in her friend's step as she approached CCC's parking garage entrance.

The parking garage was their designated meeting spot for girls' night out, which usually consisted of either pizza or Mexican food. Tonight, it was the latter. It'd been LaVon's idea to keep it totally casual—old jeans and T-shirts—to which Mo and Dar had readily agreed.

But the expensive jeans and crisp white jacket over a royal blue silk blouse that LaVon was wearing tonight didn't fit that agreement. And although Dar had offered to pick her up after dropping Merlin at Ethel's, LaVon had declined, saying she'd meet her and Mo at the garage.

Dar joined LaVon on the sidewalk and gave her friend a broad smile. This was going to be fun.

"Hi. I hope you weren't waiting long," Dar said.

"Nope. I just got here myself. Mo should be out soon."

Dar circled LaVon, who spun around with her. "You look exceptionally glowing tonight," Dar said with a grin. LaVon narrowed her eyes in response.

Dar waited for a retort from LaVon but when she got none, added, "Okay, who are you, and what have you done with my friend? And why did you just get here when you told me you left The Contented Canine two hours ago?"

LaVon shrugged her shoulders. "This is where Mo said to meet her, right?"

"Don't change the subject." Dar sniffed. "Do I smell cologne?" A smug smile crossed her face. After all the ribbing LaVon had given her about dating Shawn, there was no way she was going to let LaVon off the hook. "Could it possibly be the same cologne that a certain Dr. Darius Williams wears? I'm guessing his animal patients aren't the only ones who follow the good vet around."

"Fine," LaVon said with an eye roll. "You're such a snoop. If you must know, I stopped by his place after work to see his new puppy."

"Uh-huh. And did you wear the puppy costume you bought last year as a mascot for The Contented Canine so he could take care of you too?"

"You're really enjoying this, aren't you?" LaVon said, crossing her arms. Spotting Mo, she flagged her down. "Thank God you're here, Mo. Let's go. Tonight, the first round of margaritas is on Dar."

Dar nodded, unable to keep the grin from her face. "It was so worth it."

Mo looked from one to the other. "Clearly I missed something, but let's talk about it over those margaritas and dinner. I'm starved!"

"Me too," Dar said. "I'm glad the restaurant's only a three-block walk. Let's go."

The cool air brushed across Dar's cheeks as she stepped in stride with her friends. She loved their girls' nights. They had so much to catch up on, especially laughs, and with Mo and LaVon, that was never a problem.

They passed an easy banter between them, preferring to reserve their confidential stories until after the first margarita or two. The mild early evening weather had cooperated as well, adding to what promised to be a perfect girls' night out. But a block from the restaurant, Dar noticed something unusual.

"Just a sec," she said, holding up a finger to her friends as they neared an alley. "What is that doing here?"

Her question was met with protests from LaVon and Mo, who reminded Dar how hungry they were and that the restaurant was less than a block away. They suggested they could stop back after they'd eaten.

But Dar ignored their protests and entered the encroaching darkness of the alley anyway. Immediately her nose was assaulted by the overwhelming odor of competing foul smells: rotting food, urine, mold, along with a few smells she didn't care to know. She stepped from the sunshine into the shadows, pausing long enough to allow her eyes to adjust. A mistake she regretted.

Filthy debris from overflowing dumpsters littered the length of the alley, the rusted containers staggered against brick buildings that formed the alley's sides. And laying on the ground, in stark contrast to it all, was a white shoe. Dar squatted down to get a closer look. Mo and LaVon caught up to her and peered over her shoulder.

"Hey," Mo said. "That looks like a nurse's shoe. I think half the nurses at CCC wear those, including me. But what's it doing here? It doesn't look that old."

Dar couldn't think of a single good reason. She turned the shoe over.

"What are those brown spots on the side?" LaVon asked.

"It looks like dried blood," Dar said with a frown. "Maybe we should check to see if the owner of this shoe is in the alley. If she's hurt, you could help her, Mo."

"I'm not sure that's a good idea," LaVon said, taking a step back. "If you really think it's blood, then we should call the police."

Mo examined the brown spots closer. "It looks like dried blood to me," she said, "but we can't call the police yet. What would we tell them? Hey, I found a shoe that might have blood on it, but there's no body to go with it."

"I guess you're right," LaVon said.

"I'm sorry," Mo said, "but if there's a nurse in this alley who's hurt, I've got to see if I can help her."

"Fine," LaVon said. "But remember I was the one who told you this was a bad idea."

"Great," Mo said. But when she peered into the dark alley, she shoved Dar in front of her. "You lead."

"Gee, thanks," Dar said.

She led her two friends farther into the darkness, shivering at the sudden drop in temperature. The fading sunlight, along with its warmth, was blocked by the three-story buildings that formed the sides of the alley.

"Let's hurry," Mo said. "It's cold back here." She wrapped her lightweight cardigan sweater around her, pulling it closer to her body.

Dar squinted into the darkness, then turned on her flashlight app, sweeping the beam back and forth across the alley, highlighting piles of trash. They passed three well-used dumpsters without seeing another white shoe or a person. Dar thought it was like looking for Cinderella, but in a creepy kind of way.

She shone the beam of light farther ahead, illuminating a worn brick building where the alley came to a dead end. That left two more dumpsters, one on each side, left to clear.

Dar focused the light on the dumpster to her right first. A white object near a stack of half-rotted crates seemed to sprout from the moldy garbage. It reminded her of the mushrooms behind The Contented Canine, pushing above the layers of decayed leaves. But unlike the mushrooms, this was an unnatural urban decay.

She moved closer to investigate, then wished she hadn't. The white object was another shoe. Just like the first one they'd found.

LaVon peered over Dar's shoulder at the shoe. "Oh, hell no," she said. She took several steps backward, shaking her head.

The beam of light quivered in Dar's hand. She gasped at the dark blood covering the top of the once-white shoe, and the streaks down the sides from where it had spilled over.

"Oh shit," Mo said. "Maybe it's time to call the police."

"But we still haven't found the person these belong to," Dar said. "We're almost to the end of the alley. We can call the police when we've finished our search. After all, what if the person who wore this shoe is still here? If they're hurt, Mo can help them while we get an ambulance."

LaVon moaned. "Are you serious?" When Dar nodded, she moaned again, shifting from one foot to the other.

Mo blinked. She studied the ground in front of her as though the answer was written in the dirt. "I know too many nurses who wear shoes like these. We have to do this."

Dar began to move her flashlight along the ground, working outward from where the shoe lay on the ground. She'd only gone a short distance when her light reflected off a trail of blood. It led to the last rusted-out dumpster at the end of the alley. Piles of garbage bags had tumbled out of it and split wide open, their putrid contents splayed across the ground.

With Mo and LaVon close behind her, she continued to search, stopping as the beam shone on a collection of garbage bags along the far side of the dumpster. They seemed oddly out of place in the cluttered alley. Unlike the rest of the bags, which had been slung haphazardly in the vicinity of the dumpsters, these eight bags were lined up neatly in two rows, each row stacked directly above the other. Four bags made up the top row, their dark plastic openings gathered with wire twists.

Dar retrieved a couple tissues from her pocket.

"I don't think those are going to help much with the stench," LaVon said.

"Not what I had in mind," she said. "Mo, hold my phone and shine the light toward these bags." She pointed toward the tidy rows of bags.

Dar handed her phone to Mo, whose hands were trembling so much that, for a split second, Dar thought she'd set it on vibrate. The tissues felt damp from her sweaty hands as she used them to grab one of the carefully placed bags. She held it at arm's length, then gingerly moved it to the side. When she lifted the next two bags, she gagged as the putrid smell intensified. She could hear LaVon gagging behind her too, but she didn't dare turn around for fear of heaving.

"I've gotta say, I've smelled some pretty bad shit as a nurse," Mo said, "but this is by far the worst. And if you two don't stop gagging, I'm going to lose it."

Dar retrieved fresh tissues from her pocket and tore off small pieces, wadding them up and shoving a wad up each nostril. Though the foul smell still penetrated the tissues, it blocked the odor enough to allow her to reach for a bag off the second row. Like the top row, these bags were also crammed together neatly.

"Anyone else think this is strange?" Dar asked.

Mo nodded. For once, she was speechless.

LaVon squirmed and began pacing. "I don't hear anyone calling for help, or see anyone in need of an ambulance. Maybe we should leave."

Dar looked at Mo for a majority rule.

"Go ahead," Mo said solemnly.

Dar looked at LaVon, hoping for a unanimous vote, but her friend paced again, crossing her arms. Dar and Mo waited until she stopped.

"Fine. Go ahead," LaVon said, "but I've got a nasty feeling that we won't be needing that ambulance." Mo and Dar said nothing.

More than anything, Dar wanted to take a deep breath to steady her nerves, but she knew she'd only be filling her lungs with a stench so powerful she'd be unable to continue. Instead, she reached for another bag of garbage, but as she began to pull it away, two of the remaining bags shifted apart. Fabric with cheerful Disney characters on it poked out from between them. Dar felt her stomach churn.

Her world moved as though in slow motion. Turning around, she gave Mo a pointed look.

"I work with a lot of nurses who wear those scrubs." Mo clutched her chest and squeezed her eyes shut. Dar and LaVon feared she was having a heart attack, but within seconds Mo opened them again. "I have to know if it's one of them."

Dar nodded, and LaVon looped an arm through Mo's, the two supporting each other for whatever they were about to see. Then, as though disabling a bomb, Dar reached for the two remaining garbage bags. Bracing herself, she lifted them.

Dar gasped at the gruesome sight, sucking in the fetid air. A scream caught in her throat, as though to allow its release would be to allow the harsh reality in. She could only stare at the two shoeless feet. Though socks covered them, their color was no longer visible through the dried blood. Scrubs, intended to be a cheerful distraction for children, were also soaked in the brownish-red blood that seemed to be everywhere. And over the woman's face lay a sweater. Like the socks, it was hard to make out the color. Dar fought the bile rising in her throat.

"I'll call 911," she said.

The blood drained from Mo's face, and she staggered. Dar reached to help her, but Mo shook her head. Then, in a raw voice, she said, "I have . . . to see . . . her face."

"Mo," Dar said. "Are you sure? We can let the police identify her."

Mo edged closer, shaking. She bit one corner of her lip. "I'm sure," she said.

"We've gone this far," LaVon said. She touched Mo's arm, then pulled out a handful of tissues from her purse and thrust them into Dar's hand before taking several steps back and closing her eyes.

They were making a disaster of what would be considered a crime scene, but all they could think about was that this was probably someone they knew. And that person had been the victim of some horrendous murder. It only felt right that they should be the ones to identify her, rather than a police officer with no connection to her.

Dar felt both hot and cold at once, and her mouth went dry, as though she'd indulged in too many glasses of wine the night before. Flies buzzed around her head and around the body in front of her, searching for the ideal place to lay their eggs. Dar swatted them away with the full force of her frustration and anger.

She tried to calm herself. Then using the tissues again, she eased the darkened sweater back. Her face crumpled. She sat back hard onto the filthy ground, finding it hard to breathe.

Who could do such a thing? Maybe that monster is watching us now, Dar thought. A scuffling noise came from behind her. Fear clenched at her heart, freezing her reflexes, though her mind raced with rapid-fire questions. *Is it the killer? Has he returned to the scene of the crime? Will he murder us just like he murdered this poor woman?*

Dar jerked her head around as Mo slumped to the ground with a thud.

CHAPTER TWELVE

Dar took a step back from Detective Mike Shafer, whose red face reminded her of an over-inflated balloon about to burst. Even with the sirens wailing in the background, she had no trouble hearing his words or deciphering their meaning.

"This crime scene has been contaminated, thanks to all of you!" Mike shouted, causing bright red splotches to appear on his neck as well. "You should have called 911 the second you found the bloody shoe. Now your footprints are everywhere, making it next to impossible to find those belonging to the killer, unless one of you would like to confess."

Silence.

"Uh-huh," Mike said. "And what were you thinking—touching and moving everything from the victim's shoes, to the bags, and even the sweater covering the victim's face?" His rage had shifted into full gear by now. "Trust me, since the three of you have seen fit to be your own damn detectives, you'd better be prepared to be grilled with questions!"

Feeling like a scolded child, Dar cringed as Mike continued to rant after Mo and LaVon left with the paramedics. She tried not to focus on his anger, no matter how well justified, but stared past him, half tuning him out.

She spotted Mo on the back step of an ambulance, holding a bag of ice to the back of her head, her eyes puffy from crying. Physically, she'd be okay, thanks to a bag of garbage that had broken her fall when she'd fainted. The bag had split open on impact, surrounding Mo with fetid scraps of old food and containers. Her head, though, had landed on a container made of hard plastic, giving Mo a nice goose egg. On the plus side, the stench had worked quicker to revive her than any smelling salts ever could. Emotionally, though . . . Dar knew it would take time to get over the gruesome murder of one of her colleagues.

Dar saw Mo give her a heartfelt look. Apparently, she had no problem hearing Mike's rantings, along with everyone within a block radius, and she mouthed the word "sorry" to Dar.

Continuing to avoid eye contact with Mike, Dar searched for LaVon next. She was relieved to see her sitting on a nearby curb with a blanket over her shoulders, taking sips from a water bottle, and appearing stronger than she had minutes earlier. Not surprisingly, she, too, had heard Mike's booming voice. Dar could read her lips mouth the word "sorry" as well. *Friends*, Dar thought. She felt conflicted, wanting to hug them, comfort them from this nightmare they'd shared, but also wanting to smack them for abandoning her with Mike.

She looked back at Mike, who had an angry scowl fixed on his face, and was waiting for a response to his question. She stuttered, having no clue what he'd asked, but then a woman from the forensics team approached, saving her from further humiliation.

"Sorry to interrupt," the woman said. "You asked me to update you if I found anything unusual."

"And?" Mike snapped, obviously still on a short fuse.

"We found stomach contents on the side of one of the nearby dumpsters," she said. "I did a quick check of the victim's mouth, and I don't think the contents came from her. Maybe our killer had a bit of remorse for what he'd done?"

"That's good," Mike said. "Collect a sample and see what you can learn about our killer."

"Um, actually, that won't be necessary," Dar said. She tried to fake a smile, but it came out as a sheepish grin. "You know how everyone responds to shock differently?" She dropped her head, and they all stared at the spatters on her shoes.

Mike threw his hands in the air. "I don't suppose any one of you three ladies at least know the name of the victim?"

Dar nodded. "Everyone at CCC knew her as Spike, but I think her name is, er was, Myra." Her mind felt foggy as she tried in vain to remember more. "I forget her last name, but Mo probably knows. Go easy on her, Mike. This was someone she worked with on a regular basis."

"Shit," Mike said, rubbing his neck. "I still need to get details from the three of you, and it can't wait. Meet me at Merv's Diner on High Street in half an hour. It's near the police station. I'll finish up here then join you. This is not a request. Be there."

Dar headed toward the street, but she couldn't help but glance back at the crime scene, where she knew Spike's body still lay. The image of the nurse's body, all the blood, popped into her head, and guilt threatened to overtake her.

This was all her fault. She wished she could turn back time.

***

Merv's Diner was an unassuming restaurant with typical grill fare and strong coffee. Two couples sat near the front, so Dar asked to be seated at a booth away from them.

As Dar scooted into a booth near the back, she felt the weight of all she'd seen that night settle into her shoulders, head, and neck. It was as though her entire body was about to cave in on itself. Every ounce of her being wanted to go home, stand under a stream of hot water, then curl up in bed with the comforter over her head. She would pretend that tonight had been nothing more than a nightmare, and she would choose more pleasant dreams as she drifted off to sleep.

LaVon and Mo joined her, looking equally glum as they slid into the booth. A waitress appeared and took their orders of coffee and sandwiches, leaving all three sitting in silence until she was back with their food.

Dar felt sick at how her highly anticipated girls' night out had turned into a disaster before the night had even begun. If only she had listened to her friends' initial protests, if she hadn't entered the alley, she could have spared them from the horror they'd seen. If she had, they'd have spent the evening laughing at each other's stories and drinking margaritas, not this.

But then, who knows how long Spike's body might have lain hidden beneath those garbage bags before being found? She couldn't believe that someone had so brutally murdered such a kind-hearted nurse. Dar kept seeing Spike's milky eyes staring back at her. She slid her sandwich back.

Mike arrived and ordered a coffee. He studied each of their ashen faces as he sipped it, then sighed. "I'm sorry about yelling at you back there," he said. "And I'm sorry about your coworker, Mo." He paused. "Still, you've made my job of catching whoever did this that much harder. That being said, I'm going to need your full cooperation."

Silently, each nodded ascent, and Mike continued his inquiry. "Let's start with as many details as you can recall, beginning with when and where you all met tonight, up until I arrived."

Together, Dar, Mo, and LaVon filled in details of their night, beginning with their meeting outside the CCC parking garage. When Mo and LaVon told him how Dar carefully removed the bags with tissues, Dar saw a vein in Mike's neck swell, but he stayed silent.

Mo told Mike she thought that she could help if someone had been hurt, but once they'd seen the scrubs, they were desperate to confirm whether or not it was someone they knew.

There was silence when they finished speaking.

Mike paused a beat, then moved on. "How well did each of you know the victim?"

"Not at all," LaVon answered.

Dar dropped her eyes to the table, so Mo went next. "Her real name is . . . was Myra Evans, but everyone called her Spike because of her hair. I worked with her at CCC. I float to different floors, but I was assigned to her floor often. I didn't really know her outside of work, but what I do know is that the kids loved her. She was a responsible and compassionate nurse, and seemed to get along with everyone—staff, patients, and their parents. And trust me, that isn't always easy."

Mike spoke to Dar. "What about you? Did you know her?"

"A little." Dar shook her head as tears rolled down her cheeks. "This is all my fault."

Mo and LaVon gaped at her.

Mike leaned forward. "Exactly how was the death of Myra Evans, aka Spike, your fault?"

At the same time, LaVon asked, "What are you talking about?"

Tiny stars danced in Dar's vision. She felt like she might slither down the booth's seat and onto the floor beneath the table at any moment. She'd prefer it to facing Mike, who was scowling again and demanding an explanation. But how could she explain it? Her pulse raced as she searched out objects one by one to calm her breathing.

LaVon hugged Dar. "Maybe you need to eat some of your sandwich. Your face has gone three shades whiter than usual. We know you couldn't hurt anyone. Unless, of course, that person was trying to kill you."

Mo added, "Mike already knows Dar can defend herself. Besides, Spike was already dead when we found her."

Dar shook her head. "Please stop talking. Both of you. You're not helping." She knew they were referring to past attempts on her life, but it felt as though they were confirming what she felt—that she'd deliberately killed Spike herself.

Mike's nostrils flared as he pressed his lips into a thin line. "Okay. Then suppose you tell us how this is your fault."

Dar's words tumbled out. "I should've insisted. I should've made Spike understand what she needed to do."

"Insisted what? Made her understand what exactly?" Mike said, the vein in his neck about to burst.

Dar chewed on a fingernail. When she finally spoke, her words came out fast, and she found it impossible to control her remorse. Her voice quivered. "I should've insisted that she file a police report on Bruno yesterday, or at least done it myself. But she was so scared he'd retaliate that she begged me not to do it. If I had, maybe none of this would've happened. Maybe she wouldn't have been killed and left in that alley like garbage. She didn't deserve that."

Dar hid her shaking hands in her lap.

"Whoa, back up," Mike said. "Are you saying Spike had an altercation with this Bruno guy yesterday?"

"Yes," she said. "And I could've—*should've*—prevented this from happening."

Mike rubbed the pulsing vein at his temple.

"How did I not hear about this?" Mo asked.

Dar summarized Bruno Rossi's unwelcome visit to CCC and his confrontation with Spike. Mo was quiet. LaVon's mouth hung open, but after the initial shock, she switched to annoyed. "Why didn't you tell me? Does Shawn know? How do you manage to end up in the middle of chaos like this?"

"I didn't tell you because I thought that was the end of it. And yes, Shawn knows. You could say he wasn't too happy about me jumping into an argument, even if it was to defend Spike from a bully." She shrugged her shoulders. "And as for ending up in the middle of chaos, it's like Mike said before, it just seems to find me."

"Why didn't you tell me all this when I spoke to you yesterday?" Mike asked.

"Spike didn't want the incident reported. Besides, it was all I could do to answer your questions about Mr. Reece's murder," she said.

Mike puffed out his cheeks, then exhaled. "I'll issue an APB on Bruno Rossi. One more question. You didn't say which floor of the hospital this altercation took place on."

"Second floor. Same as Shawn's office. It's why. . ."

Mike interrupted her, alarm evident in his voice. "That's the floor Sarah's on." Grabbing his phone, he was soon barking orders for extra police protection on the second floor at CCC. Next, he called his sister, Jackie. Feigning a calm voice, he said, "Hi, sis. Just calling to see how Sarah's doing. You brought her home? That's fantastic!" Mike let out a sigh of relief.

But as Mike continued to listen to his sister, the smile he'd displayed moments earlier vanished. Deep furrowed lines formed across his brow.

Dar wondered what disturbing news his sister had for him. They'd all had enough bad news for one day. She leaned toward Mike, trying to eavesdrop, but her movement caught his attention, and he quickly pulled away. She watched with concern as he hurried outside to speak in private.

When he returned, she said, "Sorry, I didn't mean to pry. Is everything okay?"

"No," Mike said, making no attempt to explain. "I have to go." He withdrew a couple bills from his wallet, then stared at them as though in a trance before he crumpled them up in his fist. He then blinked, threw the wadded bills onto the table, and without another word, rushed out the door.

CHAPTER THIRTEEN

Two murders. Both employees of CCC. No suspect in custody. Ruminating on those three facts, Dar feared for Shawn's safety. CCC was the common denominator in both murders, and because of that, her nerves were on edge. She had to see with her own eyes that Shawn was okay. He usually worked late on the days when he had a new patient admitted in critical condition, so she was apt to find him at the hospital.

She made an excuse to leave Merv's Diner, telling her friends that she needed to pick up Merlin from Ethel. It wasn't exactly a lie. She did need to pick up Merlin, just not until morning.

Dar hugged her friends before leaving. They each promised a raincheck on their girls' night out, but no one suggested a date. Dar suspected they felt as she did; they had no desire to repeat anything too soon that would remind them of this night.

***

Dar's mind shuffled from bad- to worst-case scenarios for Shawn as she drove back to CCC. Maybe whatever Shawn was trying to remember from Mr. Reece's office the morning he'd found him dead was a clue. If so, did the killer suspect Shawn knew something? If he did, Dar feared Shawn could be in grave danger.

Though Bruno was at the top of everyone's suspect list for Spike's murder, Dar didn't want to rule out the possibility that it could be someone else. The killer could even be a disgruntled parent of a patient who was targeting CCC employees at random. She'd heard stories from Shawn and Mo about parents who'd lost their tempers and exploded in verbal rages under the stress of nearly losing a child. But she'd never heard of anyone getting physical.

Another alarming thought occurred to her. Had she mentioned Shawn's name when telling Bruno that security had been called? Though she tried to replay the whole scene of Bruno harassing Spike, that detail eluded her.

Dar didn't see the downed parking gate arm until it was directly in front of her. Slamming on the brakes, she managed to miss it by mere inches. She sucked in air and froze with both of her hands glued to the steering wheel.

She sat like that for a moment before she exhaled, then scanned her volunteer pass and drove past the gate. When she found Shawn's reserved parking spot on the second level, she was relieved to see his vintage mustang there. She pulled into a nearby spot and parked, then hurried to the elevator.

Arriving at the second floor, she rushed toward Shawn's office, but her heart sank when she didn't find him there. Stacks of papers, medical journals, and sticky notes remained scattered about on his desk, yet she knew Shawn often dashed out without tidying up.

She went behind his desk to check his computer, but he had logged out. At first, she thought that meant he'd gone home, but then she remembered him telling her that he was in a habit of logging out of his networked computer whenever he left his office due to the confidentiality of patient charts stored there. He also would've locked his office door before going home, so he must be in the building—but where?

Dar hurried down to the nurses' station. One of the nurses who worked closely with Shawn's most serious cardiac patients was sitting behind the desk.

"Kim, hi. Do you know if Shawn is still here?" she asked.

"I'm sorry, Dar," she said. "You missed him by at least half an hour."

"Did he say where he was going?"

"No. He usually stops at our desk to chat before leaving, but tonight we only got a wave from him as he passed. Is everything okay?"

"I hope so," Dar said.

She tried Shawn's cell, hoping that she'd somehow missed him while in the elevator, but it went straight to voicemail. After leaving a message for him to call her, she began to wonder where he could be, especially if he'd left that long ago and his car was still in the parking garage.

Rushing down the hall to the elevator, she stepped in and repeatedly pounded the button for the parking garage level. Muzak played inside the slow-moving elevator, and she couldn't decide which annoyed her the most. In fact, it was how she imagined hell to be; trapped alone in a non-stop elevator that inched along, while forced to listen to a single Muzak song on a continuous loop. Dar waited for what felt like an eternity as she chewed on her last fingernail, the sole survivor of a life-long habit. At last, the digital red numeral "2" changed from a "1" to a "P." Not waiting for the elevator doors to completely open, she squeezed between them and exited the elevator.

An image of Shawn lying dead, his body discarded in some deserted location, flashed through her mind. Why hadn't she called him instead of trying to see him in person? She tried his cell phone again, but again, it went straight to voicemail. Leaving a second message, she could hear the desperation in her voice.

Uncertain what to do, she called Mike but got his voicemail as well. "Mike, this is Dar. I'm at CCC, and I'm worried Shawn might be missing. His car is still in the hospital parking garage, but his nurse said he left at least a half hour ago. He's not answering any of my calls, either. Call me."

Next, she called LaVon, who had planned to give Mo a ride back to her car in the parking garage. After explaining the situation, Dar asked her to stay on the phone while she checked out Shawn's car.

"I'm giving the phone to Mo so I can drive. Stay put. We're getting in the car now."

Dar couldn't wait. She approached Shawn's parking spot, but she strained to see clearly in the dim lights. As she got closer, she could make out the outline of a figure in his car. It didn't move, and the head was tilted in an odd position, facing away from her. Dar stopped. Her heart jack-hammered in her chest and ears. If it was Shawn, why wasn't he answering his phone? Then the figure moved.

Dar's mind raced. Was this the murderer waiting for Shawn to return to his car, or had Shawn already returned and been shoved into the trunk, or worse?

The car door latch clicked, and Dar screamed, the sound echoing throughout the garage. She whirled around, dropping her phone in the process. She tried to run, but her legs didn't seem to get the message, and then it was too late. Two arms clamped around her from behind, pinning her arms to her sides.

Everything happened at once, blurred together like a carnival ride that spins faster and faster until you realize you're about to be sick. Her stomach churned. The air from her lungs escaped and refused to return as she panicked.

Unable to breathe, unable to scream, she was at the killer's mercy.

Through her hazy vision, she thought she saw two police officers with their guns drawn and aimed directly at her. No. They were aimed behind her. She prayed they wouldn't miss.

CHAPTER FOURTEEN

"What the hell?" Dar heard the voice behind her say as her pinned arms and chest were released, sending her into coughing spasms. While one officer kept his gun on his target, his partner approached with a set of handcuffs, walking past Dar. She spun around to see her assailant, ready to bombard him with questions as to what he'd done with Shawn, but the words dried up in her throat, and she could only stare in confusion at the man behind her.

A bungled mess didn't begin to describe the situation. More than anything, she wanted to reboot her life, or better yet, start over as someone else. Even falling into a deep coma for a few years was preferential to this.

The officer snapped a cuff on first one wrist, then the other. The man furrowed his brows, his blue eyes darting about the parking garage. With his hands cuffed securely behind his back, he finally looked at Dar, his blue eyes now tinged with flaming flecks of red-hot rage.

She opened her mouth to speak, but again words failed her, and her jaw fell slack.

"Are you okay, ma'am? Did he hurt you?" The officer was scanning her for signs of injury. When Dar shook her head no, he spoke into his mic. "Suspect in custody, and victim seems unharmed. Detective Shafer has been notified, as requested."

Dar tried to process it all. When her brain caught up with the present, she wished it hadn't. There was no life reboot, no coma, only a strong desire to vanish. She swallowed, but the lump in her throat made her cough again, delaying the inevitable reality—and Shawn.

"I-I'm fine," she sputtered. "But you need to uncuff him. He did nothing wrong. I'm the one responsible for this mess."

The officer stared at her in disbelief while Shawn's face grew redder by the second and contorted into a glare aimed directly at her. He appeared every bit the hardened criminal that she'd mistaken him for earlier, and she squirmed now, regretting that she'd asked the officer to remove his handcuffs.

A second car sped through the parking garage, its tires squealing until it came to a halt next to the squad car. Mike jumped out of it, gun in hand. Another car followed close behind him and came to a grinding halt alongside Mike's vehicle. LaVon and Mo both clambered out, despite Mike's motions demanding them to stay put. He scowled, then refocused his attention on the officer who had Shawn's wrists firmly shackled behind his back.

"Would someone care to fill me in on what's going on?" Mike bellowed. "And why the hell do you have Dr. O'Reilly in handcuffs? Where's our suspect?"

"Yes, sir." It was the officer's turn to look confused. "This is our suspect. I was patrolling the hospital parking garage, as you instructed, when I heard a woman scream. When I arrived on the scene, I found this man grabbing her from behind."

"Put your guns away," Mike said. "I can vouch for this man. Get those handcuffs off him, then you can leave. I'll handle this." His jaw clenched and unclenched as Shawn's handcuffs were removed. When the patrol car had exited the parking garage, he turned to Dar. "How in the hell did this happen?"

But before she could answer, LaVon and Mo had already pounced on Shawn and Dar, asking both if they were okay. LaVon hugged Dar, then smacked her in the arm. "I told you to stay put and wait for us."

"Yeah," Mo added, "when I heard your phone drop and your blood-curdling scream . . ." Mo waved her arms in frustration. "Well, you can only imagine what I imagined."

LaVon raised her eyebrows, then crossed her arms. "What she said, only better."

Mike interrupted them, his pointer finger aiming with rapid-fire movement at Mo and Lavon. "I need the two of you to shut up." Then he pointed his finger at Dar. "You, start talking. I want an explanation, and I want it now."

"I'd love to hear this, too," Shawn added. He rubbed his wrists where the cuffs had been too tight, then took a step back from Dar.

Mike glared at Shawn, who fell silent.

Dar scrunched up her face, plastering a fake smile on it. She knew it was cheesy, but she wanted them to see that it was all a silly mistake.

"A coworker was murdered, Shawn," Dar said, "and I had to see you in person tonight to know you were okay."

She glanced at Shawn to see if any of the heat had left his face yet. It hadn't. She gulped and began rambling.

"I saw your car in the parking garage, so I went to your office, but you weren't there. Then the nurse at the desk said you'd left a half hour ago. And when your phone went straight to voicemail, I couldn't help but think the worst. I was afraid the murderer had gotten to you, too. That's when I decided to check your car again." Dar left out the part about her fearing he might be lying dead in the trunk of his car. No need to give everyone any more reason to think she was hysterical.

"When I got off the elevator and walked toward your car, I saw the outline of someone inside with their head at a funny angle. At first, I thought it might be you, but then I remembered you hadn't been answering your phone. When the person moved, I thought it had to be the killer. I thought he'd murdered you and was trying to hot wire your car to make a quick getaway. Among other things," she muttered under her breath.

Heat spread up Dar's neck to her face as everyone stared at her, and she began to chew on a fingernail. Hearing her thoughts spoken out loud, she felt like the biggest idiot.

"So that's why you tried to run when I opened the car door," Shawn said. "When I heard you let out that banshee wail, I threw my arms around you to stop you and make sure you were okay. But before I could say a word, two officers showed up, pointing their guns at me. The next thing I knew I was wearing a set of handcuffs that were a size too small." He rubbed his wrists.

Dar's forehead wrinkled. "Why didn't you answer your phone?"

"Don't try to turn this around on me," he said. "I had an exhausting day and one of my patients nearly died on the operating table. I needed a few minutes of peace and quiet before I went back to my office. But as soon as I sat down in my car, the stress of the day caught up with me. I put my phone on mute and must've dozed off until all hell broke loose."

"Oh." So that explained the odd angle of his head. Dar placed a hand over her heart. "I'm so sorry."

Shawn ran a hand through his hair. "I'm definitely awake now."

Dar tried to approach him. "I really am sorry, Shawn." He stepped away from her.

"We're just glad you're both okay," LaVon said.

"And at least we know security is quick to respond, thanks to Mike," Mo added.

"Yeah, that's great," Mike said. "I really appreciate the practice run, not to mention the shitload of additional paperwork I get to fill out now on top of trying to solve two homicides."

"Two?" Shawn asked. "When you said a coworker was murdered, I thought you were still talking about Mr. Reece. There was another?"

"We found Spike's body in an alley tonight," Mo said.

Shawn was speechless. He shook his head and looked at Dar with eyes that reflected his exhausting day.

"I'll tell you about it later," she said.

"Tomorrow," he said. "I've had enough stress for one day, and I still have some work to finish before I can leave. After that, all I want to do is go home and get some sleep." Then he gave a piercing look at Dar. "That is, if it's okay with you. I wouldn't want you calling the police again." And with that, he turned and walked back toward the hospital.

Dar watched him leave, a knot forming in her stomach. She'd made a mess of everything. If she thought she'd been afraid to have a serious conversation with him before, tonight had made it nearly impossible.

The whole incident got her thinking about what Mo had said about security. "Spike could've been attacked anywhere between the hospital and the alley we found her in, but after tonight, I doubt it happened in the parking garage," she said to Mike. "Other people would have seen or heard something."

"That depends on a number of things," he said.

But Mo jumped in, ignoring his comment. "So maybe she wasn't assaulted here. Maybe it was between the parking garage and her bus stop. It could have been either a stranger..."

"Or someone who knew her routine," Dar said, finishing her sentence. The same fear she'd had shortly after learning of Mr. Reece's death circled back to the forefront of her mind. What if she, too, had met the victims' killers? Or worse, what if it was someone she knew?

CHAPTER FIFTEEN

On Monday morning, Dar woke with a determination to put one foot in front of the other. Ethel had called Saturday and asked to keep Merlin an extra day since he and Buddy were getting along so well, and Dar agreed without hesitation. Feeling like one of the smash burgers she'd seen grilled by a local chef, she took the remainder of her weekend to lie in bed. She'd needed it. After waking to a new week, she showered, dressed, then drove to the farmhouse to pick up Merlin. It did her heart good to see Ethel's smiling face, and she hugged her a little longer than usual. Ethel eyed her curiously, but said nothing. Dar turned her attention to the dogs, avoiding any questions about news of a second murder connected with CCC or the fiasco with Shawn. If Ethel knew about either, she didn't let on. As she brushed her hand over Merlin's soft coat of fur, she smiled at the thought of having him by her side today. Though it would've been comforting to have had Merlin with her yesterday, she was glad he'd had fun instead, playing with his pal, Buddy.

Thanking Ethel again, Dar led Merlin out the door, but when Buddy's tail fell motionless, Dar stopped and squatted down to give Buddy a hug. She promised him that he and Merlin would play together again soon. Then she retrieved a treat from her pocket and held it out to Buddy, who snarfed it up, wagging his tail double time in appreciation.

Dar left and made the short drive next door to The Contented Canine. Still early, she settled in at her desk while Merlin circled into his favorite spot on the braided rug near her feet. Though she tried to delve into her to-do list for the day, intruding thoughts popped into her head; she couldn't shake Mr. Reece's murder, discovering Spike's body, or the fiasco with Shawn and the police. It was all she'd thought about yesterday as well.

Her only consolation was knowing that Shawn was alive and well. Though she hadn't heard from him yesterday, he had called her on her way to pick up Merlin. She didn't know if it had been the result of him getting some much-needed sleep, but the anger had left his voice. After Dar had apologized again, Shawn said he appreciated that she had acted out of concern for him. He'd even shown signs of his humor returning when he offered to text her when he left work in the future, "so I won't have to worry about police guns being aimed at me as I leave." She had a feeling she was not going to hear the end of this for a very long time.

Her thoughts were interrupted as LaVon walked toward her carrying a document. LaVon never came in this early. Dar figured she wasn't the only one who needed a distraction today.

She gulped down some coffee, praying the caffeine would kick in before her friend reached her desk. After the stress of Saturday night, she was astounded to see a huge smile cross LaVon's face. She took a second swig of coffee.

"Good morning!" LaVon greeted her.

"Mmm," Dar said. "How about taking the morning person down a notch?"

"Maybe later," LaVon said, waving her hand dismissively. "I've got something to show you, and I think it'll do more for your mood than your precious caffeine." LaVon thrust some papers in front of Dar's face. "It's our quarterly report."

Dar snatched the papers, lowering them to her desk. "Thank you?"

"You're welcome," LaVon said, a huge grin on her face.

Dar tried skimming the report, but like every other financial document she ever tried to read, the numbers all blurred together. She opened her eyes wide.

"You don't see it, do you?" LaVon pointed to a number at the bottom of the second page. "Notice the color of that number? It's black, just like me. Beautiful, isn't it?"

Dar stared at the bottom line that had been red for far too long. "That's amazing!" She double-checked it again. "Really? Even though we hired Nalini back along with one of her classmates?"

When Nalini had quit work there to enroll in classes at a local college with the goal of becoming a veterinarian, Dar thought they'd lost one of their best part-time employees. But then Nalini asked if she and a classmate could job share a full-time position to help cover some of their school expenses. Dar and LaVon had been determined to find the funds to make it work, and now that decision had proven to be a win-win for all of them.

"Yes, really," LaVon repeated. "I took advantage of the lower interest rates and refinanced our mortgage. Combined with the steady stream of regular customers we've acquired, we are officially in the black!"

"We did it!" Dar shouted. She ran around her desk and hugged LaVon. They jumped up and down, laughing and clapping as though they were nine again and had just found out they'd be in the same class. Merlin barked, not wanting to be left out of the excitement.

Dar was still grinning when LaVon's face turned serious. "There's something else I need to talk to you about." Dar's cell phone rang, and LaVon motioned to it. "You better answer that first. We can talk later." She hurried off, leaving Dar in suspense.

Her phone rang again, and she glanced at the caller I.D. "Hi, Daniel. What's up? Are you checking in on me again? It's crazy how you'd sensed something was wrong Saturday night. I was happy to hear a friendly voice on the phone when I got home."

"No problem," Daniel said. "It was a strange feeling. I kept getting vibes about two different events, neither of them good. I had to be sure. I was worried, which seems to happen a lot since we reconnected."

"Hey, what are sisters for?" Dar teased.

"If I'd known a sister could make my hair turn gray, I'd have stayed in a coma," Daniel laughed.

"Very funny," Dar said. "Is there a reason you called other than to heckle me?"

"Actually, there is. I interviewed a guy to help Knuckles at the stables," he said. "Now that we have another horse, and hopefully a pony soon, there'll be more work than Knuckles can handle on his own."

Dar liked the idea of having another individual working alongside Knuckles, at least until he proved he could control his anger issues. Still, they needed a thorough background check on him. Even though he wouldn't be working directly with the children, his job would put him in close enough proximity to them that she couldn't afford to take chances.

"The guy's name is Owen Jay," Daniel continued. "He seemed down on his luck and anxious to work. I thought we could hire him on a trial basis, especially since we have Joe to oversee them both."

Joe had worked for the Montgomery family for years before Dar and Daniel had inherited the estate. His experience with horses was exactly what they needed, and he was willing to stay on and help guide them through the difficult process of choosing the best horses for the new equine therapy program. He was in charge of ordering their food, equipment, training, and vet care, as well as overseeing what was soon to be two stable hands.

"I feel like we might be asking too much of Joe," Dar said. "I don't want anything to take time away from his training the horses. Have you talked to him about it?"

"I did," Daniel said. "He told me he likes a challenge—that's why he's a horse trainer."

"That sounds like Joe," Dar said. "Does this Owen Jay have any other employment history or recommendations?" She trusted her brother, but she also knew he had a weakness when it came to helping someone in need.

"Sort of," Daniel said. "Owen told me he worked briefly at Connor's Stables. After about three months, he took a better paying job at a construction company called Newok Construction, but the company recently closed down. I tried to reach Connor's Stables for a reference, but the owner is out of state for a horse show. I'll have to wait until he returns to verify Owen's employment there."

"See if he can bring in a check stub from Newok Construction," Dar suggested.

"Already asked him," Daniel said, "but the construction company paid him in cash. He was hired as temporary help for a big project that the company was trying to complete. He gave me the number of the woman in charge of their HR department, though. I'll give her a call next."

"The sooner, the better," Dar said.

"Right. And if it's okay with you, for now, I'll have him muck the stables with Knuckles. There's fencing in the paddock and around the pasture that need repairs as well."

"I guess that's fine. Remember, we can't have Owen around the children until he has a complete background check," Dar said, not quite sold on hiring him yet. It was hard enough for Joe to keep an eye on Knuckles, let alone a second stable hand. Neither were exactly experienced, but if they proved to be motivated, it could work. Now that Knuckles was more comfortable with his job, he was already showing signs of improvement, and Joe had commented that he was a hard worker.

Still, she wished she shared Daniel's confidence about hiring Owen Jay. But seeing how enthusiastic her brother had been about helping her set up the program, she didn't have the heart to dissuade him. She made a mental note, though, to make sure Daniel followed through on Owen Jay's work history and background checks.

"Thanks for keeping the momentum going on this program," she said instead. "I wish I could be there more often to help out. I should be there this weekend, so we can talk more then."

"Great," Daniel said. "Not to change the subject, but do the police or Detective Mike have any leads on the two murders?"

"Not that I've heard," Dar said.

"And I'm guessing you haven't let Shawn in on your moving dilemma yet."

"No, but I considered broaching the subject with him while the police still had him in handcuffs."

"Uh-huh," Daniel said drily. "Don't you think that at this point in your relationship, he deserves to at least know your thoughts about it? What are you so afraid of, Dar?"

Dar chewed on a fingernail, then sighed. "Honestly, I'm afraid of messing it all up. I'm afraid that if I make the wrong decision, I could lose Shawn or my best friend."

"Wow," Daniel said. "That's a lot of pressure."

"I knew you'd get it," Dar said.

"Not exactly," Daniel said. "You're forgetting one important thing, but your pride is keeping you from seeing it."

"What's that?" Dar asked.

"You're smart. You'll figure it out," Daniel said, then disconnected.

"If only," Dar thought to herself.

CHAPTER SIXTEEN

Dar finished her morning at the kennel by signing out a poodle, a French bulldog, and a lab mix before relinquishing them to their owners. She always enjoyed this part of her job. Even though the noise level ratcheted up several decibels with the cacophony of barking dogs, it was worth it to see the dogs' tails wagging in excitement as their owners smothered them with affection. By the time the last dog was out the door, Dar had made a decision.

She detected a strain in Mike's voice when he answered her call. Maybe it was the unsolved murders, or maybe it was related to whatever his sister had told him when they'd been at Merv's Diner. More likely it was the fact that every time she spoke with Mike, she'd done something to make his job twice as hard. Rather than being helpful, she'd only added to his stress in more ways than she cared to remember.

"Hey, Mike," Dar said. There was silence on the other end. "I wanted to apologize again for everything that happened Saturday. I'm sorry that I compromised the crime scene, and I'm sorry that I caused you and the officers to respond to what turned out to be a false alarm in the parking garage. I wish I could make it up to you somehow." Mike didn't try to interrupt her. "Anyway, you said to call if I remembered anything or noticed something suspicious."

"Go on," Mike said.

"It could be nothing, but the other day when you and Shawn left the restaurant, there was a guy across the street. He was standing with a group of people waiting for the bus, but he didn't get on when it pulled up. It was like he was using them to hide, but I think he was watching you two. Even when he was on the phone, he never stopped looking in your direction until you both drove off. Then he stared right at the restaurant, as though he was trying to see who was still inside. It gave me the creeps."

"Did you see his face?"

"No, I couldn't. He had on a green camouflage hoodie, with the hood pulled over his head. Between that and the sunglasses he wore, it was impossible to see his features."

"Could be he simply changed his mind about taking that particular bus," Mike said.

"Maybe." Dar wasn't sure she'd convinced Mike that there was something off about the guy. "Anyway, I'm just reporting what I saw."

"Hold on a sec," Mike said, putting her on hold. "I'm back," he said moments later. "I just got the coroner's report. Again, this is confidential; according to her findings, Dr. Stevens confirmed two things: one, Mr. Reece was poisoned, and two, he ingested it through his lungs."

Even though she would've tried to get it from him, Dar wondered why Mike would share this information with her. It wasn't like him. Still, she didn't want to push her luck by asking him why. Instead, she asked, "What was the poison?"

"Hydrogen cyanide," Mike said. "According to Dr. Stevens, when it's inhaled in a small space, it can cause death in seconds."

Dar thought about that. "Didn't Shawn say something about the fan being on in the bathroom when he walked into Mr. Reece's office?"

"He did, but at the time, we were more concerned with Shawn's fingerprints being on the fan switch," Mike said.

"Maybe," Dar said, "someone hid a device with the poison above the ceiling and used the fan to dispense it."

"There's just one problem with your theory," Mike said, "a bathroom fan sucks air in, so it would've taken any poison out of the room. Still, I'll get forensics to go over the fan, wiring, or anything else that might be connected to it."

"Even if the poison was hidden somewhere in his office or bathroom, who would be capable of rigging up something like that without getting killed themselves?" Dar asked.

"You forgot, 'why.'"

"It's hard enough to imagine Mr. Reece having had any enemies," Dar said, "let alone a person with a reason to want him dead." She shuddered.

"There's one more thing," Mike said. "I did you a favor by feeding you privileged information about the case, but I need a favor from you in return. It's a personal matter, though. Can you meet me?"

Dar hadn't expected this. So that was why he'd told her information without her asking. "Um, sure. I could take Merlin to the dog park during my lunch break. There are plenty of benches around there where we can talk privately."

"Sounds good," Mike said. I'll meet you there in a couple hours."

Before Dar could ask any more questions, he disconnected. Mike had never asked her for a favor before, and it felt strange, especially since he was usually the one to help her out of scrapes. Plus, he was a proud man; Mike asking for a favor must be like him asking his boss to clean his gun for him. She couldn't imagine what could cause him to go through the humility of doing so now.

CHAPTER SEVENTEEN

Dar finished returning phone calls from customers and was about to leave to meet Mike when she remembered LaVon had wanted to speak with her. She caught LaVon in her office. Apologizing, she told LaVon she had an important errand to run that couldn't wait. "Do you want to meet tonight to talk?" she asked.

LaVon shooed her away. "There's no rush. We'll talk when you're not chasing bad guys."

Dar wanted to explain that it had nothing to do with chasing any criminals, but her meeting with Mike was a private matter. She hated to give LaVon the impression that whatever she had to say was unimportant, but she didn't know how to do that without revealing Mike's request. All she could do was mutter her thanks to LaVon for understanding before hurrying out the door.

The warm early afternoon sun brightened Dar's mood. As she passed green lawns and fruit trees with their new white, pink, and purple blooms, she could almost believe this was a world where there were no murders, no stress, only joy.

But she knew that the world was complicated and messy. It could also resemble a day plagued with torrential rain that turned the green lawns to mud, filling low areas with dark puddles, as gale-stolen petals of soft pastels got blown atop their murky waters. She'd survived the "messy" days. And just as nature sought to provide a balance, she sought to achieve a semblance of the same in her life.

When she arrived at the dog park with Merlin, she spotted Mike sitting on a bench at a distance from the pet owners. She waved when he saw her, then bent down to unhook Merlin's leash. Merlin was a whirl of motion, seeming more eager than usual to join the other dogs. When she was finally able to release him, he dashed over to a golden lab who looked an awful lot like Buddy.

"Dar, what are you doing here?"

Dar turned around at the sound of Shawn's voice. "I could ask you the same," she said. "Why aren't you at work?"

"Are you trying to get rid of me? If you must know, I decided to take a few hours off and bring Buddy here to play. I've put in so many hours lately, I needed to get out of the hospital and enjoy some fresh air. Ethel dropped Buddy off with me while she runs some errands. I never guessed I'd run into you here. My day just got even better. So why are you here? You didn't answer me before."

Dar hesitated, not sure what to do. She assumed that whatever Mike needed to discuss with her was meant for her ears only.

"You seem nervous. What's up?" Shawn asked.

Her gaze automatically went to Mike, and Shawn followed her line of sight before she could look away. *It's a good thing I'm not a spy*, she thought.

"Hey, Mike's here." Shawn said as he turned and waved.

Dar held her palms up to Mike, waiting for his cue. He dropped his head, then motioned for them both to join him.

"Sorry, Mike," Dar said when they reached his carefully chosen bench.

"You're not familiar with the word 'private,' are you?" Mike was scowling.

"What are you two talking about?" Shawn asked. "Is there a new development in one of the murders? Why the secrecy?"

"Shawn," Dar said. "Mike and I were going to talk about a personal matter. He wanted to keep it private."

"Oh, let him stay," Mike said. "He might as well hear this, too."

Dar took a seat on the bench next to Mike while Shawn remained standing.

Mike sighed, clutching his hands as he leaned forward. "That phone call I got at Merv's Diner was from my sister, Jackie. It was about Sarah. She had some good news and some bad news. The good news was that Sarah was released from the hospital, and they're thrilled to have her back home."

"That's great!" Dar said. "What's the bad news?"

"Before Sarah was released, she stopped eating and speaking. Her test results were good, and the doctor had planned on sending her home, but he wasn't sure because of her new behaviors. Instead, he brought in a social worker, but Sarah refused to speak with her too. In the end, everyone agreed Sarah might do better at home."

"I'm sorry, Mike," Dar said, recalling Sarah had seemed fine when she'd seen her last. "Did she talk when she got home?"

"No," Mike said. "Not a word. Her parents are worried sick . . . and so am I."

"Is it possible she heard about Spike?" Dar asked.

"I'm sure she knows," Shawn said. "All the kids have been asking about Spike. Trust me, they pick up on adult conversations even when adults think they can't hear."

Mike nodded. "Jackie and her husband keep reminding Sarah that she's safe." He cleared his throat. "At least she's eating a little now that she's home, but she doesn't have her usual appetite. The worst part is that she's waking up in the middle of the night, screaming. Her parents are at a loss as to how to help her."

Dar thought for a moment. "You said you needed a favor?"

"I heard you talking about a new therapy program you're starting for kids at the estate. Any chance Sarah might benefit from it?"

"Possibly." Dar frowned. "Unfortunately, the first group is full. We have four horses, so we can only accommodate four children. They're all working on anxiety issues, so it sounds like it would have been a good fit. I can put Sarah on the waiting list. It's also possible that we'll get another horse soon, but it could be a while. They have to have the right temperament."

Mike's shoulders slumped. "I guess that's the best we can do then."

"Or," Dar said, trying to think of a solution. "We can include her when the kids are introduced to smaller animals in the barn. It helps to build their confidence around less intimidating animals before they meet the larger horses. Even though Sarah won't be able to continue with the horses this time, maybe she'll feel more comfortable and further ahead when our second group begins."

"That could work," Mike said. "I'll suggest it to my sister, but I'm sure she and her husband will be open to it, especially if there's a chance it'll help Sarah."

"I don't have any business cards yet," Dar said, "but you have my number. Have your sister call me. I can explain the program to her, then if she wants Sarah to start, she can complete the forms and bring them to Sarah's first group session."

Mike looked at Shawn. "This stays between the three of us, right?"

"Of course," Dar and Shawn said in unison.

"Thank you," Mike said.

After a moment, Mike put his cop-face on. "Shawn, tell me again about the fan running when you went into Mr. Reece's office."

"Oh," Shawn said, caught off guard by the change in subject. "I'm not sure I noticed it right away because of the shock. I was listening for signs of breathing and trying to hear his heart, but it was hard because of the fan running in the bathroom. I hurried in to shut it off, but the switch was already in the 'off' position. It seemed odd since it was still running."

"Did forensics do a thorough check above the ceiling?" Dar asked.

"They did," Mike said. "And they discovered a device with a small canister wired to the fan in the ceiling, which had been wired in reverse so that it could dispense the poison. The device appeared to be remote-controlled. Forensics also found traces of hydrogen cyanide, the same poisonous gas that was found in Reece's lungs, inside the canister."

"Do you think someone locked Mr. Reece in the bathroom and released the gas?" Dar asked.

Mike nodded. "That's what it looks like."

"It must have killed him in seconds," Shawn said.

"Unfortunately," Mike said, "whoever wired and hid the device there was smart enough to wipe their prints in both the bathroom and the office."

"Leaving only my prints when I tried to turn the fan off," Shawn said.

"It also explains why the fan was left running and the office window open," Dar added. "So someone locked Mr. Reece in the bathroom, then released the gas and waited for him to collapse?" Dar asked. "Do you think he wore a gas mask or stood outside the office nearby until the air cleared of the poison? Then why drag Mr. Reece's body into the office? Was it to keep the body a safe distance from where the poison had been delivered, hoping the device in the ceiling wouldn't be discovered? But if that was the case, why not turn the fan off with the remote rather than leaving it on?"

"Maybe he intended to remove the device, but he got spooked," Mike said. "He could've planned to use the remote from a safe distance, but it jammed or something. By then he wouldn't want to risk returning to the scene of the crime. Or maybe he just got careless. I've seen my share of stupid criminals."

"What about security cameras?" Dar asked.

"There aren't any cameras near the administrative offices," Mike said. "The only ones caught on camera by the nurses' station were a nurse, a couple aides, and Shawn. The nurse and aides have been cleared, and I don't think Shawn would risk his position at the hospital."

"Then there's that little oath I took, promising to 'do no harm,'" Shawn added.

"If the killer had used the elevator, we'd have seen him or her on camera. I'm guessing our killer used the stairs. For one, it's closer to Mr. Reece's office, and two, there's no security camera in the stairwell."

"Makes sense," Shawn said. "So, am I still a suspect?"

"Let's just say we have a more promising suspect," Mike said.

"Speaking of suspects, have you found Bruno yet?" Dar asked.

Mike nodded. "I received a call before you arrived. Bruno was picked up at the airport, ready to board a plane for Mexico. He's being detained for questioning, which is why I need to go. Hopefully, the two murders will soon be solved and everyone can relax—especially Sarah."

Dar watched Mike walk away, then turned to Shawn. "Although I really want Bruno to be the killer, something doesn't feel right about that."

"Oh, Miss Detective?" Shawn said, his eyebrows raised. "Wasn't it you who saw Bruno threaten Spike the day she was murdered? Hadn't he been stalking and harassing her to the point that she was petrified of the brute? He seems a pretty good fit to me."

"Maybe," Dar said with a frown. "It's just that Bruno didn't seem all that sharp to me; more brawn than brain. I can't see him wiring a ceiling fan, much less planning a murder without being seen. He's too impulsive. Plus, why would he want to kill Mr. Reece? And the only connection we know of between the two murders is that Mr. Reece and Spike worked at the same hospital."

"Maybe he had an accomplice who had a beef with Reece," Shawn said. "Or maybe Reece had something on Bruno and threatened to go to the police with it?"

"I guess both are possible," Dar said. "Although, how would the two have known each other? I still get the feeling we're missing something."

CHAPTER EIGHTEEN

That evening, Dar sat across from Shawn, enjoying a late dinner in her home. She'd invited him with high hopes of finally having a chance to talk. They'd had too few opportunities lately to do so, and the list of concerns they needed to discuss was not going away.

Although she seldom cooked, she'd managed to prepare a simple meal of spaghetti and a salad, and had bought a bottle of Merlot to go with it. The dinner was relaxing, and they were comfortable keeping conversations to a minimum. Afterwards, Dar refilled their wine glasses and carried them to the coffee table in front of the fireplace. She sank into her couch and tucked her legs beneath her while Shawn arranged kindling inside the small stone fireplace before lighting it. As the fire took off, he added a log, and Dar listened to the pop and sizzle of the flames. Merlin and Buddy settled onto a nearby rug, swishing their tails occasionally in lazy contentment.

Shawn snuggled up next to her on the couch, and for a few moments, they were content to sip their wine and watch the flames dance. He slipped an arm around her, and Dar saw the flames reflecting in his eyes as he leaned close and kissed her until she was sure the blaze had leapt straight to her heart.

Shawn raised an eyebrow. He took her wine glass, placed it alongside his on the coffee table, then leaned toward her again.

She hadn't noticed her phone ringing until Shawn began looking for the source of the interruption. Seeing the caller I.D., he passed it to her and mouthed the word, "Daniel." Shawn shrugged and told her, "Tell him hi for me."

"Hey, Daniel, what's up?" Dar said.

"Sorry. I have the feeling I'm interrupting a moment."

Having a twin who was so in tune with her, after being an only child for so long, was nothing short of amazing. Dar couldn't help but smile. "Shawn says 'hi.'"

"Right back at him. I'll make this quick, but I thought you'd want to know."

"What is it?" Dar asked, the smile dropping from her lips. She gripped her phone tighter.

"When I got back from lunch yesterday, I found Rosie wringing her hands and pacing," Daniel said. "She thought she'd seen a stranger hanging around the stables."

"Was it the new guy, Owen?"

"I don't think so. Joe offered to take him and Knuckles to lunch, but Owen declined, saying he had errands to run," Daniel said. "Anyway, Rosie decided to check out the stables herself."

"Alone? Did she find anyone? Is she okay?" Rosie was willing to protect the Montgomery Farm Estate and its residents at any cost. She guessed it was an irrational guilt Rosie had that stemmed from her past inability to protect Dar's biological mom from being murdered, though she had no way of preventing it. Dar hoped it hadn't instilled a reckless bravery in Rosie.

"Yes, alone. And no, she didn't find anyone. She seems okay," Daniel said, answering Dar's barrage of questions. "Rosie said she could've imagined seeing someone, but she didn't look convinced."

"Maybe Rosie was frightened because she was alone at the estate," Dar offered.

"Our Rosie? Frightened?"

Dar had to laugh. He was right. After all, Rosie had once knocked out a dangerous man without hesitating.

"I wasn't convinced it was her imagination either, especially after Rosie mentioned a detail too specific to be a figment of her imagination."

"What was it?" Dar asked.

"She was sure the person was talking on a phone while pacing back and forth. That's quite the detail to have imagined."

"I agree," Dar said. "Odd, though, it reminds me of the guy in the hoodie I saw when we were at lunch. He'd been pacing while on the phone, too. Was anything stolen?"

"Not that I could find. When Knuckles and Joe came back from lunch, I had them check too."

Daniel added, "I questioned Owen when he returned a little late. He said he'd gotten stuck in a line at a drive-thru restaurant for lunch. He even lifted up his fast-food lunch bag with its greasy contents to show me. I don't like this, Dar, especially when the equine therapy program is about to start."

"I don't like it either," Dar said. "But since we don't have anything concrete to report to the police, we'll just have to be vigilant for now. I think it's time we added security cameras outside. Thanks for letting me know, and if anyone sees suspicious activity of any kind, call 911. I don't want anyone getting hurt."

"Okay," Daniel said. "And I'm sorry if I interrupted something between you and Shawn. But hey, what kind of brother would I be if I didn't ruin my sister's evening?"

"Goodbye Daniel!" Dar said with an eye roll.

At the thought of a possible intruder on the estate grounds, lines formed across her forehead. Seeing them, Shawn insisted on hearing what had happened, so Dar repeated what Daniel had told her about Rosie seeing a possible intruder. By the time she finished discussing it with Shawn, she no longer wished to get into a serious discussion about a possible move or a job change with him. Instead, she chose to salvage what was left of their evening, and as Shawn poured more wine into their glasses, she guessed he was more than happy to do the same.

CHAPTER NINETEEN

The following morning, Dar drove to the Montgomery Farm Estate to spend the day securing last minute details for her first upcoming equine group. Once there, she used her key fob to open the security gate, then drove along the winding drive and parked along the U-shaped driveway in front of the mansion's steps. As she opened the car door, Merlin leapt out and immediately ran off to explore the grounds.

She strolled around the side of the house to the stables in the rear. As she neared them, she spotted Joe at the barn door. He waved to her.

"It's good to see you, Miss Kelly," he said.

"Please, call me Dar," she said. "It's good to see you too. How's everything going?"

"Good, except for an electrical problem. I discovered a wiring issue in the bunkhouse that needs to be fixed."

"That's not good! Can you show me?" Dar asked.

Joe led her through the stables to the bunkhouse. Dar gasped as she stepped inside the cozy cabin room with its large stone fireplace. Two massive chairs with hand-carved frames and thick cushions covered in a rustic print sat invitingly in front of it. On the side walls hung two massive paintings that Dar guessed were at least seven feet high, with beautiful hand-carved frames. The horse in each painting looked majestically into the room, as if to oversee the stable hands who cared for all the Montgomery horses. But it was the black horse in the painting on the left wall that captivated her. He seemed to stare back at her, his head held high in an air of confidence.

"Is that Black Knight, the prize horse that Black Knight Pharmaceuticals was named after?" Dar asked.

Joe nodded and smiled at her reaction. "Impressive, isn't it?"

"Yes," Dar said. She took in the entire room with the vaulted ceiling. The designer had managed to capture a rustic masculine, yet cozy feel. "I haven't been in this area before. I guess I always thought this was your domain and I didn't want to intrude."

Joe smiled again. "Well, as one of the owners of this estate, I guess it's time you see the rest of the place."

They continued around the corner to a kitchenette with a hand-carved table in the same style as the massive chairs near the fireplace. Beyond were two sets of oversized bunk beds and a full bath through one door.

Though it had the ambiance of a bunkhouse, like the rest of the estate, no expense had been spared in the details.

"This is where Knuckles and Owen sleep, but the wiring issue is above the kitchenette. The canned lights aren't working. I tried new bulbs and checked the fuse, but I'm afraid that's the extent of my skills. Do you have an electrician you like to use?"

"I can take care of that for you." The voice came from behind them.

Dar and Joe turned to see Owen, the new stable hand, coming into the living area with Knuckles. Both men tugged at boots full of mud and straw and dropped them onto a mat.

"You're an electrician?" Dar asked.

"Not officially," Owen said, splaying his hands outward. "But my dad was an electrician, and he taught me everything I know. In fact, I helped him wire canned lighting in the ceiling of my uncle's house."

Dar looked from him to the kitchenette ceiling, imagining all the ways things could go wrong if she didn't hire a professional.

"Your call," Joe said.

"Tell you what," Owen said. "Those lights have been driving me nuts anyway, so I'm happy to fix them, but if I can't, at least you're not out any money."

"And what will it cost me if you can fix them?" Dar asked, crossing her arms.

"How about . . ." Owen began, then seemed to change his initial thought. "How about if I get fifteen extra minutes of break time every morning for the next two weeks?"

"Don't do it," Knuckles said.

Dar was surprised to hear Knuckles speak, but when she asked him why, he just glared at all of them, then walked away with his hands balled into fists. Dar noticed the new bruises and scrapes on his knuckles as he stomped off, and she made a mental note to ask Daniel about it.

"I don't know," Dar said with a shake of her head. "What if you get hurt? Plus, I'd never forgive myself if this beautiful building caught on fire."

"I understand," Owen said. "I only offered because I thought I could save you some time and money, but it's your call."

"It seems like too good of a deal to pass up," she said finally. "But it can't interfere with your other jobs around here. You'll have to do the work in the evening."

"I can work nights, no problem," Owen said, "long as I get my extra break time."

"The extra break time is up to Joe," Dar said, looking to the man in question.

"If he can fix those lights, then I think I can do without Owen for fifteen minutes each morning," Joe said. "Two weeks, though. No longer."

A door slammed behind them, and Dar noticed that Knuckles boots were no longer sitting on the mat.

She thanked Joe for pointing out the problem, then walked back to the house. As she did, a red truck entered through the staff gate, followed the drive past the house, and pulled along next to her. The driver lowered the window.

A woman's red ponytail escaped through the back of a baseball cap and cascaded in thick waves halfway down her back. She wore an oversized plaid flannel shirt over a green T-shirt that matched her eyes. Dar eyed the truckload of hay. The woman waved at her as though they were best friends and flashed a smile that revealed brilliant white teeth.

"Hi," the woman said. "My name is Roxanne, but you can call me Red. Are you one of the owners?"

Dar nodded. "Do you mind telling me how you got through the closed gate, Roxanne?"

"Oh, I assumed you knew. Joe let me in. Said I should call him when I was on my way, and he'd have the gate open for me when I got here. He placed an order for these bales of hay and asked that I deliver them to the stables. He seemed in kind of a hurry to get them."

Dar studied the woman, who looked too well put together to be delivering hay. "Strange, I just spoke with Joe and he never mentioned that you were coming. Did he say why he needed the extra bales? I thought he typically got his hay from someone else."

"Yes, ma'am. He mentioned four horses that required hay and straw. I'll bring the straw in my next load."

Dar felt herself relax. "Well, if Joe ordered it, then I suppose it's okay. If you pull around to the stable doors, I can help you unload the bales," she offered.

"No need," Red replied. "I'm sure you have plenty of other work to do, but I appreciate the offer." With a quick nod, she continued toward the stables.

Dar watched the old red truck rumble down the lane and park near the main barn door, as though she knew exactly where she was going. Joe came out to meet her. Together, the two of them began unloading the stacked bales from the truck's bed. Relieved at the sight of Joe, Dar turned and continued toward the house.

The sight of the home's back entrance gave Dar pause. It was the same door she'd once used to escape from being killed by Wes Shade, who she still refused to believe was her biological father. The door opened in front of her, and she jumped.

"I didn't mean to scare you," Rosie said.

Dar's hand covered her heart as she beamed at the woman who was still wearing her apron from lunch. "Sorry, Rosie. I was having a flashback when you opened the door. I think we scared each other."

Rosie hurried down the three steps to meet Dar with a huge hug. "I know what you mean. I can't pick up my cast-iron skillet without thinking of that night. Come in. Daniel's been waiting for you.

"He told me about the mysterious stranger that you saw near the stables," Dar said.

Rosie waved it off. "It was probably my imagination. Don't you worry."

Dar followed her into the house and through the back hallway, passing the conservatory and pantry before turning into the kitchen. Daniel was sitting at the island, finishing his lunch. The aroma of food made Dar's stomach rumble. Rosie's ears perked up, and without hesitating, she assembled a plate loaded with a ham and cheese sandwich, apple slices, and chips, then slid it in front of the bar stool next to where Daniel was sitting.

"Your brother can wait while you eat," Rosie said. "Then you talk." She gave Daniel a stern look. "I'll be in the basement, but when I get back, I want to see Dar's food gone."

"Hi, sis. Welcome to my world," Daniel said.

Dar laughed. "Judging by my plate, whatever she does must be worth it if you get food served at the first rumbles of hunger."

"Actually, she's great," Daniel said, his mouth full.

Dar took a couple bites but couldn't wait any longer to question Daniel. "Have you learned anything new about the trespasser Rosie saw?" she asked.

Daniel swallowed and was about to answer when a shrill scream interrupted him. It seemed to be coming from beneath the floor.

"That's Rosie!" Dar said. She jumped up and grabbed Rosie's cast-iron skillet. A string of Spanish words penetrated the floor beneath her, and she darted for the back hallway with Daniel close on her heels.

Throwing open the basement door, she tried to ignore the pounding of her heart as another flashback intruded her thoughts. *I control my thoughts and actions; no one else*, she told herself, taking the steps two at a time until she reached the basement. Feeling the weight of the skillet gripped firmly in her hand, she followed the dark hall to her left. She could hear Daniel's footsteps behind her as a dark shadow moved up ahead. Dar gripped the weapon tighter.

Rosie stepped out of the rec room, shouting a litany of words that Dar couldn't make out. The words spewed out at lightning speed, but Dar had only to watch Rosie's gestures to get the message loud and clear; she was furious. She needed to calm Rosie down if she wanted to find out what happened.

"Rosie! Are you okay? Did someone hurt you? Are they still here?" Dar realized she must have been talking equally as fast because Rosie gave her a blank stare. So much for calming her down. She rewound her own litany of questions to her first one, but slower this time. "Are you okay, Rosie?"

"Si, but it's missing. Oh, this is terrible!" Rosie began wringing her hands.

"What's terrible? What's missing?" Daniel asked.

"The painting," Rosie said. "One of the paintings is gone." She tugged at Daniel's arm and led him to a hand-carved wooden frame.

But the only thing it framed now was the wall.

CHAPTER TWENTY

Of the two paintings that had hung in the basement hallway, only one remained in its frame. Dar hadn't recognized the artist, Julian Hughes, who'd signed them, but she had enjoyed the sense of joy that he had skillfully evoked with his wistful brush strokes. In fact, the word "joy" was in the title of each of the three paintings they owned; the third hung in the tasting room of the wine cellar. But stealing what she guessed was a 24" x 30" painting couldn't have been easy, unless the thief had done this before.

"Did you see anyone down here?" Dar asked Rosie.

"No. I came down to select a bottle of wine for dinner tonight," Rosie said. "I heard a noise and thought maybe it was you and Daniel, so I thought I'd get your approval on the wine. That's when I noticed the painting was gone."

"I don't know much about art, but I liked these ones a lot," Dar said. "Still, I didn't think the paintings down here were nearly as valuable as those upstairs."

"You know Mr. and Mrs. Montgomery not only met the artist, but hosted a show for him. They would be so upset about this; God rest their souls," Rosie said, crossing herself.

"How did they meet him?" Daniel asked.

"Have you noticed the beautiful carved wood furniture around the estate?" Rosie asked.

They nodded. The skilled craftsmanship on the custom-made furniture had exquisite details, unique to the Montgomery Farm Estate, carved into each piece. It was impossible not to notice them.

"It was the artist's father, Thomas Hughes, who did the work," Rosie said. "Even these frames. He was delivering a couple pieces of his furniture one day when Mr. Montgomery told Mr. Hughes how much he enjoyed his skilled work. That's when Mr. Hughes told him his son was also an artist. Mr. Montgomery asked him to bring his son with him the next time he made a delivery, and to bring a few of his paintings. When he did, the Montgomerys bought all three of Julian Hughes's paintings, then hosted an art show for him here. After that, Julian Hughes sold many paintings."

Dar walked over to the second painting still in the hallway and read the title carved into the frame, "Evening Joy." A radiant sunset filled the canvas with vibrant yellows, golds, oranges, reds, and pinks, but it was the technique in which the paints had been applied that created the painting's joyful mood. Dar then studied the empty frame with the title, "Morning Joy," that Julian's father had carved into it.

"So, Mr. and Mrs. Montgomery had a gallery show for Julian in their home? That must've been exciting," Dar said.

Rosie nodded. "Yes. It was a big event, and anyone who had money was invited. The show was a big success, and the Montgomerys were pleased that Julian sold so many of his paintings. But Mr. Montgomery told everyone that the three 'Joy' paintings he'd bought were Julian's best."

"That must have been a turning point for the artist's career," Daniel said.

"The Montgomerys thought so," Rosie said. "They fully expected his paintings to become increasingly valuable."

"So, did they?" Dar asked.

Rosie shrugged her shoulders. "I don't know," she said.

"I'm glad they're not here to see this, then," Daniel said. "We need to report the theft." He looked along the walls and ceilings. "I don't see any security cameras down here. I wonder if it's because the stone walls would interfere with reception. I'll have to check into it."

Dar held her cell phone up and turned in a circle. "I can't get any cell reception down here," she said. "I'll have to go upstairs to call the police."

The three of them returned to the kitchen. Dar lugged Rosie's skillet over to the stove and heaved it back on top of it. She had a new appreciation for the woman's strength.

Dar pulled out Mike's card and was about to call him, then changed her mind. A homicide detective surely didn't want to be bothered with a theft when he had murders to solve. Instead, she called the Fort Wayne police and told them of the stolen artwork, though she had no idea of its value when they asked. She made a mental note to schedule an appraiser to get estimates on all the artwork and collectibles throughout the estate.

Seeing her half-eaten sandwich, Dar finished every morsel of it before turning to Daniel. "I know you think I'm loony, but isn't it possible that a custom-built home like this would have a hidden passage or two? I mean, it makes sense. And if that's the case, maybe our thief knew about it and used it to his advantage."

"But how would the thief know when we don't even know if one exists?" Daniel asked.

Dar frowned. He had a point. She turned to Rosie. "Do you think there are hidden passages?"

"I don't know for sure," Rosie said, "but your grandparents would sometimes disappear then reappear somewhere else, like they were ghosts who could walk through walls."

"I knew it!" Dar said.

"Okay, Miss Sleuth, calm down," Daniel teased.

"I don't know about secret passages," Rosie said, "but there seemed to be plenty of other secrets in the Montgomery family. Rosie leaned in closer. One night, I overheard Mr. and Mrs. Montgomery talking about some important papers when all of a sudden Mr. Montgomery started speaking in a hushed tone.

"What made you think the papers were important, Rosie?" Dar asked.

"Because he asked Mrs. Montgomery to hide them in her secret hiding place," Rosie said, her dark brown eyes wide.

She reminded Dar of someone telling a ghost story around a campfire. Maybe the secret hiding spot was just a story too. But it was one that she'd never heard before, and seeing Daniel's raised eyebrows told her that it was new to him as well.

"So did Mrs. Montgomery agree to hide the papers?" Daniel asked.

Rosie nodded.

"Rosie, do you know where her 'secret hiding place' is?" Dar asked. "It couldn't be the two safes. We've been through those and all their contents with our lawyer."

Rosie's eyes lit up. "Yes, I know where it is," she said. Then her smile fell into a frown. "But I don't know how to open it."

"One out of two's not bad," Daniel said.

Dar gave Rosie a hug. "Well, what are we waiting for?" she said. "Show us the way!"

CHAPTER TWENTY-ONE

Dar and Daniel followed Rosie to the main staircase that curved from the foyer to the second floor. They climbed the grand staircase, then walked along a wide hallway with bedrooms on either side. Dar counted eight of them. Though she'd done so before, she still marveled at how many bedrooms there were, each with its own ensuite.

When they entered the last bedroom on the right, Dar gaped at the ornate feminine décor inside. It was grander than any of the other rooms, and hard to look away from. Rosie motioned them toward a door along the left wall that opened onto a balcony, pulling Dar away from the furnishings. When they stepped onto it, Dar smiled as she gazed down into the cozy library.

Rosie smiled as well. "This bedroom was first Mrs. Kate Montgomery's and after she passed, it was Erin Montgomery's, your biological mother. Actually, your mother seldom used it. She preferred the bedroom across the hall, which she had decorated with a simpler design. But she loved the balcony, just like her mother, and read for hours out here. It was her favorite place when the weather was too nasty outside, because the heat from the fireplace below kept it warm." Rosie paused a moment, lost in memories.

"And this was her favorite chair," Rosie said, pointing to a rather unremarkable, yet comfortable, overstuffed chair with a leather footrest in front of it. "I'm not sure of the story behind it, but I once heard Mrs. Montgomery, your grandmother, mention that it had been passed down through the generations. I thought maybe she kept it here for sentimental reasons, because it was so different from her other furniture." Rosie opened the hinged top of the footrest, revealing a luxurious cream-colored throw.

Dar picked up the soft throw. As she held it to her chest, she smelled the slight scent of a lingering perfume, and once again longed to have known her biological mother. She wondered if Daniel felt the same.

"There's nothing else," Daniel said, peering into the open footrest.

"But I think there is more," Rosie said. "I think it holds a secret compartment, but I don't know how to find it."

Dar was skeptical. "This is the special hiding place where Mr. Montgomery asked his wife to hide important papers? It looks like an ordinary footrest."

Rosie wrung her hands. "Si. Yes. But I think there's more to it. I'm sure there's another compartment to open. I was delivering your mom's laundry to her room one day, and the door to the balcony was open a little. I saw her bending over an open compartment within the footrest and pulling papers out. I felt ashamed for watching her and was afraid she might see me, so I walked away."

Dar and Daniel both examined the footrest. It soon became obvious that the interior dimensions were smaller than the exterior, but neither of them could find a latch or release of any kind to reveal a hidden space.

Dar looked at the time. "We'll have to try again later," she said. "Daniel and I have a lot of details to work out for the equine therapy program, and we're running out of time."

Rosie nodded and turned to leave, but Dar stopped her.

"Thank you for sharing this with us, Rosie. And I want you and Daniel both to promise me that if you don't feel safe living here, you're welcome to stay at my place until we figure out who stole the painting and how the thief got inside."

Rosie waved a hand dismissively and thrust out her chin. "You forget, I have my cast-iron skillet for protection."

"And don't worry about me," Daniel said. "I've got Rosie to protect me, so I'm good. But thanks for the offer," he added.

Rosie's eyes glistened. "I am so blessed to have your mother's beautiful twin babies back in my life. I thought I'd never see you again after your grandfather forced your mother to give you both up for adoption. If she'd known that you had been split up, and that Daniel had been sent from one foster home to another, she would've fought to get you both back. I hope you don't hold any of it against her. Erin was so young at the time, and frightened by an abusive husband."

"Yeah, I met Wes Shade when he tried to kill me," Dar said. "Nice guy. He tried to do the same to Daniel. We were so relieved when he was convicted and sent to prison. Hopefully somewhere far away from here."

Rosie crossed herself. "I'll never forget when I discovered that he had hit your mother. But her father, your grandfather, bullied her as well, even though he loved her in his own way. It took her a long time to recover from the damage they'd both done to her, but in spite of all that, she was a survivor. And she'd have been so proud to know that both of you are survivors too, and have become amazing adults." Rosie swiped at an eye. "Excuse me."

Rosie left the balcony, and Dar and Daniel wiped at the glistening tears in their own eyes. It took a moment before either of them could speak again.

"Before I forget," Daniel said, clearing his throat, "Owen finished the wiring in the bunkhouse. The canned lights seem to be working fine again. I believe you promised Owen an extra fifteen minutes for his morning break for two weeks, as payment, starting today."

Dar shrugged. "I know it was a strange request, but I can't argue with the results."

"Guess not," Daniel said. "Now, let's go over a few details for the equine group."

"Definitely," Dar said. She sunk into the comfy chair. "Saturday will be here before we know it. I have all the forms back, except for Sarah's, but her parents are bringing hers when they bring Sarah to the first group session. Did you double-check on insurance?"

"I did," Daniel said. He pulled the footrest toward himself, then straddled it like one of their horses. "We're fully covered. I've been helping with the smaller animals, getting them more accustomed to humans petting and handling them. The rabbits were timid at first, but now they enjoy being held. It was also a good excuse to check if their cages and pens were cleaned. So far Knuckles and Owen are maintaining a clean environment for all the animals."

Dar smiled. "I had my doubts, but it seems that both are working out. Still, I appreciate Joe keeping a close eye on them." Daniel agreed.

"I also met with Annalise," she said. "Having an equine therapist with her credentials and experience is a real asset for the program, not only for the children, but as a mentor for me as well. She suggested we walk each horse around our arena and try to simulate anticipated responses that might occur with a group of anxious kids. She couldn't say enough about how well Joe had trained the horses. Getting them to remain calm when exposed to sudden noises and movements isn't easy. Of course, the kids will be the true test. When the kids actually mount the horses, each horse will have an adult lead."

"So, it will be you, Annalise, Joe, and myself as guides," Daniel said. "Annalise has been prepping us, but I'm sure I'll have more questions after my first experience as a guide. Anyway, everything sounds good. I think you're as ready as you'll ever be to launch your dream." When Dar didn't respond, he added, "Okay, I expected a smile, not a frown. What's wrong? You're staring into space."

"Sorry," Dar replied. "My mind wandered. I can't stop thinking about that footrest you're sitting on. Did you notice that the studs around the outside aren't along the bottom like most are designed? They're up higher."

Daniel stood up, and Dar knelt down next to the footrest. She began running her fingers over the row of studs, feeling for any change between them. When she got to the middle one, it gave a little. She pushed harder and heard a click. Lifting the lid, she looked inside, but nothing had sprung open. She sat back on her heels.

"Maybe, there's another one," Daniel suggested. He dropped to his knees, and pushed the center stud on the opposite side. It also gave slightly with a click, but with no results.

"Two sides left," Dar said. She moved to the adjacent side while Daniel took the side across from her. "On the count of three. One, two, three." Dar wasn't sure if she heard one click or two, but one look at Daniel's face confirmed their success.

What had appeared to be the bottom of the footrest's interior was actually the top panel to a secret compartment. Dar opened the panel wider so they could both get a good look at its contents. Peering inside, Dar's eyes widened and her mouth fell open. She glanced at Daniel. His face mirrored hers.

CHAPTER TWENTY-TWO

Rising to her feet, Dar thought about how many times she'd anticipated an answer about her past, only to succeed in finding more questions. She looked at Daniel, the large envelope they'd found hidden in the footrest's secret compartment in his hand. It had been sealed with wax, then set with an official Montgomery Farm Estate stamp. They'd broken the seal open.

Inside the large envelope were two letter-size envelopes. She looked from those down into the mansion's library, full of autographed books from famous authors. She felt an odd sense of sanctuary on the balcony. This place where she stood had been a safe place for her biological grandmother, then mother; a place that had provided an escape from the daily demands placed on their shoulders. Here, they had gained a resilience pulled from a secret core within themselves; much like the secret hiding spot tucked inside the worn footrest.

"Aren't you going to answer that?" Daniel asked her.

Brought back to the present, Dar realized her phone was ringing. It was Shawn. She answered, but he spoke so fast, she could only understand half of what he was saying.

"Whoa, slow down," she said. "All I heard was something about meeting you at CCC." Dar looked over at Daniel, who was waving his hand, motioning for her to go. "Okay, I'll be there as soon as I can." Dar disconnected. "Are you sure you don't mind?" she asked Daniel. "As much as I want to know what's in these letters, Shawn said he remembered something about Mr. Reece's murder, but he needs my help to verify it, whatever that means. But if you want to read the letters while I'm gone, I'm good with that. As long as you tell me everything later."

"Go," Daniel said. "These letters have been here this long, we can wait a little longer to read them. I won't open them without you."

"Thanks," Dar said. It seemed he'd read her mind again. "This week should be a little slower at the kennel, so hopefully, I'll be back sooner rather than later."

"Don't worry about Merlin, either," Daniel said. "He can keep Rosie and me company for a day. We'll spoil him rotten. It'll be more fun then, when I drop him off tomorrow at your place. I need to make a stop anyway at my old accounting firm in Reed."

"Great. But you know there'll be no living with Merlin after you spoil him," she said.

"That's what I'm counting on," Daniel said with a mischievous grin. He placed the letters back inside the footrest's compartment and closed it, causing the four studs to click back into place on each side.

Dar hustled downstairs and found Rosie in the kitchen. She hated telling her that she couldn't stay as planned, but promised to return as soon as she could. Grabbing her purse, she dashed out the door to her car. Her overnight bag was still sitting on the back seat, as though she'd known on some level that she wouldn't be staying long.

***

Traffic between Fort Wayne and Reed was lighter than usual, but as she approached the last four blocks before CCC, a back-up of cars snarled the street. By the time she parked, took the elevator, and made her way to Shawn's office, she found him pacing inside the small space.

"Shawn, what's going on?" she asked.

"I thought you'd never get here," he said. "I think I know what was bugging me."

He took her hand and led her down the hall to Mr. Reece's office. Standing outside the door with crime scene tape across it, Shawn looked directly at her.

"First, I want you to think carefully whether or not you saw a certain object in the room the last time you spoke with Mr. Reece."

"I'll try my best," Dar said, "but I wasn't in his office more than five minutes, I had Merlin with me."

"That's all I ask," Shawn said.

"Okay. So, what is this object that's so important?" Dar asked.

"Do you remember seeing Mr. Reece's 'Do Not Disturb' sign?"

Dar strained to take in her surroundings that day, but her focus had been on Mr. Reece, himself, not his office. "No, sorry," she said. She knew it wasn't the answer he'd been hoping for from her.

Shawn's shoulders slumped. "It's okay. It just would've been nice to have someone corroborate what I recalled."

"Which is . . ." Dar prompted.

"The morning I found Mr. Reece's body, his 'Do Not Disturb' sign was hanging on the back of his office door."

"Shawn, how is that significant? The guy probably used it when he needed to get work done, and when he wasn't using it, he hung it on the back of his door for convenience."

"But that's just it," Shawn said. "That's not how he used the sign."

She frowned, not sure where he was going with this. "Okay, so how did Mr. Reece use his sign?"

"He always kept it in the center of his family photos." Shawn glanced up and down the hall then ran a hand through his hair. "I asked him about it once, and Mr. Reece told me he hung the sign on the wall with his family photos as a reminder to not to let his work disturb his family time."

"That's sweet," Dar said. "But isn't it possible he took the sign off the wall and put it on his door when he didn't want to be disturbed?"

"I asked him that same question," Shawn said. "He just laughed and said that took too much effort, that if he wanted privacy, he just shuts the door. So why would he have it hanging on his door when I found him?"

Dar wasn't convinced. "Maybe he changed his mind and decided to use it on his door that day."

"Well, if he did, that was a first," Shawn said. "Not once did I see that sign on his door. It was always on his wall."

"So, you think someone else hung the sign on the door," Dar said. "You need to share this with Mike. It could've been the killer."

While Shawn repeated his revelation to the detective, Dar thought again about her last visit with Mr. Reece. Her back would've been to the wall where Shawn said the sign typically hung. Most people who entered his office would have had their backs to that wall of photos, which were primarily for Mr. Reece's benefit, unless they'd been either a regular visitor, like Shawn, or had spent more than five minutes inside the office. She guessed it was possible others noticed the sign when they turned to leave, but she doubted most people who were in a hurry would.

Since there wasn't a camera facing Mr. Reece's office, there was no video of the individuals who'd been in and out of his office prior to his death. But Dar had another reliable source—one that was a bit crazy, but also a lot of fun.

CHAPTER TWENTY-THREE

Dar stepped outside Shawn's office at CCC and texted Mo. *Can you meet with me to talk?*

Minutes went by before Mo's reply came back. *Can't. Working.*

Where? Dar asked.

CCC, came Mo's reply.

Perfect. I'm here, in Shawn's office.

Meet in cafeteria in 20 minutes? I've got a break then.

See you then.

Dar walked back into Shawn's office and got a recap of his conversation with Mike.

"Apparently, Bruno, Spike's ex-slash-stalker, claims he received a text from Spike the day she was murdered," he said. "He almost didn't answer it because he didn't recognize the number, but according to Bruno, it was Spike, saying that she'd lost her phone and had to use a friend's phone to text him. Supposedly, she said she was sorry about everything she'd done to hurt him and wanted to start over; could he meet her in the CCC parking garage?"

"Wow, and Bruno believed that, after all her restraining orders against him?" Dar said. "There's no way Spike sent that text."

"I think we're all in agreement on that," Shawn said. "But there's more. Mike said they have one blip of film on the garage camera that caught Bruno in the garage with clenched fists and yelling. The front of Bruno was covered with what appeared to be blood."

"That creep!" Dar said. "What did he have to say to that?"

"Bruno insisted it wasn't blood. He told Mike that some lady with a carry-out container of spaghetti sauce tripped and the stuff sprayed all down the front of him. Bruno insists he didn't have time to clean it off before he got another text from Spike saying she'd changed her mind and that she'd never get back with him."

"Did the garage camera catch this woman tripping?" Dar asked.

"No. It seems the camera had a number of glitches, including the moments when that would've allegedly happened."

"What about Bruno's phone or Spike's?" Dar asked. "Their texts could be traced."

"Gone," Shawn replied. "Bruno says he threw his phone after getting Spike's last text, but then couldn't find it. Says he was set up; he's innocent. Spike's phone hasn't been found either. And Spike's two friends outside of work had given up trying to contact her, thanks to Bruno filling her texts and voicemail. They hadn't spoken with Spike in a long time. Their calls and texts confirmed it. The police also checked with the nurses on her floor, but none of them had lent her their phone."

"His story is too convenient," Dar said. "If he's so innocent, why did he run?"

"Good question," Shawn said. "He told Mike that he returned to CCC the next day, planning to confront Spike about the texts she'd sent him. He parked on the street, and as he was walking past a coffee truck, he overheard nurses in line talking about 'poor Spike' and saying 'it's so awful that she was murdered.' Bruno figured he'd be blamed, and that no one would believe his story, so he decided to lay low in Mexico for a while."

"Hmmm," Dar said. "What does Mike think?"

"He needs more evidence."

Dar glanced at the time. "I've gotta meet Mo in the cafeteria. I'd ask you to join us, but I wouldn't want you to be bored with girl talk."

Shawn looked at her suspiciously. "Uh-huh. You're up to something, I can tell. Please leave the detective work to the professionals like Mike, who happens to be excellent at his job." Shawn's pager went off. He kissed Dar slowly then added, "Gotta give you and Mo something to talk about," he added with a smoldering look.

Dar gulped. She was contemplating leaning in for more when suddenly her phone buzzed with a text from Mo. *Coming?* Dar quickly texted back. *On my way!*

CHAPTER TWENTY–FOUR

Dar spotted Mo in the cafeteria without any trouble. Not only did her flaming red hair stand out among the others there, but in true Mo fashion, she was standing next to a table, waving her hands in the air as though flagging down a firetruck in front of a burning building.

"And here I was afraid I wouldn't find you," Dar said with a chuckle.

"You're welcome," Mo retorted. "As thrilled as I am that you wanted to meet, I get the feeling you're on a mission. If it's about Spike's murder," she said, lowering her voice, "I'm all in."

"Actually, it's about Mr. Reece's murder."

"Since the two might be connected, let's hear it."

"Okay. Who at CCC would be most likely to know everyone's business?" Dar asked.

Mo sat back in her chair, frowning. "Hello, have you met me?"

Dar laughed. "All right, since you're the expert on everything that goes on around here, any chance you noticed who had been in and out of Mr. Reece's office within the last couple weeks before he died?"

Dar knew the question was a long shot, and one that Mike might have already asked Mo. She also knew that Mo was a hard worker, probably too busy hustling up and down the halls caring for the patients to have taken note of such things.

"I don't know the answer to that, but I have heard some gossip that may or may not be relevant," Mo said.

Dar leaned forward. "Go on."

"One of the nurses from the first floor said she'd seen someone from construction going in and out of Mr. Reece's office numerous times in the past few weeks."

"But if she worked on another floor, how—" Dar started to ask.

Mo interrupted. "She commutes with another nurse who works on the second floor. Jan usually waits near the second-floor nurses' station until her friend finishes her shift, so they can share a ride home.

"Anyway, Jan was upset one day. Said she'd been trying forever to get the lock replaced on her floor's supply closet, but she noticed that Mr. Reece seemed to be getting priority on his repairs from one of the construction crew members. Jan thought it was odd, though, that Mr. Reece often left before the construction dude and would tell the guy to lock the door behind him when he finished.

I asked her if he was handsome, you know, to find her a date, but she just gave me a look."

"Wait. Why did she want the lock replaced on the supply closet?" Dar asked.

"Really?" Mo asked, looking at her like she was crazy. "That's your question?"

"Yes. And I'd prefer you answer it sometime today, if that's possible for you to do without constantly getting sidetracked," Dar retorted. "It's like watching a squirrel running all over trying to find the nuts it buried."

"Me? Squirrelly?" Mo said, feigning hurt. "Anyway, to answer your question, Jan said she discovered the count for some expensive medical supplies was off. When she called the company, which wasn't her job, they insisted the correct number had been sent and delivered. She was hoping to talk to Mr. Reece about it, but he died before she had a chance."

"Strange," Dar said. "Shawn mentioned being short on medical devices on the second floor and was going to talk to Mr. Reece about it the morning he found him dead. Maybe there's a connection. Maybe someone was stealing from the supply closets, and that same person had something to do with Mr. Reece's murder."

"But why kill Mr. Reece? Surely he didn't have anything to do with the possible thefts. He seemed like a nice guy," Mo said. "The same goes for Spike. How could she be connected to all this?"

Dar wondered the same. "Back to the construction guy," she said. "Do you think this nurse could describe him?"

"I doubt it. She wasn't even positive it was the same guy each time. I can ask her again if you think it's important. I'm sure she'll be more than happy to talk about it again," Mo said. "I may have met my match with this lady."

"One of you is plenty," Dar teased. "Seriously, though, let me know what you find out. And thanks for meeting with me on your break. How's that boyfriend of yours, by the way?"

"Ceps is fine. Actually, he's better than fine," Mo said with an exaggerated sigh, "but that story will have to keep for another time. I've got to get back to work." Mo gave Dar a hug, then rushed out.

As Dar watched her leave, her cell phone rang. "Hey, Daniel. You and Rosie miss me already?" When Daniel didn't answer immediately, she changed her tone, "What's up? Is something wrong?"

"You could say that," Daniel began. "I'd brought Merlin into the house after you left and gave him one of those bones with a treat inside that I'd bought to spoil him for you."

"And you're calling to rub it in?" Dar asked.

"Another time. Anyway, Merlin was chewing on his new treat when all of a sudden, he started barking. I thought maybe he needed to go out, so I led him toward the back door, but he wouldn't go out. I hadn't noticed that the basement door was slightly ajar, but Merlin did. He squeezed through and bolted down the steps. I found him whining near the electrical room. I didn't see anyone there, but when I looked down the hall, I noticed another empty frame. We've been robbed—again."

CHAPTER TWENTY-FIVE

Dar was tired of all the questions spinning around in her head. Though she knew robbery wasn't Mike's department, she wanted her friend's help. After all, wasn't it implied that he owed her a favor for working Sarah into the equine therapy group? She would have tried to help Sarah regardless, but Mike didn't need to know that. She decided to cash in on the favor.

"What's wrong?" Mike asked, skipping right past the pleasantries.

"It's not an emergency," Dar reassured him, "but I have a favor to ask."

Silence hung on the other end of the call.

"I knew getting Sarah into your program was going to bite me in the ass one day," Mike said, "but I didn't expect it to be so soon." He sighed. "Okay. What kind of favor are we talking about? You do know I have two homicides to solve."

"Maybe this was a bad idea. I'll call the guy who handles thefts again."

"Again? What thefts?" She could practically hear the frown in his voice.

Dar told him about the two stolen paintings with no signs of a break-in. "The only ones in the house have been Rosie, Daniel, and myself. It's like the thief has found an entrance we don't know about."

"Hell, my niece will be at the estate soon, and I don't want some burglar roaming the place while she's there. I'll stop by there to see what I can do."

"Thanks, Mike. You're the best!" Dar said.

"It'll have to wait until tomorrow, though. I have an appointment with Mrs. Reece. I'm sure she'll be thrilled that I have so little to report on her husband's murder. Talk to you later." Mike ended the call abruptly.

Next, Dar called Daniel to let him know that Mike would be at the estate the next day to inquire about the stolen paintings. "I'll try to stop by tomorrow as well," she told him. There was still the matter of reading the hidden letters. Then, if she had time, she wanted to search for a secret passage within the mansion. There had to be one, though she knew the search would take time. The mansion wasn't called a mansion for nothing. She thought about starting her search with the outbuildings, but soon realized that it would take just as much time to find a passage there as in the house. At least she was more familiar with the house.

She left the hospital and drove to The Contented Canine. A feeling of guilt swept over her. She'd been there so little lately. She quickly called LaVon to let her know she was on her way, but was surprised by LaVon's response.

"Take your time," LaVon said. Her voice was surprisingly calm. "Everything's fine here. We have two new boarders today, both from one owner, so they get along great."

Now Dar was suspicious. "Who are you, and what have you done with my friend?" It seemed she was asking LaVon this question a lot lately. "Normally, you'd be flipping out and calling me every ten minutes asking when I'd be back. What gives?"

"Like I said, everything's fine here. Take your time. I'll see you soon."

"Right," Dar said before ending the call. There was something going on with LaVon. She was sure of it. Maybe it had something to do with whatever she'd been wanting to talk to her about. Normally, Dar could tell if LaVon was hiding bad news, but lately she hadn't been able to read her friend at all. But that was on her. She hadn't exactly found time for LaVon recently, and that needed to change. As she pressed harder on the gas pedal, Dar felt herself being stretched thin like a piece of taffy. If she didn't make some decisions soon, she was afraid she'd continue to stretch until the inevitable occurred, and that thin piece of taffy would snap. And she feared it wouldn't be pretty.

CHAPTER TWENTY-SIX

Dar hurried into The Contented Canine, expecting to witness a chaotic scene in her absence. But instead, she was greeted by LaVon, who was all smiles and sunshine, motioning toward something shiny near Dar's desk. Dar's mouth dropped open at the sight of a stand with a small coffee bar featuring a gleaming new stainless steel coffee maker.

"I love it," Dar said. Her eyes lit up in anticipation of the readily available caffeine jolt. But then her eyes dimmed. "Wait. I can't believe I'm asking this, but can we afford such a luxury?"

"No worries," LaVon said. "How about we take our newest residents out for a walk? I still haven't had a chance to talk with you, and I really hate to keep putting it off."

"Sure," Dar said. Though she tried to sound enthusiastic, she feared the coffee bar had been meant to butter her up for some bad news. Maybe her good fortune with the kennel was about to end, and her best friend and business partner was going to tell her she had found a better offer elsewhere. She felt as though her feet were made of lead as she walked to the hooks near the door and grabbed a leash.

Following LaVon into the kennel area, she helped her open the cages to a basset hound and cocker spaniel, whose excited greetings lifted her mood. When the dogs spotted the leashes, their tails beat in double time, and then triple time when they caught sight of each other. Dar had to laugh. LaVon wasn't kidding about their two new guests being best buds.

Once they were out in the fresh air, Dar felt herself relax a little. "Let's take the path through the woods," she suggested. "It'll block the wind that's picked up."

"Good idea," LaVon agreed.

They walked for minutes in silence, enjoying the sights of fresh spring-green colors budding on the trees. Moss phlox blanketed areas in shades of purple and pink where the sun shone through the early spring branches. Along the path, white trillium was abundant, rising out of last fall's decaying leaves.

Dar welcomed nature's change of seasons, and decided she would try to do the same and welcome any changes LaVon was about to reveal. Taking a deep breath, she asked the dreaded question.

"So, what is it you wanted to talk about, LaVon?"

Dar caught LaVon's sideways glance at her, and once again, she struggled to read her friend's mind. It used to be so easy for both of them to know what the other was thinking, but a lot had changed in the past few years.

"You know I love working with you here, right?" LaVon began.

"Of course," Dar answered. "And your accounting skills have helped make The Contented Canine a successful business." She stopped while the basset hound searched out new smells. "Look, if you need to move on, trust me, I understand completely."

"But . . ." Before LaVon could reply, both of their phones buzzed repeatedly, and they paused to check their messages.

"It's Nalini. 911," they said in unison.

Dar and LaVon exchanged worried glances, then turned and ran with the dogs back through the woods. When they reached the clearing, their fears revved up a notch. A Reed police car was parked in front of the building.

Though relieved not to see smoke coming from the building, Dar decided it best to keep the dogs outside. LaVon offered to stay with them, so Dar handed her leash to LaVon and promised to let her know once it was safe to bring them in.

Dar found Nalini inside, talking to a young male police officer and pointing at the kennel door that led back to where the dogs were kept. *Something happened to the dogs!*

"Excuse me," she said, walking over to the officer. "I'm Darla Kelly, one of the owners. What's going on?"

"We received a 911 call saying someone threw a brick through one of your windows," he replied. "My partner is outside checking for footprints on that side of the building."

Dar looked at Nalini and began firing off questions. "Which window? Was anyone hurt? Were any of the dogs hurt? Are you okay?" She grabbed Nalini's arm and quickly checked her for signs of cuts.

"I'm fine, but one of the dogs, Mrs. Johnson's dog, Roxie, was cut by the broken glass. My friend is trying to keep her calm until Dr. Williams gets here to examine her. I hope it's okay that I called him before checking with you."

"It's more than okay. I appreciate your quick actions in contacting the police, us, and the vet. Can you show us the window?" Dar asked.

Nalini led her and the police officer to a window near Roxie's cage. Though the brick hadn't been able to penetrate the bars on the cage, shards of glass had flown inside, and at least one jagged piece had made contact with Roxie. Nalini's friend held the shivering dog, who whined in her arms as she tried to calm the injured canine.

Dar grabbed a blanket from a metal cabinet along the wall and covered both the dog and the girl. "The vet will be here soon," she said. Then she examined the area to ensure no other animals had been hit by the flying glass. She checked each one until satisfied that the rest of their boarders were uninjured. When her attention returned to the shattered window, her face glowed red.

"Who would do such a thing?" she demanded.

Not waiting for a reply, she remembered LaVon was still waiting to hear if it was safe to bring the dogs inside. Dar quickly excused herself and rushed outside.

There, LaVon and a female police officer were standing in the parking lot, engaged in a serious conversation. Dar joined them and after introductions, suggested they take the two dogs inside and continue their conversations there.

Once they had the dogs settled in their kennels, LaVon asked the police officer to tell Dar what she'd told her in the parking lot.

"No problem," the policewoman said. "As I was saying earlier, I checked the area outside the broken window but didn't find any footprints. It's stone landscaping all along that side of the building. My guess is he or she stayed on the stones, threw the brick, then ran along the stones until he or she reached the woods."

"But we were in the woods," LaVon told her. "We didn't see anyone."

"Maybe we were too focused on the dogs, the trail, and our conversation to have noticed much else," Dar said. "Or the vandal saw us before we saw him."

The male officer finished taking pictures of the window, brick, strewn glass, and finally Roxie's injury. "We'll cruise the area," he said, "though, whoever did this is most likely long gone by now. I'll also file a report of vandalism and call you if we have any further questions or if we find anything."

Dar and LaVon thanked them before they left. They were discussing what they should do next when LaVon's phone buzzed.

"Darius, er Dr. Williams is here," she said, looking at her phone. "I'll bring him back."

"Good," Dar said. "I don't want to call Mrs. Johnson until Roxie's been examined. That poor dog. Who would do such a thing?" she asked again.

Dar spent the remainder of the evening taking her own pictures of the vandalism, then worked with Nalini to clean up the shattered glass. They'd just finished when LaVon returned with a sheet of Visqueen and a roll of strong tape.

"That should work," Dar said.

Together, they spread it across the window's gaping hole and taped it in place until repairs could be made. By then, Dr. Williams had cleaned Roxie's wound and given her a thorough check for other injuries.

"Fortunately, it was nothing serious, only a scratch," Dr. Williams said. "No stitches needed."

He offered to help them give Roxie a bath so he could check further for any tiny pieces of glass that might have been missed. Once he was satisfied their furry friend was free of glass, he turned to leave, but not before he told Dar and LaVon that he would waive his fee on the visit.

"I can't believe someone would do something like this," he said, his hands balling into fists. "Let's hope the police catch the culprit soon, and when they do, I'd like to personally wring the guy's neck."

After Dr. Williams left, Dar tried placating Roxie with treats to keep her calm. Then, LaVon helped her move Roxie and Foxie into a larger, new cage where they could be together and have zero chance of being exposed to a missed sliver of glass from the clean-up. They pulled the two dog's beds, which Mrs. Johnson had insisted on bringing, close together. The dogs positioned themselves on the beds so that their noses touched. Dar placed their toys close by, and soon both dogs were snoring softly.

Mrs. Johnson was initially frantic when Dar called her, but when Dar sent her a picture of them sleeping peacefully side by side, she calmed down. Mrs. Johnson agreed with Dar that instead of coming immediately to pick them up, it would be best if she waited until morning. Then she could take them directly to be examined by her own vet. Though Mrs. Johnson didn't blame Dar or any other staff member for what had happened, Dar wondered if the woman would ever trust them again with her precious babies.

CHAPTER TWENTY-SEVEN

The following morning arrived too soon for Dar. Half awake, she stood in her kitchen groggily searching for the "strong" button on the coffee maker. She sighed with relief at her success. While waiting for the coffee to brew, she filled Merlin's water and food bowls, overflowing both onto the surrounding floor area. Merlin was all too happy to clean it up.

Dar was grateful to have her friend back. When Daniel had called her and learned of the vandalism at The Contented Canine, he'd offered to keep Merlin another day, but she had missed her furry friend far too much.

As she ran through a list of things in her mind that she needed to accomplish that day, she grabbed her coffee and absently took a big gulp of it. Sputtering and choking, she ran to the sink and spit it out, then turned on a stream of cold water and stuck her tongue in it, half expecting to see steam rise off it. It was a sad fact that she needed a caffeine jolt before she could manage to drink her coffee without burning her entire mouth as she'd just done.

Today, both shower and coffee had failed to produce the alert feeling she'd hoped to achieve, so she filled her thermos with more coffee before grabbing her purse, keys, and Merlin and heading to her car. It was only as she was pulling away from the house that she realized she'd forgotten the thermos. Going back for it delayed her further, but some things she felt were worth it. As she backed out of her driveway for the second time that morning, she slammed on the car's brakes, then twisted to check the back seat of her car. Merlin barked at her as if to let her know that at least she hadn't forgotten him.

Dar blamed her less-than-perfect start to the day on her attempt to get to work earlier than usual. She had to see for herself that Roxie was still doing okay, and that the kennel was in pristine condition before Mrs. Johnson arrived to pick up her dogs. Though Dr. Williams assured her Roxie would be fine, stating that the dog had been more frightened than hurt, Dar wanted to be certain. Nalini had offered to stay through the night and promised to call if Roxie so much as whimpered. Then Dar thought of one other thing that she needed to check on today.

As Dar walked through the door of The Contented Canine, Nalini was putting on her coat to leave. One look at her, and Dar forked over her coffee.

"You need this more than I do, and that's saying something," Dar said.

Nalini waved a hand. "I helped myself to your new coffeemaker. I hope you don't mind."

"Of course not! I completely forgot we have that now. How's our girl, Roxie, this morning?" Dar asked. She planned to look in on the dog herself, but she valued Nalini's opinion, especially since her loyal employee had spent a very long evening constantly checking on Mrs. Johnson's cherished dog.

"Roxie slept much better than I did," Nalini said, moving awkwardly in an attempt to work out kinks. "She's fine. I think she's already forgotten the whole ordeal, unlike the rest of us. Who would do such a thing?"

"I don't know, but I intend to do some investigating of my own."

"Normally, I'd try to stop you, tell you to be careful, yada yada, but I'm too tired. I'll talk to you later, after a hot shower, food, and twenty-four hours of sleep."

Dar thanked her again profusely, then made sure Nalini made it safely to her car. After she saw Nalini's car turn onto the road, she hurried back to the kennels.

While she filled the dogs' bowls with fresh water, Roxie began to stir, along with many of the other dogs. She opened Roxie's cage and gathered her into her arms, gently stroking her fur while examining her for any signs of bleeding from last night's scratch, but found none. Roxie covered her face with wet kisses, her tail wagging constantly. Foxie was not about to be left out, though, and jumped on Dar's legs until she received the same attention.

Dar sat down cross-legged on the floor with both dogs, each nudging her hand to pet them whenever she stroked the other. She smiled.

In that moment, she felt she had the world's best job. But she couldn't deny the twinge of longing she also had for pursuing her second dream, to start an equine therapy group. Unfortunately, doing both well was next to impossible, no matter how hard she tried to make it work. As much as she hated to admit it, she knew she had to choose between the two.

Dar frowned at having ruined what had been a pleasant moment. She stood up. Grabbing leashes for the two dogs, she led them into the gated grassy area, then yawned and stretched in the early morning sun. As she did, something in the woods caught her eye. It almost blended in with the budding leaves at the edge of the woods, except for its unnatural hue. The wind caught it, causing it to flap, as though struggling to escape the twig it hung from at an odd angle.

Gathering up Roxie and Foxie, she returned them to their kennel, fed them, then added a bone for each to chew on. Satisfied that they were content, she grabbed her phone and rushed outside to get a closer look at what she'd seen in the woods.

Walking a wide swath around the building to the woods so as not to disturb any prints that might have been missed, Dar again spotted the object. She approached for a closer look.

A scrap of green material hung from a tree branch, where it'd been caught and ripped from someone's clothing. The police must have missed it somehow. Maybe the late afternoon sun had shaded the area enough for it to have blended in better as opposed to the morning sun that now shone on it. Dar snapped a picture of it, sensing something familiar about it. She tried to remember where she'd seen it before. Then it clicked.

Mike answered on the second ring.

"Well, what murder did you walk into already this morning?" he growled.

"Sorry, I called before your fourth cup of coffee," Dar said with impertinence, "but be nice, I only had one so far myself." She'd tried to match Mike's growl, but it was a lame attempt. "Did you hear about our vandalism at The Contented Canine yesterday? Someone threw a brick through a window. One dog was injured, but thankfully it was no more than a scratch. It could have been worse."

"Yeah, a Reed patrol car with two officers responded, right? So why call me?" Mike asked. Then a crack seemed to form in his armor. "You okay?"

"I'm mad, but other than that, I'm fine," Dar replied. "What kind of low-life would risk injuring animals? Anyway, the police didn't find any clues yesterday, but this morning I spotted a scrap of cloth caught on a branch near the edge of the woods."

"Why are you telling me and not the officers who investigated?"

"I know you don't believe in coincidences any more than I do," Dar said. "The piece of material I found is green camouflage, and the guy who was lurking across the street from the Twin Forks restaurant was wearing a green camouflage hoodie."

"How can you be sure it's from the same guy?" Mike challenged. "Green camo isn't necessarily uncommon."

"Doesn't it seem strange to you?" Dar asked. "First there's a guy in green camouflage who acts like he's spying on you and Shawn, and then we find a torn piece of the same material near the spot where a brick was thrown through our window. If it is the same guy, why would he want to vandalize The Contented Canine? Maybe he's trying to send me a message."

"Like what – 'I don't like dogs?' I think you're imagining things," Mike said. "It was probably just some punk doing it for the thrill, trying to see what he could get away with. Leave the investigating to me. I'm the professional, remember?"

"How could I forget with you reminding me constantly."

"At least Shawn has the sense to call me when he remembers a clue."

"Hey, I'm calling now," Dar protested. "Besides, I was the one who told Shawn to call you about the 'Do Not Disturb' sign. You're welcome. And there's one more thing I learned from Mo."

Dar filled him in on their conversation regarding the shorted medical supplies, and the nurse who'd seen a construction man coming and going late from Mr. Reece's office.

"Okay. I'll interview this nurse Jan that Mo told you about and see what else she can recall. I'll also get our forensics accountant to take a closer look at the recent orders of medical supplies."

"If someone's been stealing from the hospital," Dar said, as she tried to sort it out, "I can't see how that's connected to the two murders, unless they actually saw the thief in action. Otherwise, I don't see how Mr. Reece or Spike could be involved."

"That's why the police collect evidence and facts, rather than loose theories. We call that justice. Gotta go." Mike disconnected.

Dar sighed. Mike needn't worry. She had no plausible theory for the hospital thefts and murders. But the timing of it all, so close to the vandalism to her business, and the art thefts at the estate, felt strange and overwhelming. Was it a coincidence? Even if it were, too many people she knew worked and lived within the confines of the crimes' locations, and she didn't want any of them hurt. She had to learn the truth behind each crime.

CHAPTER TWENTY-EIGHT

Dar let Merlin into the back of Shawn's old mustang in The Contented Canine's parking lot, where Shawn was waiting for them. She hopped into the front passenger seat, leaned over the console, and gave Shawn a kiss. It was already five o'clock, but now she wished she wasn't in such a hurry.

"Thanks for doing this," she told Shawn. "I know this isn't exactly what you had in mind when you said you wanted to meet for dinner."

Shawn locked his gaze on her. "No, but I'm happy that for once you've included me in your plans instead of leaving me behind to worry. Now, remind me why we're driving to Fort Wayne in such a rush? After having a brick thrown through your business, I guess I expected you'd be spending more time here tonight, but then you always keep me guessing."

"Is that bad?" Dar asked, hoping she'd like his answer.

"It drives me crazy, but in a good way." Shawn did a low tiger growl, raising his eyebrows up and down.

Dar laughed, then squeezed his hand. "Well, you don't need to guess how much I love you." It rolled off her tongue without hesitation and felt right. Shawn's gaze made her realize it was what he'd been waiting to hear. Though Shawn had spoken those three words to her often, she wasn't sure she'd ever reciprocated. She'd thought it, but out loud, she'd only danced around it, saying how much he meant to her, or how special he was to her. Her previous relationship had been a disaster, leaving her so guarded that she'd avoided saying 'I love you' to Shawn—until now.

"This would be an excellent time to have a hands-free car," he said, leaning forward with a slow tender kiss. He cleared his throat as he pulled back from her, then put the car in gear. "So, you didn't answer my question. Why are we driving to Fort Wayne in such a hurry?"

"After Mrs. Johnson picked up her dogs this morning, I kept thinking about the vandalism. Maybe it was meant to be a warning."

"What kind of warning?" Shawn asked.

"Just a feeling, I guess," Dar said. It was one thing to have Mike dismiss her gut feelings, but she couldn't handle the same from Shawn. She'd keep those thoughts to herself from now on. She decided to tell him about the reason for this trip instead. "There's something you should know before we get to the Montgomery Farm Estate."

"I'm listening," Shawn said, sliding a sideways glance at her as he drove.

"When I was at the estate last, Daniel and I found a hidden compartment in an old footrest that contained letters that Rosie had overheard Mr. Montgomery tell his wife to hide there. The problem is, Daniel and I were interrupted before we had a chance to read the letters. But now I have a nagging suspicion that we need to read them as soon as possible. I only wish I knew why."

"Another gut feeling?" Shawn asked her.

Dar heard no mockery in his question, and saw no glimmer of ridicule in his eyes. She looked at him, and felt safe enough to reply, "You know me too well, Shawn O'Reilly." Silently, though, she hoped for his sake, that it wasn't a bad thing.

CHAPTER TWENTY-NINE

When they arrived at the Montgomery Farm Estate, Shawn parked in the circular drive at the base of the mansion's main steps. Dar got out of the Mustang first, followed by Merlin and Shawn. As she took in the height and span of the building, she felt dwarfed by the enormity of her biological mother's childhood home. She couldn't imagine what it must have been like growing up here.

The trio climbed the steps to the grand double-door entry, and Shawn opened one of the substantial doors for Dar and Merlin. Once inside the massive foyer, Shawn stared at the custom-made crystal chandelier and the curved staircase with its intricately hand-carved banister.

"I don't think I'll ever get used to walking into this opulence," he said.

Dar wanted to tell him how important it was to her that he consider doing exactly that because of the home's connection to her and Daniel's family history. But her thoughts were soon forgotten as Rosie appeared from the hallway and rushed toward her. She felt Rosie tremble as she embraced her.

"I'm so glad you're here!" Rosie exclaimed.

"Rosie, what's the matter?" Dar asked.

"There's been another theft—another painting!" Rosie clasped her hands together over her chest. "Daniel and I still don't know how they're getting inside when the doors are locked."

"We'll figure this out. I brought reinforcements with me." Dar gestured toward Shawn.

"I'm sorry for my manners, Mr. Shawn," Rosie said. "It is good to see you again. I'm so glad you're here to help."

"I'm not sure how much help I'll be, but I'm happy to be here," Shawn said.

"I hate to be rude, Rosie, but is there any coffee? It's been a long day. And did Daniel call the police?"

"Yes, to the coffee. Come into the kitchen, and I'll pour you some." Rosie led them down the hallway toward the kitchen. "Also, yes, Daniel called the police. He said he'll be down in a minute. I think he's on the phone with someone. In the meantime, let me fix you something to eat. There's nothing you can do right now anyway."

Rosie busied herself serving coffee, while Dar and Shawn settled themselves on chairs at the kitchen island. They agreed to wait until Daniel joined them before discussing this latest theft. Rosie prepared plates of sandwiches and fruit, along with a vegetable tray and blueberry muffins that smelled divine. Merlin busied himself at their feet, picking up every morsel that fell to the floor whether on accident or for his benefit.

Dar gratefully sipped her coffee and helped herself to one of everything from Rosie's offerings. She hadn't realized how hungry she was until the food was in front of her. She noticed that Shawn was not shy either about helping himself. They each thanked Rosie between mouthfuls of food. When they'd finished, they both sat back and moaned.

"I take it Rosie's been taking good care of you," Daniel said.

Dar smiled at her brother as he walked into the kitchen. "And then some."

"I think my grandmother has some sweet competition with Rosie's blueberry muffins," Shawn said, rubbing his mid-section.

"Put me down as a judge for that," Dar and Daniel said in unison.

Shawn shook his head. "Are you sure we need to discuss anything tonight, since you two are clearly on the same wavelength?"

"The connection is one we're still trying to figure out," Dar said, "We definitely need to discuss everything, especially so we can benefit from your brain power, Shawn."

"And here I thought you loved me for my body," Shawn said.

"Before I gag," Daniel said, "I should tell you Detective Mike was here today regarding the first two stolen paintings, so after this latest art theft, I called him back. He spoke with a good friend of his with the Fort Wayne police, and then called me back. The Fort Wayne police agreed to post a police officer outside for a couple nights. Come on. I'll show you where this theft occurred."

Daniel led them down the staircase to the lower level. When he flipped on the lights, Dar grimaced at the sight of the two empty frames in the hall, evidence of the first two thefts. Now that the two Hughes "Joy" paintings with their vibrant colors were gone, the joy seemed to have vanished from the hall as well.

Daniel continued down the hall into the wine-tasting room. Once inside, he pointed to their left, and there above the stone fireplace hung a third empty frame.

"I vaguely remember the painting," Dar said.

"It was titled 'Afternoon Joy,' also by Julian Hughes," Daniel said. "I found a file in the office that our biological mom must have used. It had some of the receipts and papers on other pieces of art throughout the house, but oddly enough, there was nothing on these three paintings."

"That is strange," Dar said.

"Do you know when it was stolen?" Shawn asked.

"Not exactly," Daniel said. "But it had to have been sometime after two a.m. because I came down here when I couldn't sleep. I got a bottle of wine from the cellar. The painting was still in its frame above the mantel when I left."

"What about the video at the gate? Was there anyone who entered the property unexpectedly?" Dar knew that there were other ways for individuals to slip onto the estate grounds, though she doubted few would attempt trespassing through the heavy landscaping on its perimeter. It would be extremely difficult to do so unscathed from the briars.

"I checked. Only staff and two others, but both of them were expected, including the vet. And before you ask, the horses are fine. Joe asked Dr. Darius to check them out because he thought they had seemed a bit high-strung and jittery the last two days. And no, Merlin hasn't done anything to cause any problems with the horses. In fact, he and the horses have become best buds, so no worries there. And Dr. Darius couldn't find anything physically wrong with them." Daniel rubbed the back of his neck.

Dar was quick to notice. "What else did he say?"

"He asked if the horses had any change in routines." Daniel hesitated a moment before adding, "Or if there were new staff working with them."

Dar's eyebrows raised.

"Knuckles and Owen both seem to be finishing all their chores along with anything else Joe asks them to do, and the horses love Knuckles. Maybe they're still adjusting to Owen, our latest hire. Let's give it more time. Joe promised to keep a close eye on both the horses and the men."

"Good," Dar said. "Did you say there were two who came through the gate that weren't staff. Who was the other?"

"The lady who delivers the straw and hay. She seems nice enough, though," Daniel said.

"Not to mention pretty," Dar said with a raise of her eyebrows. Her brother's face turned crimson.

"I couldn't really say," he retorted. "She had the brim of her baseball cap pulled low, covering most of her face. There was something familiar about her, though."

Dar thought it was strange that her experience with the woman nicknamed 'Red' had been different from Daniel's experience. When Dar had met her, the woman had been outgoing and seemed to enjoy showing her face, flashing Dar a bright smile as she spoke. So why would she be different with Daniel?

"I think the déjà vu moment was when she rolled her window down, and a gust of wind knocked her hat off," Daniel said. "She had blond wavy hair." He shook his head. "But the feeling disappeared when she tucked it back under her cap and drove on to the barn."

Dar decided to have a talk with Joe just the same. It seemed odd that they would receive deliveries two days in a row, but until she heard from Joe, she didn't want to scare Rosie and Daniel, or presume something that didn't exist.

"Rosie," Dar said, "were you the one who discovered the painting was missing?"

"Yes," Rosie said. "I thought I heard a scraping or grating sound coming from the basement, so I decided to check every room. I tried to listen for that noise again, but after a minute or two, the furnace kicked on. It made a clank and groan. That's probably what I heard; either that, or it was these massive stone walls settling."

"But if the grating sound was the furnace turning off, it's not likely it would kick on again in such a short span of time," Dar said.

"So, how did you know about this third art theft?" Daniel asked. "I hadn't called you yet."

"Rosie told us when we got here," Dar said. "I came so we could read the hidden letters we found. Do you have time to do that now? I'm hoping we can find an answer to one of our mysteries instead of more questions."

"I like your optimism, sis. Let's do it," Daniel said. Then he looked at Shawn. "And I think you'll get a kick out of seeing where the letters are hidden."

"I do like a treasure hunt," Shawn said, "except you two have the unfair advantage of having already found it. At least we'll all have a chance to be surprised when you two read the letters."

"Oh, so you're assuming we'll let you listen when we read them out loud," Dar said. She could hear Daniel laughing and Shawn's footsteps close behind her as she raced for the stairs.

CHAPTER THIRTY

Dar was still laughing when Shawn caught up to her at the top of the stairs and threw his arms around her. By the time Daniel appeared around the curve of the staircase, they were no longer winded, though still locked in an embrace. Daniel rolled his eyes and walked past them and down the hall toward the last bedroom on the right.

"Let's go," Dar said. She stepped out of Shawn's embrace, then took his hand and pulled him with her down the hall.

As they slipped onto the balcony, they found Daniel waiting for them deep in thought. Dar couldn't believe her brother had been able to wait to read the letters together. She wondered if she'd have been able to do the same.

Without a word between them, Dar stepped to one side of the footrest while Daniel moved to the opposite side. They knelt down and Daniel opened the lid, revealing the cream-colored throw, which Dar placed gingerly to one side. She glanced first at Shawn, then back at Daniel.

"Ready?" she asked him.

Daniel nodded. Together, they pressed the center studs on each of their sides, which gave slightly before releasing two soft clicks. They turned the footrest ninety degrees and did the same on the other two sides. Another set of clicks sounded, and the inside bottom panel sprang open.

"Wow," Shawn said. "Where can I get one of those?"

Dar and Daniel peered inside the secret compartment, then looked at each other with wide eyes.

"They're gone!" Dar said. "Are you sure you put them back in here?"

"I'm positive," he insisted. "The only other person who knew their location was Rosie, and we both know that she wouldn't take them."

"This is my fault," Dar said. "If I hadn't left in such a hurry, we could have read the letters right away. At least then we'd know their contents and what was important about them."

Dar let out a sigh. "Daniel, do you mind calling Mike while I call LaVon? I'm going to take a few days off until we can get this resolved. With our equine therapy program starting soon, I can't take any chances that there's a stranger lurking about the property who might endanger the lives of the children."

When Dar called LaVon, LaVon reassured her that she was more than willing to cover for her after she explained the mysterious thefts. "Don't worry, Dar," LaVon told her, "I've got everything under control here, and I've no doubt you'll figure out who stole the paintings and the letters. Just be careful, okay?"

Dar promised. She'd expected some resistance from LaVon at having to be responsible for additional work at The Contented Canine. Though grateful, she hadn't thought LaVon would agree so readily, especially if she was planning on leaving her job. Putting extra time and effort into the business had to be the last thing LaVon wanted to do. A better explanation was simply that she was a good friend who was helping her out—the best friend, actually.

"Earth to Dar," Shawn said, waving a hand in front of her face.

"Sorry," Dar said.

"I was trying to tell you that I've decided to stay for the night," Shawn said.

"I'd love for you to stay, but what about work?" she asked.

"I don't have anything scheduled until early afternoon," he said. "Maybe the more people who are here, the less the thief will feel like taking a risk of stealing anything else."

"Our thief is getting bolder," Dar said. "I can't believe he was able to sneak upstairs without being seen. There has to be a passage somewhere, maybe more than one, that we don't know about. But what's bothering me the most is how this person not only knew about the letters, but where they were hidden as well. And they must have known the contents too, otherwise why steal them? But we didn't even know what those letters contained, so how did they?"

"It's as though they know this place better than we do," Daniel said. "I have to agree with you, Dar, there has to be a secret passage that the thief is using to get access to the house; we just haven't found it yet.

"First thing tomorrow, I'll start a search for every employee who has worked here, as well as any outside businesses or services that were utilized by the Montgomery family. The thief had to have a connection to the Montgomery family in order to gain this kind of inside information."

"Rosie might be able to help with that," Dar said. "In the meantime, Shawn and I can search for a secret passage. And I think I have an idea where we can start."

"You know I'll follow you anywhere," Shawn said. Then, with a wide grin, he added, "Especially into dark hiding spots."

Dar gave Shawn a second glance after his remark about following her anywhere. Had she imagined it, or had Shawn's tone been unusually serious? It was as though he caught himself and tried to cover it by adding a humorous comment. Or maybe she was projecting too much of her own wishful thinking into what he said. She was determined to talk to Shawn about the future, but whenever she thought the time was right, there always seemed to be another murder or theft to solve.

CHAPTER THIRTY-ONE

The following morning, everyone awoke early at the Montgomery estate. Rosie insisted they all eat a hearty breakfast before starting their tasks, but it would be another ten minutes before it was ready. Daniel mentioned something about talking to Joe, and left for the barn, but only after promising Rosie he would be back in time for breakfast. To pass the time, Dar suggested to Shawn that they take a short stroll on the grounds.

She led Shawn to a path around the pond, where a light fog had settled. Clumps of yellow and red tulips bloomed in bunches, still holding droplets of water on their delicate petals. Even the willow tree branches dipped low, laden by the heavy dew.

As she enjoyed the scenery, Dar marveled at the great care taken to ensure that the flowers and trees planted throughout the grounds showcased each Indiana season. She wondered if her biological mother had been involved in its artistic planning or if she had left the gardens entirely in the hands of a professional landscaper. She winced at the reminder of how little she knew about the woman who'd given birth to her and Daniel.

"Are you okay?" Shawn asked.

Dar nodded. "As much as I'm enjoying myself, we should probably get back."

Shawn put his arm around her shoulders, pulling her in close before kissing her gently. "I definitely could get used to this," he said.

"Which part?" Dar teased. "Strolling around the beautiful grounds, kissing me, or Rosie's cooking?"

"All of the above, but right now it might be a tie between kissing you and Rosie's cooking. I'm starved!"

Dar hit him playfully on the arm before admitting she was hungry too. They raced back to the house and found Daniel already eating at the kitchen island. The aroma of bacon, eggs, and blueberry muffins wafted in the air. They filled their plates and didn't talk until the last crumb had been devoured. When they'd finished, they thanked Rosie profusely before bringing up business.

"I learned something interesting from Joe today," Daniel said. "He told me that the new guy, Owen, recommended Red for the hay and straw deliveries. Owen told Joe that Connor's Stables, where he'd previously worked, had used her services with no complaints. Plus, she had the best prices."

"Has Joe had any problems with her deliveries, or the quality of the hay and straw?" Dar asked.

"No, but I still feel like I've seen her before," Daniel said. "Anyway, I meant to tell you that I also got in touch with the HR lady from Owen's last employment at Newok Construction. She said he'd been a reliable employee and a hard worker. She was glad to hear he'd found another job and thought he'd make a great stable hand." Daniel frowned. "Strange. I don't remember telling her what position I'd hired him for here, but I guess I must have since she knew it."

"Thanks for checking Owen's reference," Dar said. "If you have any doubts about it, though, let me know. It seems like a bit of a shift to go from construction worker to stable hand. At least he's worked as a stable hand before, but we still have to wait for that former employer to return from his trip before we can call for a reference. Since there's nothing more we can do about that right now, Shawn and I plan to search the house for a hidden passage, beginning in the basement's wine cellar and working our way toward the rec room."

"Good luck with that," Daniel said. "While you're doing that, I'll start a computer search on the employees hired to work at the Montgomery Farm Estate over the years. Maybe we can find someone who would know about some type of hidden passage. Rosie has agreed to help me by compiling a list of anyone she can recall who has worked here or had reason to pass through these gates. It seems like a long shot, but you never know."

"Thankfully, that no longer includes our biological father," Dar said. "If I didn't know that Wes was safely behind bars, I'd tell you to put him at the top of the list." She thanked Rosie for the amazing breakfast, then headed to the wine cellar with Shawn.

Starting with the tasting room, they checked behind every painting that remained, and under each piece of furniture. They found nothing. Next, they entered the wine cellar where an impressive collection of wines had been sorted on racks by types and dates. After combing the room's every nook and cranny, Dar stretched her back.

"Does it seem strange to you that the thief didn't steal a single one of these expensive bottles of wine?" she asked. "Some of them have to be worth more than one of the paintings, so why leave them untouched?"

Shawn thought about it. "Maybe it would be more difficult to steal a bottle that could easily break than a painting that could be rolled up."

"I guess I could see that, but what about the letters? Why take those?" she asked.

Shawn shrugged. "I guess we'll never know until we find them." He walked over and kissed Dar. "Ummm," he said. "You taste like blueberry muffins."

Distracted by the kiss, Dar didn't notice Rosie walked in.

"I'm sorry to interrupt, but someone from Currie Children's Center is trying to reach you, Dr. O'Reilly. They said for you to call them back right away; something about new complications with one of your patients."

"Thanks, Rosie, but please call me Shawn. It's a good thing you gave me the heads-up about the lack of reception down here."

"I suppose you need to leave," Dar said.

"I'm afraid so. I'll call them back, but I want to be there to examine the patient myself." He kissed Dar again. "Would you be offended if I called you my little muffin?"

"What do you think?" Dar said with a scowl. Her expression changed quickly, though, as she thanked Shawn for staying and offering to help with the search. "I'll text you if I find anything."

After Shawn left, Dar made her way down the hall and into the utility room. Memories of fighting for her life came flooding back. The evil look in Wesley Shade's eyes as she tried to send an S.O.S. still gave her the chills. She closed her eyes, trying to shut out the memory and the terror Wes Shade had inflicted on her.

Recalling something else from that day, her eyes flew open. She'd been hiding behind the second row of shelving units and thought she'd caught a glimpse of a much smaller third unit almost hidden in the far end of the L-shaped room. She hadn't noticed it at first because the ceiling lights didn't illuminate that portion of the room.

Dar entered the utility room and walked through the shortest part of the L-shape, then turned right, making her way along the longest section of the room. She passed a long shelving unit on her left and a water heater to her right before reaching the deep shadows at the end of the room. A huge furnace extended from one corner, its ductwork reaching out like massive arms.

She turned on her phone's flashlight app. Next to the furnace, she could make out the shelving unit she'd seen while hiding that day. It sat so close to the furnace that she could barely see the stone wall behind it. She shone her light on it. It appeared shorter than the other units, though just as tall, and stacked with dusty boxes of various sizes. Gray cobwebs stretched between the boxes sitting on the top two shelves, the stone wall visible above them.

Dar shivered. This end of the room felt cold and uninviting to her. Seeing nothing remarkable, she rubbed her arms for warmth and then left the gloomy area. But something on the cement floor caused her to slip. Her arms flew about her as she tried to catch her balance, nearly dropping her phone in the process. Having regained her balance, she aimed the light at the floor to see what had caused her to slip.

In the halo of her light were several pieces of straw. She focused the beam outward from the straw but found no trail of it in any direction. Strange.

Dar moved to search another section of the room when a cobweb drifting slightly between two boxes caught her eye. She stopped and swung the beam of light in its direction but could see no apparent source of the breeze. It must have been her own movement that had caused it, nothing more.

She stood motionless to test her theory, but the cobweb still floated toward her. She moved her phone light back along the shelving unit, this time along the bottom shelves, but all she could see were large boxes shoved close together.

Dar made her way to the far end of the unit, away from the furnace. The dense shadows had prevented her from discerning where the shelving unit ended and the two walls formed a corner. But on closer inspection, she could see that this end wasn't flush with the wall.

She aimed her flashlight into the dark space and saw the same cold stone wall she'd seen above the shelves. Stepping around the end of the unit, she swept the light across the massive stones, but froze when a section of the wall disappeared.

Dar gaped at what appeared to be a three-foot-wide black hole. As she moved the light toward the bottom of the black hole where the floor should be, her light went out, plunging her into darkness. She gave her cell phone a smack, as though it would revive her dead batteries. She sighed, knowing it was pointless to explore any more until she recharged her phone. If she wasn't mistaken, what she'd glimpsed in that brief moment before her phone died could change everything.

CHAPTER THIRTY-TWO

Dar took the steps two at a time as she raced from the basement to the main level of the estate. She was so lost in thought, she nearly slammed into Rosie at the top of the stairs. Rosie gasped, covering her heart with her hand.

"I'm so sorry, Rosie," Dar said. "I didn't mean to frighten you."

"I was . . ." Rosie said, "looking for you." She took a moment to finish catching her breath from the fright. "Your friend, the detective, is here, and he has a little girl with him. I think they wanted a tour of the stables, so Daniel offered to show them around."

There was no way Dar could talk to Detective Mike or Daniel about her new discovery—not with Sarah listening. It would have to wait.

She thanked Rosie for the message, plugged her phone into the charger, then headed to the stables to find them. When she got there, she found Sarah sitting on the floor petting their largest rabbit, Fluffy. It was good to see Sarah smile again, though she gave no verbal response when Dar said hello. Instead, Sarah's focus turned to the balloons next to the rabbit's cage.

Dar asked her, "Did you know that today is Fluffy's birthday?" Sarah shook her head but didn't ask how old. *Baby steps*, Dar thought. "I was going to give a balloon to everyone in our group on Saturday, but since you're here now, would you like one?"

Sarah nodded again, and Dar separated a neon pink mylar birthday balloon from the bunch and handed it to her. Sarah struggled to hold it while still holding the squirming rabbit, so Dar tied the balloon loosely around the young girl's small wrist. "There, now you can enjoy the balloon and the animals." Sarah gave her a faint smile, then returned to petting Fluffy. She ran her fingers slowly along the bunny's long velvety ears.

Dar followed the familiar sound of Mike's voice around the corner to where he and Daniel were talking. When she walked over to them, Mike explained, as he had to Daniel, that he'd hoped bringing Sarah to visit their stables in advance would help ease her fears about the upcoming equine therapy program. Dar suspected it was to ease his own anxiety as well.

"That's great, Mike," Dar said. "I just wished you'd have called first."

Sarah came around the corner, holding Fluffy, and stood by the wall, keeping her distance. Dar guessed she was listening to every word they said, so she gave Mike a brief description of the program that Sarah would be participating in with the smaller animals, much like she was doing today. As she finished, Knuckles and Owen entered the stables with two of the horses. Dar was about to offer Mike and Sarah a closer view of the horses when she heard a strange noise, similar to the sound of a frightened kitten.

Dar glanced around, confused, before hearing the pitiful mews again. They were coming from Sarah, whose previously rosy cheeks had gone white. She was staring in the direction of the horses, but before Dar could comfort the panicked child, Sarah ditched Fluffy and ran off.

"You didn't tell me she was afraid of horses," Dar said, alarmed.

"She never was before," Mike replied with a frown. He called for Sarah but got no reply.

Joe entered the stables, scanning the area. He saw the two horses left abandoned. "Where the hell are Knuckles and Owen?"

"They were with the horses a minute ago. I didn't see them leave, but it must have been about the same time that Sarah ran off."

"Who's Sarah?" Joe demanded.

"When Sarah first got here, she ran over to one of the horses near the fence," Daniel said, ignoring Joe's question "She didn't seem frightened at all. In fact, she reached out to pet him on her own."

"We need to find Sarah. Now!" Dar said, her voice rising in alarm. "If it wasn't the horses that scared her, it had to be one of the men standing next to them!"

"Split up!" Mike ordered. Daniel took a confused-looking Joe with him to search the indoor arena, promising to explain on the way.

"I'll help you search the horse stalls," Dar told Mike.

"Good. I'll search the last one, while you search the first one. We'll work our way toward the center."

Mike left and Dar raced to the first stall. She moved the bedding straw around with her foot while calling Sarah's name just loud enough for Sarah to hear, yet soft enough so as not to spook the horse. Seeing no sign of Sarah, she did the same in the second stall, also with no luck. She was about to check another stall when she heard a commotion coming from the last stall.

Her feet slipped on the straw as she ran toward the stall. She could hear Mike's shouts along with the horses he'd managed to upset; they snorted and stomped in protest. Dar entered the stall as calmly as possible, but it was pointless, because Mike continued to shout at Knuckles, shoving him against the wall.

"Where is she?" Mike demanded. He clenched Knuckles's shirt in his balled-up fists. But Knuckles remained silent, infuriating Mike even more. He slammed Knuckles against the hard wall, but still Knuckles said nothing.

Daniel and Joe came running into the stall, having heard the commotion as well. Joe grabbed the horse's bridle and began speaking softly. Daniel rushed over to Mike, then pushed both hands onto his heaving chest in an effort to force him off of Knuckles. "Mike, stop!" Daniel said.

But Mike ignored Daniel's order, coming at Knuckles again. This time it took Joe as well as Daniel to pry Mike off Knuckles, but not before Mike gave Knuckles one last unexpected shove. Knuckles stumbled and sat down hard on the floor at the back corner of the stall. He glowered at Mike with his chest heaving, but he didn't retaliate.

Dar worried Mike's aggression had proven too much for Knuckles's mental state. It was as though Knuckles's anger had transferred to Mike, who was still seething under Daniel and Joe's restraint.

"He has to know where Sarah is," Mike insisted. "Why else would he run?"

Neither Dar, Daniel, nor Joe could provide the answer. Only Knuckles could, yet he remained silent on the stall floor, surrounded by bales of straw.

Dar thought she saw Knuckles's expression change to one of curiosity or puzzlement. She followed his focus to a particular bale of straw in the corner near where he sat. Knuckles looked at Daniel and then back to the bale. Dar could have sworn he was mulling something over, but what? Was he going to confess?

After what felt to Dar like an eternity, Knuckles glanced at Mike as if to ensure he was still firmly restrained by Daniel and Joe. Dar expected he'd found a chance to rush Mike and knock him out. Instead, Knuckles slipped his arm into the end of the bale of straw he'd been focused on. As he slowly withdrew his arm, Dar noticed the bloody knuckles on his hand. In that hand, he held a canister that had fit neatly into the hole. It was like watching a magician pull a rabbit out of his hat.

A hiding place in plain sight, Dar thought. *But why are his knuckles so bloody? What or who had he hit?* She hadn't heard of another incident of him losing his temper since he'd slammed his fist into the wheelbarrow. He'd been doing so well, yet something had obviously caused him to lose control.

Knuckles handed the container over to Daniel, who also noticed his injured hand as he did so. But before anyone knew what was happening, Mike slipped out of Daniel and Joe's grips. He lunged at Knuckles and slapped a pair of handcuffs on him. Mike and Knuckles both puffed out their chests, nostrils flaring, as though they were two alpha bucks about to lock antlers. Knuckles glared at Mike in silence. Mike, however, didn't wait to speak.

"Knuckles, I'm placing you under arrest for theft, and possible kidnapping."

CHAPTER THIRTY-THREE

Dar couldn't believe what was happening. She moved to Daniel's side as he opened the canister, allowing her to reach in and pull out the canvas. She unfurled it just far enough to confirm her suspicions as she read Julian Hughes's signature on his painting titled "Morning Joy." She looked at Daniel, whose face registered the same disbelief that she felt.

Had Knuckles stolen the painting from their house, then stashed it in the stables, in a spot they'd never think to look—in the center of a bale of straw? After everything Daniel had done to help him, paying for his mental health care, befriending him and giving him a job, could Knuckles be so cold as to steal from him? Had he kidnapped Sarah as well? But why? And where was she now?

"Wait!" Daniel said to Mike, who was about to lead Knuckles away in handcuffs. "Why would Knuckles hand one of the stolen paintings over to me if he was the one who stole it?"

"Because he knew he'd been caught," Mike growled. He swung Knuckles around. "You might as well hand the other two paintings over, too. But first, tell me where you've taken my niece. Tell me, or I swear I'll beat it out of you!" Knuckles remained silent, and Mike balled his hands into fists.

Dar felt she had to stop Mike from doing something he'd regret later. "Mike, what if you're wrong about Knuckles?" she asked. "You could be questioning the wrong person. We need to focus on finding Sarah."

At the mention of Sarah's name, Mike grew more anxious. He grabbed Knuckles and shoved the big guy out of the stall. "Let's see what's in the bunkhouse. Keep an eye on him," he barked at Joe.

Unaccustomed to being given orders in such a manner, Joe replied, "Not my job. Besides, I need to calm the horses down; all the shouting has them so worked up, I'm not sure how long it'll take me."

Mike undid one of Knuckles's handcuffs and attached it to the handle on the stall door. He then gave Knuckles a threatening look and said, "I'll be back for you later. You better pray we find Sarah before then."

Dar, Daniel, and Mike left for the bunkhouse. Dar was the first to arrive, and called out for Sarah. Something in the corner reflected light into her eyes, and she hurried toward it. "Over here!" she shouted over her shoulder. She raced to the pink Mylar birthday balloon she'd given Sarah, but Sarah was nowhere in sight. Dar examined the balloon's string that had once been tied to the little girl's wrist.

"It's been cut," she said.

"We'll find her," Daniel reassured Mike.

"If she's been hurt in any way, I'll kill whoever's responsible," Mike vowed.

"Maybe Sarah ran back to the house," Dar suggested.

All three hurried toward the house and were surprised to find Owen standing outside the back door.

"Where've you been?" demanded Daniel.

"And where's my niece?" Mike asked, getting in Owen's face.

Owen put his hands up. "Whoa," he said. "I was looking for the little girl, and thought she might have run back to the house. But Rosie already checked the house, so I thought I'd go back to the stables to help Joe search there again." He shook his head. "Do you think she could be somewhere on the grounds?" Owen motioned in the direction of the pond. "Like I said, I'll go back to the stables and search for her there."

Dar saw the panic in Mike's eyes as he stared at the pond centered in the wooded area. His eyes darted back and forth as a million scenarios raced through his mind, none of them good.

"She doesn't know how to swim," he said to no one in particular. Then, with a crazed look, he turned on Dar, pointing a finger at her. "I asked you to help her, not get her kidnapped." Pivoting on his heels, he swiped at his eyes with one hand while pulling out his phone with the other. Within seconds, he was on the phone with the Fort Wayne Police and began the dreaded task of issuing an Amber Alert for a missing child, his own niece.

Dar could hear him providing a description of Sarah and the pink shirt she was wearing with the word "Princess" on the front. Once Owen had left to go back to the stables, Dar knew what Daniel was about to say. "I know, I know," she said. "Mike didn't mean what he said. He's lashing out at me because it's safer than blaming himself."

"I'd say that's the gist of it," Daniel agreed.

"Daniel, would you mind staying with Mike?" Dar asked. "The next call he'll be making will be to his sister. He's going to need support, and I'm the last person to give him that right now."

She stared into the distance. Though she tried not to take Mike's comments personally, it still hurt. But then she reminded herself how much Sarah meant to Mike, and she let it go. This was no time for a pity party. Her focus needed to be on finding Sarah.

That's when Dar realized she'd been staring at a truck parked on the far side of the stables. Only the front of it was visible from where she stood, but she could see no driver inside it. Daniel turned to see what she was so intent on.

"What's Red doing here?" she asked him.

"I don't know," Daniel answered. "You'd have thought we'd have seen her while searching the stables."

"Strange," Dar said. "Joe never mentioned Red making a delivery today."

But Dar had an idea of where she might find Red. And suddenly, she realized someone was lying, and they'd all missed it. "I'll check the house again," she offered, "while you and Mike check the grounds. I think Sarah's smart enough to stay clear of the pond, but she was scared, and accidents happen. Let's pray that's not the case."

Dar watched Daniel jog over to Mike, who was pinching the bridge of his nose. She guessed he'd spoken to his sister already. When she was certain the two of them were hurrying toward the pond, Dar pressed her lips together and thought about the lie. How did Owen know Sarah was missing? He had disappeared the same time Sarah had run off. Even if he had somehow overheard them when Sarah vanished, Rosie didn't know Sarah was missing, so why would she have told Owen she'd already searched for her?

Dar entered the back door of the estate and called for Rosie. There was no answer. Rushing to the kitchen, she shouted again, but Rosie was nowhere to be found. Adrenaline surged through her as she feared that both Rosie and Sarah were now missing and possibly in danger.

There was one place left that she could think of to check for them.

Hurrying to where her phone was plugged into the charger, she unplugged it and then raced downstairs. At the bottom of the steps, she blinked at the sudden darkness. Not wanting to use her phone's battery just yet, she allowed her eyes to adjust to the dim emergency lights along the steps before finding the basement's light switches. She flipped them all on. That was a mistake. The stark change in light was now too much, and she groped for the switches again, flipping half of them off.

The world's worst detective, she thought. If someone was holding Sarah down here, she'd clearly announced her presence. Trying to be more careful, she continued to make her way down the hall, listening for sounds as she went.

As she entered the utility room, she made a beeline for the back corner, where she'd found the dark hole in the wall. Turning on her flashlight app, she slipped behind the shelving unit and focused its beam on the wall. The gaping hole hadn't been a figment of her imagination after all. As she moved toward it, something crunched beneath her feet. Swinging the beam down, Dar peered at remnants of straw and mud, smashed by a previous visitor to the tunnel. Bringing the beam up, she shone it ahead of her creating a halo of light into the otherwise dark void. She checked for large spiders lurking in webs, but they'd already been swept away by humans. Humans who gave her more cause for fear than any spider could.

Dar took a deep breath, then let it out slowly. Feeling only slightly calmer, she bent low to clear the top of the tunnel's entrance, and forged ahead into its inky darkness.

CHAPTER THIRTY-FOUR

Daniel tried to comfort Mike, though after his verbal attack on Dar, his heart wasn't in it. But as they made their way around the pond, Mike's calls for Sarah grew increasingly distraught, and Daniel tried harder to reassure Mike that they would find Sarah alive and well. They'd nearly made a complete loop around the pond when Daniel stopped short.

"I knew she looked familiar!"

"Knew who looked familiar?" Mike asked. "Never mind. I don't care. I only care about Sarah."

"But it might be important, maybe for Sarah, and maybe regarding Mr. Reece's murder," Daniel said.

"Talk and walk. I'm listening," Mike said.

"Red, the lady who delivers hay and straw in the truck—the truck that Dar saw parked near the stables a few minutes ago. It bothered me that I couldn't place her, but I was sure I'd seen her before. I think the fact that her hair was red, not blonde, threw me at first. She tried to hide her face from me under a ball cap, but her red nails should have been a dead giveaway. Not too many people deliver hay and straw wearing red nail polish." Daniel stood in front of Mike's path. "I know who she is now."

"Who is she, damn it?" Mike's face was gathering splotches of crimson.

"She's the same lady who was at the accounting conference. She's the one who was seducing Mr. Reece. I'm sure of it."

"So, what's she doing here, and where the hell is she?" Mike paused. "Sarah ran away at the sight of Knuckles and Owen, and then they disappeared too. Now we have Red nowhere in sight. I'm really not liking this."

"What do you think is going on?" Daniel asked.

"I don't know," Mike said, "but trust me, I'm going to find out."

CHAPTER THIRTY-FIVE

With every other step Dar took inside the dark tunnel, the ceiling became lower and lower—which Dar learned the hard way. Swearing, she paused to rub her head when her light fell on a ninety-degree turn in the tunnel up ahead. She followed it and soon discovered that the ceiling rose higher until she could once again stand upright. Lanterns that hung from hooks along the tunnel's wall spilled light out in both directions. She turned off her flashlight app, then stretched her neck from one side to the other, trying to work out the kinks. As she tilted her head to the right, she spotted another dark, gaping hole up ahead.

Thinking it was another tunnel, Dar moved closer. She turned on her flashlight again to see it was a small alcove. Shadows of something stacked against the back wall caught her eye, and as she neared, she discovered a stack of round canisters, each about three feet long, standing on end. They matched the canister that Knuckles had pulled out of the bale.

She opened one but found it empty. She then shook several others, but they were empty as well. Swinging her beam onto a side wall, two canisters sat apart from the others.

Dar pried the top off one. She peered inside, then slid out the curled item and unfurled it. The name Julian Hughes was written along the bottom right corner of "Evening Joy," the second stolen painting. Carefully rolling the artwork, she placed it back into the canister, then opened the one next to it. She pulled out another painting, this one "Afternoon Joy."

The thief had obviously entered their home via the tunnel, but she still had no clue from where, or who that person could be. She had to find the other entrance to the tunnel.

As she slipped the painting back into the canister, a slight rumble vibrated along the ground. Dar stood motionless. It felt as though the tunnel might collapse around her. Recalling the day's weather forecast for rain, she hoped it would pass quickly. Though some might think a tunnel to be one of the safer places to be during a severe storm, she didn't share their thinking or trust the walls of clay.

Anxious to exit the tunnel, Dar stashed the two canisters behind the stack of empty ones. As she reached back to set the canisters down, she spotted a large envelope tucked into the space there.

Dar stared at the familiar Montgomery Farm Estate's broken seal. When she looked inside, she sucked in the dank tunnel air. There were four letters separated into two bundles. But there had only been two letters in the footrest that she and Daniel had found. One of the bundles didn't look familiar. She'd give anything to open them right then and there, but there was no time. Her priority had to be finding Sarah and Rosie, and to do that, she had to learn what was at the other end of the tunnel. She prayed she'd find Sarah there. *The poor girl must be terrified by now.* She stuffed the letters into her jacket pocket and hurried down the tunnel. Reading their contents would have to wait.

It wasn't long before Dar came to a fork, where the tunnel diverged in two different directions. She tried to get her bearings, starting with where she'd entered the tunnel from the utility room. After careful consideration, she resorted to guessing, and chose to follow the tunnel's right branch.

She wondered how many branches were inside the tunnel and where they all led. Maybe it was one huge maze, and she'd spend forever wandering about seeking an exit. No, there was no way she was going to let that happen. But then the branch she'd chosen came to a dead end, and she chided herself for wasting precious time.

This end of the tunnel was farther from any light, so Dar clicked on her phone's flashlight again, moving the beam along the wall. A reflection caught her attention, and she stepped closer to its source—a small metal ladder that appeared to lead nowhere.

Tucking her phone into her back pocket, she tested the ladder's bottom rung and found it held her weight. She climbed the remainder of the rungs until she reached a landing. Using her phone as a flashlight, she soon found a door with a small metal latch.

The latch felt cool in her grasp as she opened it and pushed out on the door, just far enough to peek through the opening. She now understood why she'd seen straw and mud at the tunnel's entrance.

A massive painting of a brown horse with a white star on its forehead stared directly at her from across the room. Next to it was a hole in the wall the size of a large fist. She started to open the door further, but the sound of boots on the bunkhouse floor caused her to freeze. The heavy *clump, clump* seemed to be getting louder.

Dar quickly turned off her light and slipped her phone into her back pocket. She shrunk back, closing the door that she guessed was hidden behind the Black Knight painting. Through the final crack of light in the door's opening, she'd seen a leg jut out from around the corner. The bottom hem of a man's jeans was visible above a pair of boots caked with straw and mud.

Mike had handcuffed Knuckles in the stable, so it had to be either Joe or Owen. But what if Knuckles had somehow gotten free of his handcuffs? She hated not knowing who she could trust, although presently, fearing she'd been seen by someone she couldn't trust was worse, much worse.

Her heart pounded as she skipped half the rungs descending the ladder. She landed with a thud on the tunnel's floor. The impact sent bursts of pain through her feet and ankles, causing her to hobble-run down the dimly lit corridor. If only she could make it back to the house before anyone followed her. But as she again passed the alcove that held the canisters, she caught the scent of perfume drifting through the tunnel ahead of her, along with the sound of footsteps, too light to belong to any man.

Dar slid to a stop, causing her cell phone to fall out of her pocket to the ground. Its impact echoed, carrying the noise down the tunnel. Dar listened as the footsteps slowed, then stopped. She held her breath, her heart pounding. If only she had told Daniel or Mike about the tunnel and her plan to search for Sarah there. But it was too late for regrets now. After a long second, the footsteps returned with more urgency, each step growing louder and louder.

Snatching her phone off the ground, Dar turned and ran back in the opposite direction. Though she knew the right branch led to the bunkhouse, footsteps came from that direction as well. Searching for the fork again, she prayed she could find the left branch before the owner of the footsteps found her.

CHAPTER THIRTY-SIX

Dar hurried back to the tunnel's fork and ducked into the left branch this time. It could either lead her to freedom or into a trap.

From somewhere behind her came the sound of not one, but two angry voices. They seemed to be near the fork she'd just left. Realizing the voices weren't far behind, she clicked on her phone flashlight, figuring it'd be faster if she could see where she was going. She ran until the light reflected off something shiny on the floor. Dar took a split second to scoop up a green button. Twenty feet further, another green button lay on the floor. Its color matched the green of a sweater she'd seen earlier that day. Rosie was dropping bread crumbs, or in this case, buttons, for her to follow. And that could mean only one thing—Rosie was in trouble.

Three buttons later, Dar reached another dead end with yet another ladder. She stuck her phone back in her pocket and hoisted herself up the rungs. There she felt the rough outline of what seemed to be a hatch this time. She lifted the hatch, but unlike the opening at the previous dead-end, she couldn't see anything. Dar pulled out her phone and hit the flashlight app. Nothing happened. She hit it again. No battery.

A clap of thunder caused her to nearly drop her useless phone. She jammed it into her back pocket and lifted herself out of the tunnel and into what she sensed was a small space. Crawling on all fours, she felt a solid object in front of her. Thinking she'd come to a wall, she stood upright, her heart thumping. She felt like a mouse who'd missed a turn in a maze that led to cheese, and instead had become trapped at a dead-end, fair game for any creature higher up on the food chain.

Turning to her right, she felt what she thought was another solid wall, but then noticed a thin line of light near the bottom of it. It was a door. She slid her hand sideways along its surface until her fingertips touched a cool round doorknob.

Dar pressed her ear against the door. When she was convinced that there was no one on the other side, she threw the door open and stepped out into an unfamiliar bedroom. She glanced out the window and saw the stables and main house lit by a streak of lightning in the distance. That could only mean she was standing inside one of the guesthouse bedrooms and had entered it through a small closet.

Searching the guesthouse for Rosie and Sarah would take too long, so she had to buy herself more time. Spinning around, she spotted a dresser near the closet that would work. It was heavier than she'd expected, but she leaned into it and pushed it in front of the closet door. Whisking an item off the top of it, she hurried out of the bedroom, but as she did, the stolen letters spilled out of her pocket and onto the floor. She picked them up, not wanting to risk losing them again, or give whoever was following her a chance to take them from her. Deciding she could retrieve them later, just as she planned to do with the paintings, she tucked them under the mattress and prayed the thieves wouldn't find them. She could only hope she'd live long enough to read their contents.

Dar exited the bedroom, glancing to her right and left down a hallway. She started to go right but stopped when she caught the glint of a green button to her left. Dar added it to the others in her jean pocket. She figured Rosie couldn't have many left.

Her ears on full alert, she tiptoed down the hall. A muffled sound came from somewhere, but another clap of thunder drowned it out, shaking the guesthouse. Standing in the center of the hallway, she waited and listened. This time, she heard sounds coming from the last room on the left. As she moved toward the room, a floorboard creaked beneath her. She stopped. Even if she found Rosie or Sarah, or both, there could be someone guarding them. She listened again. Silence. Dar white-knuckled the hand-held mirror she'd snatched off the top of the dresser. Rosie had her skillet; she had a mirror.

Arriving at the last room on the left, she opened the door, and her breath caught. Both Rosie and Sarah were tied to chairs in the center of the room, strips of duct tape covering their mouths. Rosie let out a huge sigh of relief, while tears escaped down Sarah's cheeks.

Dar gently peeled the duct tape off Sarah first before doing the same for Rosie.

"Thank you, Lord!" Rosie said with her face lifted upward. "I thought that awful man and lady were coming back to . . ." Dar interrupted her with a cough and flashed her eyes toward Sarah. Rosie picked up on her cue. ". . . make sure we hadn't escaped."

"They're not far behind," Dar said, struggling with the zip ties that bound their hands and feet. She tried to hide the anger that flared within her at whoever had done this to a little girl. Scanning the room, she realized they were standing in someone's personal office. She raced to the desk and opened the center drawer, tossing aside items until she found scissors. A scraping noise came from somewhere back down the hallway.

"That's them," Dar said. "We've got to hurry."

CHAPTER THIRTY-SEVEN

Dar cut the zip ties as fast as she could without injuring Rosie or Sarah's wrists. She couldn't believe the bastards had pulled Sarah's binding so tight, it had cut into her skin. Finally, she had both Rosie and Sarah free.

"We need to hurry," she warned again. "I tried to block the tunnel opening with a dresser, but it won't hold long, especially with two people pushing on it."

Rosie and Sarah each gave her a quick hug. It was in the middle of one of those hugs that she saw it—a green camouflage hoodie slung over the back of a leather chair in the corner.

"Where did that jacket come from?" she asked before peering into the hall to see if it was clear.

"It belonged to the man who brought us here," Rosie said. "After he tied us up, he took it off. His lady friend must think she's some kind of fashionista because she pointed out the hole in the sleeve and asked him why he was still wearing 'that ratty thing.'"

Dar rushed back and snatched it off the chair. She thrust it into Rosie's hands, saying "Evidence."

"It's him," Sarah whispered, taking Dar's hand. "The man who killed Nurse Spike."

Dar exchanged a look with Rosie as they ran out of the room. *Had Sarah witnessed Spike's murder?* That didn't seem possible, but this was not the time to question her. Dar gripped the child's hand tighter.

Leading Rosie and Sarah down the hall, Dar paused at the sound of the closet door slamming repeatedly against the dresser. It pumped up her adrenaline full force. She rushed Rosie and Sarah past the room, making it to the foyer. Dar's hopes of escape rose, along with her confidence, until a loud crash dampened those hopes. Her number one priority was to get Sarah and Rosie both to safety.

She took Sarah's small hand out of hers and placed it in Rosie's. "Run!" Dar ordered Rosie. "Find Mike. He's out in the woods by the pond."

She feared Rosie would protest, but at the sound of angry voices approaching, she signaled Rosie to go. Rosie flew out the door with Sarah in tow, soon soaked by the heavy rains. Halfway to the mansion, Rosie looked back over her shoulder as though she were a momma rabbit leaving her baby to fend off a pack of wolves.

Scanning the foyer, Dar's heart sank. She'd left her mirror weapon in the bedroom. Her eyes fell on a heavy marble statue on an antique table. She grabbed it with two hands, then raced out the front door. Outside, she dodged to the left and pressed her body against the cold stone of the house. Rain pelted sideways, drenching her, as she raised the statue above her head. She shivered from both the cold rain and fear, and waited.

A woman with fire in her eyes came through the doorway first, and Dar caught the glint of a gun in her right hand. Dar swung down hard, dropping Red to her knees, but not before the gun went off. She leveled a second blow to the woman's head and watched as Red crumpled motionless to the ground. Dar scurried for the gun as it slid across the slick porch deck.

She felt his breath on the back of her neck seconds before his large hands grabbed her from behind and placed her in a choke hold. She stomped on his foot repeatedly, but his steel-toed boots foiled any chance of doing any harm. His grip on her tightened, making her gasp for air. Not about to give in to the brute, Dar jabbed a sharp elbow into his side. His grip loosened slightly, allowing her to spin around, only to find herself looking into a face contorted with rage.

Owen's hands flew to her throat again, but Dar focused her own rage to retaliate. With every ounce of strength, she thrust her knee to his groin in one swift motion. He dropped his hands from her, grunting in pain, and Dar saw her chance to escape. She turned to make a run for it, but out of the corner of her eye, she saw an object coming toward her. She tried to duck, but she was too late.

Pain exploded on the right side of her head, and her legs went weak. Stars filled her vision, blacking out anything else from her sight. She could hear herself gurgle as she fought for breath. Choices she'd made and choices she regretted having avoided, flashed through her mind. Her last thoughts were of Shawn before the world around her transformed into a dark abyss.

***

Dar felt life-saving air begin to seep back into her lungs, though her mind remained foggy. A pair of strong hands shook her shoulders, and a voice called her name from what seemed like a distant planet. Instinct told her to fight, but as she tried, she sucked in too much air. It threw her into a coughing fit that sent fiery signals of pain to her brain, letting her know that she was miraculously still alive.

Bits of memory returned—memories of rough hands squeezing her throat, choking her, then hitting her with a solid object. That must have been when she'd blacked out. Maybe Owen had thought she was dead, and now realized he'd failed to kill her. Maybe he was trying to finish what he'd started.

Blinking, she tried to clear the tiny pixels of black that dotted her vision. The pressure on her shoulders disappeared as a deep male voice assured her that she was okay; she was safe. It made no sense.

Soaked from the cold rain, her whole body shivered as she tried to move, to escape, but her head screamed in protest. She closed her eyes and reached for her head to keep it from falling off. Her hands touched something warm and wet.

She opened her eyes again and looked at her hand covered in blood. Glancing around, two motionless bodies came into focus on the porch floor. A disheveled man knelt beside her, peering down at her with deep creases in his forehead. He raised both of his hands in the air, palms out, a pair of handcuffs dangling from the wrist of one. Squinting, she saw concern in his eyes rather than menace.

But just as she was letting her guard down, the man balled his hands into fists, fists that revealed rows of bloody knuckles. Dar cringed away from him. She was too trusting, and now she'd pay for that with her life.

The expected impact of Knuckles's fist never came. Instead, Owen, whom she had thought was out cold, wrenched his hand around her ankle, pulling and twisting. Without hesitating, she gave a swift kick with her free leg, aiming for his head. It missed its mark, making contact with a shoulder instead. The fist with the bloody knuckles did not miss, though, and Dar heard the crunch of her attacker's nose as Knuckles punched him. She felt the grip on her ankle release.

Scrambling, Dar tried to scoot herself away from both men, but her feet and hands slipped on the wet porch with each attempt. Her face stung from the pelting rain. The wind egged the rain's torment on, and she tugged at her soaked hair, which had become plastered to her face and neck. She blinked, not trusting what she saw through the deluge. Two men who had worked side-by-side at the stables were in front of her: one knocked out cold by the other. She tried to force her mottled brain to put the pieces together.

The rain began to subside, and she began to see things more clearly as she heard the sound of steps coming onto the porch. A woman wearing a green sweater with missing buttons stood, her lips pressed tightly together. She had a solid grip on a heavy black object she carried at her side. Alarm shot through Dar as she saw Rosie raise her weapon and aim her swing at Knuckles.

Words of warning failed to come out of Dar's throat, but she managed to raise her arms to stop Rosie. Rosie halted mid-swing. Unflinching, Knuckles remained calm, and in his bass voice, let Rosie know Dar was okay. Dar added a shaky thumbs-up to prove it.

A loud ringing in Dar's right ear made it difficult to understand a word Rosie was saying as she spouted off a barrage of questions. Dar placed her hand along the side of her head and winced as she found a gash there oozing blood. When she saw the marble statue lying next to her smeared with blood, she surmised that what she'd used as a weapon on Red had been used against her, as well.

Red lay near the front door of the guesthouse, and Owen was out cold near her feet. Dar shifted her weight and considered trying to stand, but the wet porch still proved too much for her groggy state.

Out of the corner of her eye, Dar saw movement. She wasn't the only one trying to stand. Red had come to and had succeeded in lifting herself to her hands and knees. But she got no further as Rosie responded with her cast-iron skillet, laying Red out flat.

"And stay down," Rosie said.

The scene on the porch, with everyone soaked to the skin, was one Dar would never forget. Especially seeing Rosie standing over two bodies with her skillet and buttonless green sweater, as though daring either of the attackers to move a muscle. Dar wasn't sure, but she could have sworn she witnessed Knuckles actually grin at Rosie.

This time, Dar managed to stumble to her feet. "Rosie . . . Knuckles, Knuckles . . . Rosie," she said, making the introductions with a raspy voice. She tried to swallow before continuing, burning her throat with the effort. "He saved my life." She mouthed the words "thank you" to Knuckles.

A small motion came from behind Rosie that put Dar on alert again. But when Sarah peeked her head out, she relaxed and smiled. She prayed the young girl had not witnessed the violence, fearing it could traumatize her all over again. Such a reaction wouldn't be surprising after everything Sarah had been through recently.

Sarah took cautious steps forward. Dar's eyebrows raised as she watched the young girl approach Owen and point to several zip ties that stuck out of his back pocket. Dar grabbed them as Knuckles rolled Owen onto his stomach and pulled his arms behind him. Despite Dar's throbbing head, she readily slipped a zip tie around his wrists.

"Put his on extra tight for Nurse Spike," Sarah said.

Dar was about to tighten the zip tie when Knuckles stopped her. "Let her," he said with a nod to Sarah.

Dar looked at Sarah, uncertain if this would prove too much for her. But to her surprise, Sarah marched over and knelt next to her. When she froze, Dar thought she'd changed her mind, but then Sarah grabbed the zip tie and yanked on it, binding Owen's wrists with all her might.

"You're not going to hurt anyone ever again!" Sarah said in a defiant tone.

"Impressive," Dar said. "Maybe there's a future for you in law enforcement." She secured a zip tie on Red as well, then added with a smile, "Just don't be as surly as your Uncle Mike."

"Who are you calling surly?"

"Uncle Mike!" Sarah said, running into his outstretched arms. He picked her up, embracing his niece in a bear hug until she insisted she couldn't breathe. Laughing, he set her back on her feet.

"I helped catch the bad guy," she told him, holding her chin high. Then she looked at the others and shrugged her shoulders before admitting, "Well, they helped too."

Mike took her hand as he surveyed the sight. "It looks like you did a fantastic job, Detective Sarah!"

Daniel joined them on the porch as Mike stepped aside to place a call. His clothes clung to him, dripping and forming a puddle around the spot where he stood.

"We heard the gunshot and came as fast as we could," he said, "but we were on the far side of the pond. We could see Rosie running to the guesthouse with Sarah right behind her. With all the rain, we couldn't be sure what we were seeing. I'm glad everyone's okay, well, sort of," he said, looking at Dar.

When Mike rejoined them, Dar moaned then half whispered, "Can we go back to the house before you ask questions?" Hearing her own raspy words, she wanted to add that she could also use a strong drink when she got there, along with plenty of aspirin to tame the pain in her throat and head.

"The ambulances should be here soon," Mike said, "and I've insisted that one of the EMTs examine you, but I guess they can do that at the house, if you're sure you're okay to walk." When Dar nodded, he added, "In the meantime, I'll stay here with these two idiots until the ambulance and transport arrive."

Again, Dar glanced around at the unusual gathering of people on the porch. There was Knuckles, who, with his bloody hand and rough features, could easily have been mistaken for the criminal, and yet he'd saved her life. And Rosie, who stood in her green, button-free sweater, who had finally set the heavy skillet weapon down onto the porch floor. Then there was sweet Sarah, who'd surprised them all with her bravery and courage, not only by securing the zip ties, but also by speaking once again. Mike and Daniel stood there as well, both with clothes clinging to them and matching frown lines.

      She wanted to verbalize her thanks to each of them, but a lump formed in her throat, or maybe it was the swelling from the bruises, that kept her from doing so. Instead, she did the only thing she could, and smiled in gratitude at her wonderful, odd group of rescuers.

CHAPTER THIRTY-EIGHT

Hearing Sarah go from refusing to talk to jabbering nonstop was music to everyone's ears. When Mike had called her parents, they announced they were already on their way, and not far from the estate. It wasn't long until they arrived at the house, and like Mike, hugged Sarah until she insisted her ribs were going to break.

Shawn and LaVon arrived directly after Sarah's parents, but after scanning Dar's battered appearance, they held back on their enthusiasm as they hugged her. Shawn left one arm around Dar, while running his free hand through his hair. But it was LaVon who repeatedly told Dar how relieved she was that she was okay, before confessing that she and Shawn had both assumed the worst.

"You weren't far off," Dar admitted. "But how did you two know there was any trouble here? I don't think any of us had time to call you when Sarah ran off, then vanished."

"I knew you wouldn't quit snooping into the painting thefts," Shawn said. "When I left you earlier, I was afraid that you might stumble across the thief, or worse, go looking for them. And after talking to LaVon about it, we decided to call Daniel. I didn't call you because I didn't want you to think I was worried. Daniel told me about the kidnapping, but when I asked to talk to you, he said they couldn't find you. And with you, that almost always means you're in some kind of danger. I shared the news with LaVon, and of course, she insisted on coming with me."

Relieved to see Dar was going to be okay, though very sore, everyone began asking questions all at once. That was when Mike stepped in, insisting that no one talk about the kidnapping until he got official statements from Dar, Rosie, Knuckles, and Sarah.

Dar smiled at Rosie gratefully as she placed a cup of coffee and a bottle of Irish crème in front of her. Sarah was rewarded with a cup of hot chocolate, complete with miniature marshmallows for her bravery, while Knuckles was given a large mug of steaming coffee and a plate of chocolate chip cookies. Rosie giggled when he thanked her and told her it was his favorite cookie. Dar couldn't believe the unlikely connection that seemed to be forming between the two.

Finding a blanket, she wrapped it around herself. Now that the adrenaline rush was gone, she couldn't stop shaking. She accepted the refill of hot coffee from Rosie, who then gave both her and Knuckles bags of ice for their cuts and bruises. Shawn refused to wait for the EMT and began examining her throat and head. He determined the cut would require stitches. As if on cue, Mike entered the kitchen with an EMT. Shawn accepted the medical supplies to first numb, then stitch her head wound, while the EMT supplied her with a couple strong pain pills. She felt silly being fussed over, but knew it was useless to refuse. Plus, the sooner they finished with her, the sooner they could get through Mike's inquiries. When the EMT and Shawn were satisfied that Dar would recover, the EMT left, but Shawn stayed by Dar's side, insisting that she keep her activity and talking to a minimum.

"Can I go first then?" Sarah piped up, surprising everyone again with her newfound confidence and voice.

Mike glanced around the kitchen at everyone gathered, then asked, "Are you okay with all these people being here, because normally when I would chat with you for something like this, I'd only allow your parents to be with you. I want you to feel safe when you answer my questions and tell your story."

Sarah gave a quick look around the room as well. "Nope. They can stay. I'm not afraid anymore."

"All right," Mike said, "but if you change your mind at any time, I can ask everyone except your parents to leave. If you're ready then, go ahead and tell me what

Owen and Red did to you. Please start with the first time you saw either one of them."

Sarah nodded. "The same day Nurse Spike went missing," she said, "I was in the hospital, and she came into my room. Dar was there too, but she left, and then it was just Nurse Spike and me." Sarah paused, her eyes watering. "She was so nice. I miss her already."

"We all do," Dar said, putting an arm around her. Sarah nodded, then took a sip of her hot chocolate. "What happened after I left your room that day?" Dar asked.

Sarah scowled. "That bad guy who tried to hurt us today, Owen, was talking in a mean voice to Nurse Spike in the hallway. At first, I could only see her, but I knew he was there too because she looked so scared. I didn't know what to do. I was scared too, so I put my head under the covers and tried not to hear his angry voice. He sounded like a mean old bear. I don't know how long I was hiding under the covers on my hospital bed, but it felt like a long time. Then I thought about Nurse Spike, and I had to see if she was okay, so I peeked out." Tears rolled down Sarah's cheeks.

Dar wiped at her own tears. She could only imagine how frightened and helpless Sarah must have felt.

Sarah's parents both hugged her tight. "You're safe now, honey," her mom said.

"Take your time, Sarah," Mike said. "It's important for you to tell your story, but if you want to do it later, we can wait."

Though Dar always suspected Mike capable of such compassion, it was heartwarming to witness. Still, she doubted his love for any other child could quite match his love for this little girl who sat, shaking her head stubbornly.

"No. I've wanted to tell somebody for a long time," Sarah said, "but he told me he'd kill me if I said one word about what I saw. I'm sorry I didn't tell you, Uncle Mike, but I really thought he'd kill me." Then she half-whispered with her eyes wide, "I didn't want to die."

This time, it was Mike who hugged her. "You have nothing to be sorry for, Sarah. That man was a bully and should never have threatened you like that."

Dar knelt next to Sarah. "I think you're the bravest girl I've ever met." She gave Sarah a moment to let that sink in before she continued. "You said that you peeked out from under the covers to see if Nurse Spike was okay. What did you see?"

Sarah lowered her head then took another sip of her hot chocolate. "I saw that bad man," she finally whispered. "Owen. Except he had on different clothes when I saw him at the hospital."

"What do you mean 'he had on different clothes'?" Mike asked.

"Like he fixed things," Sarah said. "I think he was one of those guys who works at the hospital to make it look newer or build new parts of the hospital."

Dar nodded. So that's how he had access to all the floors in the hospital.

"He grabbed Nurse Spike's arm. At first, she went up on her tipee-toes, but whatever he did after that must've hurt because her knees kind of bent when he did it. She tried to pull her arm away, but she couldn't.

"That's when he saw me," Sarah said. "He started to come into my room, but Nurse Spike stood right in front of him, and told him to leave me alone. I thought he was going to hit her. But Nurse Spike said she'd go with him if he didn't hurt me. They started to leave, but he turned around and pointed right at me. When he did, I saw a scary tattoo of a snake on his arm."

Dar glanced at Mike and knew he'd made the same connection. It sounded like the guy she'd run into that day outside Mr. Reece's office. No wonder Merlin growled when he tried to pet him.

"That's when he told me he'd kill me if I said anything about what I saw. Then he poked something shiny in Nurse Spike's back and made her walk in front of him. At first, I thought it was a gun, but when he turned to go down the hallway, I could tell it was a knife." Sarah looked up at Dar. "I never saw her again. He's the one who killed her, isn't he?" she asked.

"Let's let your Uncle Mike do his job first before he answers that question," Dar said.

Mike took the cue and also knelt to be at eye level with Sarah. "You're doing great, Sarah," he said. "I'm hoping you can answer a couple more questions for me. Think you can do that?" Sarah nodded, and Mike continued. "What happened after you ran away from us at the stables?"

"I was trying to get as far away from that man Owen as I could get, but I wasn't fast enough. When he caught me, he cut the string to my balloon with the same knife he had at Nurse Spike's back, then made me go down that dark tunnel behind the horse painting."

"We'll get you ten new balloons, if you like, sweetie," her mom said. "Go on, honey."

"It was scary down there," Sarah said, "and we walked through the tunnel all the way to the basement of the big house. That mean lady was already in the tunnel, and she started arguing with the man. She was so mad, she called him by three different names. I think she must've forgot his last name, but she always called him Owen first. It was his last names that were different."

"Can you remember any of those last names?" Mike asked. "It's very important."

Sarah scrunched up her face, trying to remember. "Uh-huh, because it reminded me of when Mom calls me by my full name when I've done something really bad. Only Mom never gets as mad as this lady. I think she said 'Owen Camo, Jay, Kane, or whatever your latest name is,' except she used some really bad words when she said it."

Mike thanked her and wrote the names down. "You're being very helpful, Sarah. What happened next?"

"Then the lady told the man that he'd made a mess of everything. She said he should've taken care of me when he had the chance." Sarah looked terrified reliving that awful moment. "She was holding a gun. I thought she was going to kill me." This time Sarah's dad held her in his arms as she sniffed back tears.

How many times had this little girl thought someone was going to kill her? It made Dar livid. Yet Sarah sat there, telling them all the details of everything she'd kept bottled up inside her, too afraid to speak out of fear that she might be killed. If Owen hadn't been caught, she might still be a frightened, quiet child.

"Rosie must have heard them fighting, because she found the tunnel, but the bad guy heard her coming. He grabbed her when she got inside the tunnel." Sarah turned to Rosie. "I'm sorry I couldn't warn you. That lady had her hand over my mouth real tight."

"It's okay, sweetie," Rosie said. "There was nothing you could do. I should have been more careful. But we're okay now, right?" Sarah smiled and nodded.

"Is that when they took both of you to the guesthouse through the tunnel?" Dar asked.

Sarah nodded again, then whispered to Dar. "I think Rosie was as scared as I was because she kept pulling buttons off her sweater all the way there."

Dar smiled at Sarah's interpretation of events. She especially loved that Sarah was trying to save Rosie any embarrassment by whispering her thoughts to Dar.

"We went down a different tunnel than the one we took from the stables," Sarah said. "It ended at that other house. When we got there, they took us to a bedroom and tied us to the chairs and left. We couldn't scream for help because they put something over our mouths." She looked at Dar. "I was so glad to see you. I was so afraid those two people had come back."

"Me too," Rosie added. "You saved us."

"I know you told us to run to safety and find Uncle Mike," Sarah said to Dar, "but when we got to the big house, we heard a loud noise that Rosie said sounded like a gunshot. She said it wasn't fair, two of them against only one of you. She grabbed a heavy pan from the kitchen and tried to make me stay back at the house, but I didn't want to be left alone. So, we ran all the way back to the other house where we'd left you, but you'd already hit the mean ol' lady called Red. She looked like she was sleeping. But Rosie saw her wake up, so she hit her with her big pan, and the mean lady went right back to sleep."

Everyone chuckled at the last part, imagining the scene of an angry Rosie. The levity seemed to help Sarah continue.

"When we first got there, the man I heard Dar call Knuckles hit the bad guy who was trying to grab Dar. Then Dar told us Knuckles saved her twice. Once when the bad guy was choking her, and once when the guy woke up and grabbed her leg. The second time, he didn't get back up, just like the lady. The best part was when I got to pull the zip tie real tight on his wrist. I hope they go to jail forever."

Sarah finally took a breath. Her parents wrapped her in their arms and told her over and over how proud they were of her. Everyone agreed. When her parents asked Mike if they could take her home, he nodded and thanked Sarah again for being such a brave girl. She beamed. Then she turned and gave Rosie and Dar big hugs. She started to leave with her parents, but then whirled around and ran back to Knuckles. The big guy seemed to melt as her small arms wrapped around him in a hug, and he embraced her back, bloody knuckles and all.

CHAPTER THIRTY-NINE

Once Sarah and her parents were gone, Mike stood up and faced Knuckles. Knuckles, who moments earlier had revealed a softer side with Sarah's hug, set his jaw. Mike cleared his throat.

"I owe you a huge apology, Knuckles. I wasn't seeing clearly when I thought you'd kidnapped Sarah. It was unprofessional of me to rush to judgment like that without all the facts."

Knuckles relaxed a bit and gave a slight nod, which Mike seemed to read as a sign to continue. Mike cleared his throat again.

"I don't understand, though, how you knew the canister that contained the stolen painting was inside the bale of straw if you didn't put it there," Mike said.

Knuckles swallowed hard. "I never liked Owen from the day he started here. He reminded me of some of the con men I'd met on the streets when I was homeless. Then when the paintings came up missing, I knew it was him and that lady friend of his who delivered straw and hay, but I had no proof. One day I saw him carrying a long object into one of the stalls, but when he came out, he didn't have it. So, after he left, I checked the stall but didn't see anything. When Owen took his long morning break the next day, I followed him to the bunkhouse. I watched him go inside, so I waited a minute, and then I went inside, too. But he was gone. I got so mad; I punched the wall." He looked at Daniel and Dar. "I'm sorry. I'll pay for the damage. Anyway, when the detective shoved me to the floor in the horse stall, that's when I saw the hole in the bale of straw. I had a feeling one of the missing paintings was inside that canister that they'd hidden there. All I could think about was getting it back for you," he said, looking again at Daniel. "You gave me a break when nobody else would."

  Daniel dipped his head in a welcome gesture, too choked up by Knuckles's thanks to say a word. He left the kitchen, returning a few minutes later with a couple bottles of wine from the wine cellar's vintage selection. Pouring a glass for everyone gathered in the kitchen, Rosie then helped him pass them out. Mike was the only one to decline, saying he was on duty.

  Dar hesitated for a split second, but feeling the weight of the day throughout her body, she chose to accept a glass as well. After a couple sips, the wine's calming warmth spread through her, and she began to relax. She glanced sideways at Shawn and LaVon, whose wine had already disappeared from their glasses. They both appeared visibly shaken, and she understood. It had to be unnerving for them to hear details of the kidnapping for the first time.

Dar let Shawn check the stitches on her head again, mainly because she knew he wished he'd been there to prevent her from being hurt. At least this gave him a way to help her. She suspected the bruises on either side of her throat were growing darker, and she winced as Shawn touched the ugly finger marks. Seeing his face redden, she tried her best to act as though her throat didn't feel swollen and painful, and took another sip of wine to prove it. But she soon regretted it, and her stomach rumbled in protest to the mix of wine with the pain medicine the EMT had given her. She was setting the glass aside when she recalled something that she thought everyone should know, especially Daniel and Mike.

"When I was inside the tunnel today," she said, "I found a stack of canisters. In one of them was our stolen Julian Hughes paintings inside, 'Evening Joy.' I'm pretty sure 'Afternoon Joy' is there too. Since I couldn't carry them at the time, I hid them."

"That's great!" Daniel said. "And we know the other painting was hidden inside a bale of straw in one of the horse's stalls, so now we have all of the Hughes paintings back."

"I almost forgot," Rosie said, turning to retrieve something from a hook outside the kitchen. "You said it was evidence." As she handed the green camouflage jacket to Dar, a heavy object fell from the pocket. Daniel offered to pick it up for her.

As he did, Dar examined the wet jacket, showing Mike the hole where fabric had been ripped from it. "Guess I wasn't imagining things," she said smugly.

"You might want to see this, Mike," Daniel said. He passed a small phone to him.

After hitting a couple buttons, Mike muttered, "I hate it when she's right." He looked up at the others. This is a burner phone, and I believe it belonged to Mr. Reece. The last text he received says, 'Your office. Tonight. 11pm.' A picture was attached of a woman coming out of a doctor's office. The caption below it says, 'I hope your wife's good health continues. Maybe you'd like to reconsider your change of heart. See you at 11 sharp."

"So that's why he was there late at night," Dar said. "He felt he had no choice."

"It sounds like there's enough evidence for Owen and Red to be charged with theft and kidnapping, is that right, Mike?" Dar asked.

"Our tech guys will need to see what else is on this phone, including names," Mike said. "I have a feeling, once we have a search warrant, two other burner phones will turn up. Owen got sloppy hanging on to Reece's phone and the jacket. I suspect something had him off his game.

Anyway, we'll definitely have no problem charging both of them with the kidnapping of Sarah and Rosie,"

Mike said. "We have at least two eye witnesses, three counting you. And Owen will be charged with the attempted murder of you, which is why I had someone from the department take pictures of your head laceration and those bruises on your throat. The prosecutor might ask you and Knuckles to testify. Sarah and Rosie can add their testimonies as to what they saw when they arrived, but hopefully, it won't be necessary for Sarah."

"Something tells me she wouldn't hesitate to testify if it meant Owen and Red going away for a long time," Dar said. "And you might want to include an attempted murder charge for Red. She came after me with a gun but dropped it when I hit her over the head with a statue." Dar saw Shawn squirm.

"But why the vandalism to our business?" LaVon asked.

Dar shrugged. "Maybe it was a warning. Maybe he thought I knew something." Her throat ached from speaking too much.

"That's a lot of maybes," Mike said.

"Sarah told us tonight that she saw a snake tattoo on Owen's arm when he pointed at her in the hospital," Dar said. "Which means he could have been the guy I saw coming out of Reece's office. He had a snake tattoo too."

Mike nodded. "It's not enough, but it's something," he said. "At least, thanks to Sarah, we have Owen's aliases. "I'll have our I.T. guy research each name she gave us."

"I suppose his references were fake, too," Daniel said. "How could I have fallen for it? I used to be able to spot a con a mile away when I lived on the streets. Either I'm losing it or they're that good."

"I'm guessing the latter," Mike said.

"What about the murders of the two CCC employees?" Shawn asked. "Were Owen and Red responsible? We know they're thieves. They stole the paintings from the estate. Maybe that's the connection; they were stealing from the hospital, too."

"That's a pretty big leap," Mike said.

"But we also know that Owen had the skills to wire the poisonous canister to the fan in Reece's bathroom," Dar said. "He did an excellent job repairing the wiring in the bunkhouse kitchen."

"By the way, why did he offer to fix that?" Daniel asked. "If he did kill Mr. Reece, wouldn't he have preferred no one know he had that skill?"

"Maybe he thought that if he fixed the bunkhouse light," Dar said, "he could keep anyone else from getting too close to the tunnel entrance, or see him enter it. Plus, by fixing the light, he earned extra time on his break, which meant a larger window of time for him to slip in and out of the tunnel undetected. He had a hard enough time making sure Knuckles or Joe didn't see him entering the tunnel, and he probably didn't want to risk having anyone else get in his way."

"But that still doesn't prove either Owen or Red murdered Reece," Mike said. "All we have is a working theory at this point, along with bits and pieces that need to be sorted out. But based on Sarah recognizing Owen as the man who took Spike from her hospital room at knifepoint, he's a solid suspect for Spike's murder. And to make a case, we need to establish a motive."

"I can't imagine anyone with a reason to kill Spike, even Owen," Dar rasped. She accepted the glass of water that Rosie offered her and took a sip.

"Let's say Owen and Red were involved in thefts from the hospital," Dar said, "and killed Mr. Reece, who we know Red appeared to have seduced at the accounting conference, maybe to provide some kind of blackmail. If that's true, how does Spike fit into all of it? Why kill her? It doesn't make sense."

"What about the video of Bruno in the parking garage with blood all over him?" LaVon asked. "I thought he was the prime suspect for Spike's death."

"He's still a suspect," Mike said. "But with Sarah's firsthand account of seeing Owen holding a knife on Spike, Bruno has been moved to second place, behind Owen."

"The two murders were so different," Dar said. She spoke more to herself than the others, still trying to process it all. The pain meds had kicked in, easing her pain but making her mind foggy. "Reece's murder seemed so methodical, yet Spike's seemed more personal, more violent. It's hard to believe the same person could have done both."

"What about the man I saw by the stables? Was that Owen?" Rosie asked.

"It could have been," Mike said. "I'll know more after I question them both."

"I still feel like we're missing something," Dar said.

"You may be right, but we can't solve anything more tonight," Mike said. "It's late. Get a good night's rest, and I'll be back to talk to everyone tomorrow afternoon. Hopefully, I'll have a few more answers for you by then."

CHAPTER FORTY

Dar didn't think it possible, but she actually felt worse than she had the night before. Every muscle in her body ached, and with each turn of her head, pain radiated up and down her neck. Even the gash on her head seemed to throb more today. She reached for Shawn but felt only the cool sheet instead. Reaching for her pain pills on the nightstand, she spotted a note lying next to them. Sitting up, she grabbed the pills, wincing with the movement. After she swallowed a couple, she picked up the note. Shawn had been called back to the hospital and hadn't wanted to wake her, but said he'd try to be back at the estate by late afternoon. Dar sighed. She'd barely spoken two words to him last night before she'd fallen sound asleep.

Hearing mingled voices drifting from downstairs, Dar showered and dressed then slowly made her way down. Though her mind felt revived by the sleep, her body seemed to be doing just the opposite.

LaVon was at the bottom of the steps, smiling up at her. "I won't even ask how you're feeling," she said. "I think my grandmother could take the stairs faster than you."

"Very funny," Dar said. "I don't suppose Rosie has any coffee made?"

LaVon nodded. "And everything you could possibly want for a brunch. In fact, I was coming to check on you before there was nothing left."

"Ha! Like that could happen," Dar said. She could smell a mingling of the most wonderful aromas wafting from the kitchen, and her stomach growled in response.

In the kitchen, she mumbled a soft "mornin'" to Daniel and Rosie as she filled a coffee mug with hot coffee. As she ate and drank, she slowly began to feel more human. Gratefully, LaVon and Daniel kept the conversation to a minimum, as though they'd agreed to wait for her cue to talk more. When she'd finished eating, some of the pain had subsided.

"Have either of you heard from Mike today?" Dar asked.

"He called about a half hour ago," Daniel said. "He sounded tired, but still plans on coming by this afternoon."

"In that case, how about we relax until he gets here. Maybe a slow walk about the grounds will do us all good."

The three agreed and Dar felt her mood lift as she breathed in the fresh air. Yesterday's rain had brought every flower, tree, and shrub to life, some still glistening from tiny captured droplets.

They were returning from having given LaVon a tour of the stables, where she'd fawned over each horse, when Shawn's car pulled up. They waved at him to join them, and as he did, Rosie came outside carrying a tray that held a pitcher of lemonade and glasses of ice. Amazed at her impeccable timing, they met her on the veranda and thanked her. They passed the time with small talk, knowing that the topic would turn far more serious when Mike arrived.

At almost five o'clock, Mike came out of the house with Rosie. No one had heard him drive up, so she brought him directly to the veranda. Dar noticed the bags under his eyes and wondered if he'd pulled an all-nighter. After a quick hello and a brief inquiry about Dar's head and throat, Mike cleared his own.

"I hope you don't mind if I get right to it," Mike said. "I think you'll like what I've learned, mostly thanks to our forensic accountant. He did a deep dive into the financials of Owen, Red, and Reece, along with the hospital's inventory records and the medical supplier's invoices. It turns out you were right, Shawn; they were stealing a VAD medical device from each shipment at CCC."

"That's why we kept coming up short," Shawn said. "Do you think they thought by taking one at a time, no one would catch on, that it wouldn't draw as much attention as stealing an entire delivery supply?"

"Probably," Mike said. "Plus, one device is easier to fence than an entire shipment, and one is still worth an impressive amount of money. And selling one at a time raises fewer red flags. It even worked for a while. It took the help of the FBI to track the sales on the black market, and our accountant, to follow the money trail to matching dates on Red's financial statements. He could also prove half of that money appeared in one of Owen's alias accounts the next day.

"But how did Owen steal them?" Shawn asked. "They were locked up in the medical supply closets, and the code was changed on a regular basis."

"That's where Reece came in," Mike explained. "He had the codes and gave them to Owen each time."

"Mr. Reece wouldn't do that," Shawn insisted.

"Unless he was blackmailed into doing it," Daniel said.

Mike nodded. "We got a search warrant for Red's apartment, and when we searched it, we found original prints of the blackmail pictures, which were also on her laptop. The woman in the red suit that you described from the accounting conference, Daniel, was in the first photo with Reece. They were in one of the conference hotel's rooms. The monogrammed robe he was wearing was confirmed as one of theirs. Red's suit didn't appear in the other photos with Reece, but she did, in all her glory. Reece still had copies of those photos in the locked desk drawer of his office."

"I wish I'd made the connection sooner that she was the same lady who was delivering our straw and hay," Daniel said.

"So why did they kill Mr. Reece?" Shawn asked. "Didn't they need him to give Owen the new codes?"

"Maybe Mr. Reece refused to continue," Dar said, "and they couldn't allow it because he knew too much." She looked at Shawn who appeared to be puzzling over something. "What are you thinking, Shawn?"

"I was thinking about the 'Do Not Disturb' sign again," Shawn said. "Maybe Owen put it on Mr. Reece's office door so he could wire the canister of poison to the bathroom fan, but then either forgot to put it back on the wall with Reece's family photos, or he left it on the door because he needed more time to clear the gas out of the office. He might have slipped it on the back of the door when he was hurrying to leave. But maybe something went wrong with the remote, and he couldn't turn the fan off. That would explain why the window was still open and the bathroom fan was still running. Owen must've hoped that whoever found Mr. Reece, like I did, would think he had died of a heart attack."

Mike said, "We found a remote in a dumpster in the same alley where Spike's body was found. It was smashed, but we got one fingerprint off it. It was a match to Owen's."

"That's great news!" Dar said. "Now you have evidence that links Owen to Mr. Reece's murder."

"That's not all," Mike said. "Using Owen's aliases that Sarah gave us, we learned that 'Owen Camo' was the name he gave the construction company that was contracted by CCC. That job gave him access to different floors of the hospital. Then Daniel hired him as Owen Jay here at Montgomery Farm Estate where he was able to steal the paintings and keep a close eye on Sarah and Dar. The last alias, Owen Kane, was his name when he did time in prison.

"It was Red who provided his references for the hospital's outsourced construction company, using a burner phone she carried, just like she did for Owen when he applied for the job as a stable hand here at the Montgomery Estate. We found the phone hidden inside her truck. With that number, we were able to take a look at her phone records, giving us more proof of her part in the thefts. And I'm certain a prosecutor and judge will find a long list of crimes to charge her with, beginning with blackmail, theft, selling stolen property, kidnapping, and attempted murder. We're still putting together details for a case as an accomplice to murder."

"I'm sorry, Dar," Daniel said. "I brought two murderers and thieves to our place. I should have double-checked references."

"How could you know?" Dar said. "They duped everyone."

Daniel frowned. "The name of the construction company Owen gave me as a reference was Newok Construction, right?"

"You mentioned that already," Mike said. "Tell me something I don't know."

"Newok Construction is K Owen spelled backwards. Switch those two, and you have . . ."

"Owen K, or Owen Kane," Dar said, finishing his sentence. "I wonder whose brilliant idea that was, Red's or Owen's?"

Mike got a text and paused to read it.

"What is it?" Dar asked.

"We also checked Nurse Spike's background, trying to find out how she might have known Owen previously. We discovered their paths did cross in the past. She'd worked as a nurse briefly at the Indiana State Penitentiary. And guess who else was doing a sentence there for grand larceny and assault?" Mike gave a dramatic pause, and LaVon jumped in.

"Don't tell me," she said. "It was Owen."

"Way to steal my thunder," Mike said, "but yes. I'm thinking that when Spike ran into Owen that day outside Sarah's room, she recognized him. That made her a liability. He didn't want anyone knowing he was using an alias while working at the hospital, nor that he had done time in prison. He probably assumed that if they knew, it would put him at the top of the suspect list for the thefts of the VADs and Reece's murder."

"So, what about the brief video clip of Bruno in the parking garage?" LaVon asked.

"Oh, I forgot to mention," Mike said. "It turns out Bruno's story was true. They found an empty carry-out container of spaghetti sauce in Red's trash, along with a wig. She dumped the spaghetti sauce on Bruno to frame him as Spike's killer, which distracted the police from searching for other suspects."

"So, why would Owen risk taking a job here as a stable hand?" Daniel asked.

"I'm guessing a number of reasons," Dar said. "First, he did it to steal the paintings, and second, when he learned Sarah would be participating in the equine therapy, he must've decided, 'two birds'... But what I can't figure out is how he knew so much about this place? He seemed to know exactly where the tunnels were and where each branch led, not to mention the locations of the paintings he'd stolen. How did he get that information?"

Her mind worked overtime trying to put the pieces of the puzzle together, and when it finally did, a knot began to form in Dar's stomach, and she blanched. Concerned, Shawn tried to get her to lie down, but she refused.

"What is it, Dar? You don't look well," LaVon said. "Maybe you should rest. You've been through a lot."

Dar shook her head. "I'm fine. Really." Then she turned to Mike. "Mike, how about I walk with you to your car?"

"Not necessary, but if you want to, okay by me. I need to get some shut-eye tonight."

Everyone said their goodbyes and thanks to Mike before Dar escorted him to the front door. Once outside, though, she stopped him.

"I do want to thank you for everything you've done, but there's something else I was hoping you could check on for me."

Mike gave her a knowing look. "Of course. Why else would you walk me to my car? But I'm telling you right now, I'm not doing anything else until I get some sleep in my own bed. The couch at the office last night sucked as a bed."

Dar gave Mike her requests, and he paused to think about it. "I should've thought of that myself, but let me check into it. That's why they pay me the big bucks. I'll call you tomorrow and let you know what I find out."

Once Mike had left, Dar slipped back into the house and rejoined the others who stared at her with furrowed brows. Dar knew they were about to ask questions, but she couldn't answer them. Not now. She hadn't intended to leave them out of her suspicions, but revealing this new fear was more than she could bear today.

"Maybe you're right," Dar said. "Maybe I should lie down. Stay the night, if you like," she said to Shawn and LaVon, "but if you don't mind, right now I'd like to be alone."

It was all Dar could do to put one foot in front of the other. The task of climbing the stairs to her bedroom proved nearly impossible, as though heavy weights had been placed around each ankle. But if she was being honest with herself, the weight was around her heart, and it was too much to bear.

When she got to her bedroom, she gingerly lowered herself onto the bed. Her pain meds she'd taken earlier had worn off, and her throat ached along with the wound in her head. Yet she felt numb inside.

She knew her suspicions had to be right. It was the only thing that made sense. And as much as she hated confrontation, she had to know the truth. An ocean of memories that she'd tried so hard to put out of her mind came flooding back with the force of a tsunami. How could she ever put a stop to them?

Not again, she thought. *Not again.*

CHAPTER FORTY-ONE

The next morning, Dar lifted her heavy lids, still puffy from last night's tears, then squinted as she shaded her eyes from the brilliant sunbeams that shone through the bedroom windows. The brightness contrasted starkly with her mood. Glancing about the room, Dar frowned at how the rays illuminated the room's gaudy décor, complete with an explosion of ruffles that seemed to leap from the pink floral curtains onto the edges of her comforter. The latter was a rose print so intense that she could almost smell their overpowering fragrance. It made her nauseous, which only added to the knot in her stomach, a remnant from last night's conversation.

Closing her eyes, she drew the plush comforter over her head. She longed to be in her own home in Reed, in the unassuming comfort of her own bedroom. But most of all, she missed Merlin nudging his wet nose against her neck, then licking her face if she failed to wake up. Though it sometimes annoyed her, she also loved it. She had only herself to blame for his absence, since she'd allowed him to sleep downstairs last night. She had been desperate to be alone, to think, and Merlin would have been a distraction.

Her sleep had been restless as she replayed everything from Mr. Reece's murder to Sarah and Rosie's kidnapping. But it was Mike's discovery about Spike and Owen that she couldn't let go. It had tumbled in her mind like a falling rock, unleashing a cascade of thoughts in its wake. Had Daniel felt the same? She sensed he had shared her suspicions last night.

Throwing the floral comforter off, Dar made her way to the shower where she washed away the comforter's imaginary scent of roses. She tugged on her last clean pair of jeans along with a pale mint green sweater. At the sound of her phone playing "When Irish Eyes are Smiling," she checked the caller I.D. and answered.

"Hi, Mike. You have news for me already?" she asked.

Dar listened to the new information Mike had obtained. "You're sure?" she asked. Another pause, then, "Thanks. I owe you one. Oh, and Mike, can we keep this between the two of us for now? I'd rather Daniel, Shawn, and LaVon not know about everything just yet." She paused one more time as she listened to Mike's advice before answering, "Of course I'll be careful."

CHAPTER FORTY-TWO

It was later than she'd thought when she went downstairs. Though she'd wanted to speak to Daniel alone, she was happy to see Shawn and LaVon sitting with him at the island counter.

"Any coffee?" she asked. It came out raspy again, reminding her that her throat was still swollen. She guessed coffee might not be the best choice, but it was a chance she was willing to take if she intended to join the land of the living. Expecting Shawn to protest, she was surprised when he didn't.

She accepted a steaming coffee from Rosie, who also offered to fix her eggs. Dar thanked her but politely declined. She grabbed a muffin instead. She needed something to absorb the acid that burned in her stomach. Shawn pushed out the bar chair next to him, and Dar took a seat.

Sipping her coffee, she also tried nibbling on the muffin, but struggled to swallow it. A suspicious silence came from the others while she ate. Sufficiently fueled by the caffeine, she lowered her empty cup and became even more suspicious when Shawn covered her hand with his. His typically romantic gesture had her feeling defensive for some reason. She raised an eyebrow.

"We know you have concerns connected to Spike's murder." Dar flashed her blue eyes at her brother. Maybe he had read her thoughts, as usual.

"I'm sorry sis," Daniel said, "but they were worried about you. Besides, we need to talk about the elephant in the room."

Dar wasn't sure she agreed as the knot in her stomach tightened. But maybe giving them part of the truth wouldn't hurt. She could omit the rest until she knew the facts herself.

"Remember when Mike said Owen had met Nurse Spike in the prison clinic?" Dar asked.

Shawn and LaVon nodded. "Isn't that why they think Owen killed her," LaVon asked, "because she recognized him, and he feared she'd turn him in for using a fake reference?"

"Not to mention make him a murder suspect for having done time," Shawn added.

"Exactly," Dar said. "But there has to be more. Spike's murder was brutal. It felt like there was a lot more anger behind her murder compared to Mr. Reece's." Dar rubbed her throat and Shawn quickly got her a glass of water. She took a sip.

"I talked to Mike this morning," she continued. "He has some more information for us. Well, to be honest, I asked him if he could get any details on how Owen knew Spike. Owen was in the Indiana State Penitentiary for grand theft. He met Spike at the clinic there. He had six months left on his sentence when he managed to get another two years added to it. When I asked Mike if his record mentioned the reason for it, he said Owen's additional sentence was for stealing drugs from the prison's clinic. He stole a small amount at first, but then he got greedy. Drugs sales inside prison is a rather lucrative business until you're caught. Which is exactly what happened when Spike turned him in."

"So, you think he blamed her for getting the extra time in prison?" LaVon asked. She studied Dar's face. "What aren't you telling us?"

Dar glanced at Daniel before answering. "I can't say for sure. I just have a strange feeling there might be more."

"Like what?" Shawn asked.

"Yeah, like what," LaVon chimed in. "Whatever it is, it must be serious, because you look like you've seen a ghost.

Yeah, a ghost from the past, Dar wanted to say, but she wasn't ready to accept her suspicions as facts.

"Yesterday, when I was walking Mike to his car," she said, "I asked him to find out if anyone else besides

Owen was involved in the drug theft at the prison clinic. He said it was suspected but never proven. It seems there was a commotion in the prison yard around the same time each theft was thought to have occurred. Owen worked with a partner here, so I thought that maybe he worked with a partner in prison as well."

"At least he's social," Shawn said. Everyone moaned. "Sorry, Dar, I couldn't resist. Anyway, I'd tell you to let it go, because it's only a theory, but I know it'd be pointless." He kissed her gently. "As much as I hate to kiss and run, I've got to get back to the hospital. Why don't you stay here another day and let Rosie pamper you? You really should try to get some rest."

"Getting pampered sounds perfect," Dar said. "Maybe we can talk later?"

"I'll call you after work," Shawn promised. He said his goodbyes to the others and left.

"Darius is stopping by to check on the horses again," LaVon said. "What do you want to bet that they're all much calmer now that our thieves are gone?"

"Joe's noticed a difference already," Daniel said, "but something tells me this visit from Dr. Darius was nothing more than a convenient excuse for him to see someone else."

LaVon beamed. Dar was thrilled to see her friend so happy.

"Are you going back to work, then?" Dar asked her.

LaVon nodded. "Unless you need me, I plan on going back—right after my 'doctor' appointment, that is," she said, making air quotes as she spoke the word "doctor."

Dar laughed at her friend's obvious reference to Dr. Darius. He seemed to be a good match for LaVon, and Dar especially liked how happy he seemed to make her friend.

"I'm sorry I haven't been at The Contented Canine as much as I should have," Dar said.

"Just concentrate on taking care of yourself," LaVon said, patting Dar's hand. "Maybe we can talk later, too. If you're up to it, maybe you can drive back to Reed later and catch me before you see Shawn. But only if you're feeling better."

"That will be a great incentive for me," Dar said. Glancing out the window, she saw Darius pull up in his white truck. She caught LaVon's eye, then nodded toward the vehicle. "In fact, since you're going to be busy, I'm going back to bed."

Dar headed toward the main stairs, but stopped at the bottom step. Straining to listen, she waited until she heard Daniel offer to walk out with LaVon. At the sound of the door closing behind them, she hurried up the steps as fast as her throbbing head would allow her, then slipped into her room. She downed a couple pain pills, snatched her keys, phone, and scarf, then crept down the back stairs to her car.

If she was lucky, she'd be back before anyone realized she was missing. If she'd told any one of them where she was going, they would've tried to stop her, and it might not have taken much convincing.

As she adjusted her rearview mirror, she caught her reflection in it. Even with makeup, the ugly purple bruises around her neck were still visible, along with a bald spot where the gash in her head had been stitched closed. She shoved a clump of hair over it as best she could, then tied the scarf loosely around her neck. Deciding it would have to do, she opened the employee gate, pausing to set the directions on her phone before pulling out onto the road. She let out a long, slow breath as she considered the proverbial bear she was about to poke. It was even harder for her to believe that as much as she hated confrontations, she was about to launch head-first into one—one that was long overdue.

CHAPTER FORTY-THREE

Dar turned off the highway and soon arrived at her destination. Making sure her phone was off, she swallowed hard as she took in her surroundings. The Indiana State Men's prison was even more daunting than she'd imagined. Seeing the massive buildings surrounded by tall concrete walls with rows of barbed wire and manned towers atop them, she suddenly wondered if this had been the right decision.

There was a missing piece to the murders and thefts that hadn't sat well with her; a puzzling piece that eluded her—until this morning. That link was the Indiana State Penitentiary. She was almost certain of her suspicion. Owen had to have worked with another inmate to accomplish his drug thefts in prison. And Mike had supplied her with the link to the missing piece of the puzzle.

After registering with the guard on duty, she was searched then led to a room containing a single table and two chairs. The guard ushered her to the chair without the shackles in front of it before giving her a stony look, as though she'd added one more burden to his day that he could do without. When he exited the room, Dar chewed on a fingernail, then tried to compose herself by placing one shaking hand over the other. But when the door opened again and the prisoner was escorted into the room, her nerves were instantly replaced with anger.

The man sneered at her as the guard shackled his wrists securely to the table, then stood watch near the same door. Dar gave the man who sat in front of her a cold stare in return.

"You've been busy, Wes," Dar said. "Even from the confines of prison, you've managed to screw up the lives of so many."

Wesley Shade cocked his head to one side, then glanced at the guard. "I don't know what you're talking about, but it warms my heart that my daughter took time out of her busy, busy life to visit her dad in prison."

"Do not call me that!" Dar hissed back. "You could never be a father to me or Daniel. You've always been too narcissistic for that role." She placed her hands under the table as she felt them ball into fists. The last thing she wanted was for Wes to see the anger he could evoke in her.

"Please, enlighten me," Wes mocked. "Oh, and by the way, how's that detective friend of yours? I heard his niece had a close call. I'm so relieved she's all right." He tilted his head in feigned sympathy. "And rumor has it that you and Daniel were victims of theft and vandalism." He clicked his tongue. "It seems you've been having your share of troubles lately."

Dar felt the heat rise in her face. It was all she could do to keep from flying across the table and slapping the smug look off his face. With a furtive glance at the guard, she chose to hold onto the edge of her chair, and her temper, instead.

"Thanks to you," she said. All the anger and hatred she had for this man simmered beneath the surface, yet she fought to keep the emotions out of her voice. For once, she was the one in control, not him. "Too bad Owen left a calling card, you know, a piece of his camouflage jacket, when he threw that brick through The Contented Canine's window. Witnesses saw him in that same camouflage jacket while committing another crime." Dar's eyes flashed in satisfaction that her accusations were hitting home. "You're the one who told Owen about the paintings at the Montgomery Farm Estate, and it was you who told him exactly how to access them through the tunnels."

Dar saw the slightest crack in his smug demeanor. "You became buddies with Owen when he was doing time here. Knowing you, you thought you'd found the perfect patsy. Then you devised a plan for Owen to steal drugs from the clinic. I'm assuming you even made sure to provide a distraction for him, keeping the guards busy and giving yourself an alibi in the process. That way your hands were clean if anything went wrong, which it did when Spike caught Owen and reported him. But Owen was clueless. He blamed Spike instead of you for his added sentence. All you had to do was play the part of a good friend, probably fueling his anger toward her. And being such a good friend, you got him through those extra two years by helping him scheme a string of thefts; a little something to look forward to when he was released. You knew that you weren't going to be released any time soon, so why not live vicariously through Owen."

Wes blinked. She'd gotten at least part of it right. She thought a moment. Something still didn't make sense. When she had asked Mike if his forensic accountant could check to see if there had been any withdrawals from Owen's account that matched a deposit to Wes's account, he had. But she couldn't envision Owen willingly sharing his profits with Wes. Her eyes focused back on Wes.

"You were blackmailing Owen to get a cut, weren't you? You threatened to snitch on his plans to steal the VADs from the hospital. With his probation, he knew he'd be sent right back to prison serving an even longer sentence for a repeat crime. Of course, you wouldn't do it yourself. You still have 'friends' on the outside," she said using air quotes, "who were willing to do it for you—for the right price. That's how you forced Owen to share a hefty portion of the profits with you."

Dar watched Wes squirm in his seat. She tried to remember what it was that Mike had said about the connection between Red and Wes. She'd been so busy concentrating on the name of the prison where Spike and Owen had met, that she hadn't paid much attention to the detail until now. She leaned forward.

"Red was involved in some of your previous theft charges, wasn't she?" Dar said. "In fact, she was a fence you'd used many times in the past. She kept you informed of the amount she sold the medical devices for on the black market, so you always knew what your cut from Owen should be." Dar sat back. "But Owen's share of the profits was insignificant for someone like you, and when the thefts at the hospital stopped, so did the deposits to your account. But you had another way to get money from Owen."

Dar noticed a twitch in his eyes. She was getting warm, but there was still the matter of communication. She guessed the prison kept a record of prisoner's incoming and outgoing phone calls, but for someone experienced in dealing and stealing drugs, he'd have a vast number of ways to get a message to whomever he chose. Wes could be very resourceful when it came to benefiting himself. Then she smiled.

"I'm glad you're amusing yourself." Now it was Wes who sat back. His eyes shone. "You know it's a shame that two people who worked at the very same hospital as your boyfriend were murdered. Maybe he was responsible for their deaths."

"We both know your friends were responsible for those deaths," Dar said. "When Reece refused to be blackmailed any longer, he'd served his purpose. But then Spike recognized Owen from his drug thefts at the prison clinic, and that made her a liability. So, you gave the order to have her killed. Owen probably didn't need much encouragement, as I'm sure you reminded him how she was the one responsible for him receiving two extra years in this God-forsaken place."

Wes glared at her. Dar waited, hoping he'd say something to incriminate himself. So far, he'd only mentioned what was common knowledge in the crimes. She needed to get him to refer to an unknown detail, something only someone who was involved in the scheme would know.

Wes leaned forward, shaking his head and smiling. "You really do need to stop hanging around that detective. It seems he forgot to tell you that proof is required when you make such hurtful accusations."

"Well, we have sufficient proof to put Owen and your friend Red behind bars for theft and kidnapping. Whatever will you do now? You've no one to manipulate; no one to do your dirty work for you. If you ever do get out, which you won't if I have anything to say about it, you'll be going straight from prison to the poor house."

She watched Wes's jaw clench.

"I do have a question for you, though," Dar said. Wes made a slight hand gesture that she interpreted as meaning for her to continue. "Why the paintings?" she asked. "Why steal the Hughes paintings when there were paintings on the main level that were worth more?"

"*I* didn't steal anything," Wes corrected her. "There are numerous cameras and guards that can attest to my continued presence here. I have an iron-clad alibi. And as you already mentioned, I believe the police have already arrested two people on that charge. Perhaps they simply liked what they saw. Art is in the eye of the beholder you know."

Dar knew there was more to it, but once again she felt she was missing an important piece.

"So, what was it?" Dar asked. "Were the paintings mere distractions again for a more lustrous pearl in your desired treasure trove?" Wes blinked. She was close, but unfortunately, she had no idea where to take the conversation to pin down what that pearl might actually be.

Wes slammed his palms on the table. "As riveting as this visit has been, I believe it's time for my lunch. Guard?" he called out. As the guard unlocked his handcuffs from the shackles, he added arrogantly, "Next time, though, I would appreciate it if you'd call first, or better yet, write. I do love getting letters."

Dar couldn't believe the gall of this guy. She hated the fact that she shared genes with such a monster. She'd never been more grateful to have been raised by two nurturing adoptive parents instead of this madman.

But the visit hadn't been completely in vain. She was certain now that Wesley Shade had pulled the strings in both the thefts and the murders. He was a master of deception, but she was determined to reveal his secrets. There was no way she was going to let this guy get away with what he'd done.

CHAPTER FORTY-FOUR

As Dar walked out of the Indiana State Penitentiary, she powered her phone back on, but not the locator. She didn't want Daniel or anyone else contacting her. Explaining where she'd been and why, was not a conversation she wanted to have over the phone. Besides, Shawn was at the hospital, and by now LaVon was back at The Contented Canine. Daniel was the only one who was likely to notice she wasn't at the estate.

Her phone dinged over and over, bringing up six text messages from Daniel. After counting his missed calls as well, she punched his number from her speed dial list. He answered immediately.

"Where are you?" he asked. Dar didn't answer. "You went to the prison to see him, didn't you?"

"I had to confront him," she said. "I'm sorry I didn't tell you, but I was afraid you'd try to talk me out of it."

"Did you ever consider the fact that I might want to confront him as well?"

She had considered it, but she had been selfish. It was the first time Dar had heard even the slightest hint of anger in Daniel's voice, and she hated being the one to have caused it.

"Actually, I did," Dar said, feeling like a heel, "but it could have gotten complicated. You have your own issues with him, which is why I had to do this myself. It was selfish of me, I know, and I'm sorry. I'll tell you all about it when I get back. I'm on my way."

The connection ended.

Dar sighed. As she pulled onto the road, her mind whirled at the decisions she wanted, no, *needed* to make. She prayed that the drive back would clear her head and provide her with some answers.

But as she glanced at the time, she found her visit had taken longer than she'd anticipated. Her first equine therapy group was tomorrow, and she still had details to attend to. Yet she needed to sort some things out in her head first, like the exact part Wesley had played in the thefts and murders, and how to prove it. Then there was her job, too, and Shawn. Decisions had to be made, and soon.

Dar felt her breaths growing shorter. She pulled off the road and onto the shoulder, then threw the car into park. She told herself she didn't have time for this, but she had no choice; ignoring the growing symptoms would only lead to a full-blown panic attack. So, she sat on the edge of a busy highway and ran through a gamut of relaxation methods, ending with several deep breaths. She exhaled slowly after each one, then waited.

After a couple minutes of normal breathing, she made a decision. She knew it was ironic, but her first decision was that she'd make no major decisions on her drive home. As desperately as she wanted to find answers to all her problems, it was useless to do so if it resulted in a panic attack. Instead, she found a selection of soothing music, rolled down her window, then drove home, trying to concentrate on nothing but the road and the view.

She had made one decision, though, before she'd ever left the prison's visitor parking lot. Without any hesitation, she'd promised herself that Wes would never step foot outside the confines of prison ever again.

CHAPTER FORTY-FIVE

When Dar arrived back at the estate, neither Daniel nor Rosie was anywhere in sight. The house seemed dark and forlorn as the sun slipped behind the clouds outside. It was as though her surroundings had absorbed and reflected her mood.

She found a note from Daniel on the kitchen counter saying he was at the stables and that she had a message to call Sarah's mom. Dar expected Sarah's mom would want to cancel equine therapy tomorrow, and who could blame her after all Sarah had been through. But when Dar returned Jackie's call, she soon discovered it had nothing to do with Sarah's attendance.

"Sarah mentioned something today that might be important to the police," Jackie began. "When I asked her to explain, she wanted to talk to you instead of Mike. Do you have time to speak with her?"

"Of course," Dar said.

She couldn't imagine what Sarah wanted to say to her that she couldn't say to her favorite uncle. When Sarah got on the phone, Dar engaged her in some small talk. She thought Sarah seemed a bit reluctant to move on to her reason for calling, but soon she could hear Sarah's mom coaxing her in the background.

"Mom says I'm not in trouble for what I told her," Sarah began.

"If your mom says you're not, then I agree," Dar said. "If it helps, just pretend you're talking to your mom again. Does that work?"

Sarah giggled. "Okay," she said.

Dar heard Sarah take a deep breath, and she could picture her double-checking with her mom before she continued. Sarah had come out of her shell since Owen and Red's arrest, so what could possibly have caused her to take a step back into that shell?

"I told my mom that I was glad Owen wasn't going to get paid by the old man," Sarah said at last. "Owen didn't deserve to get paid for anything. Everything he did was bad."

"What do you mean?" Dar asked.

Sarah laughed. "You sound just like my mom, except she didn't understand, because she wasn't in the tunnel with those bad people, but you were. Uncle Mike wasn't either."

"You're right, Sarah, and it was scary down there, wasn't it?" Dar recalled the shadows from the lanterns, and how the sound of voices and footsteps echoed off the walls of the tunnel.

"Ah-huh," Sarah said. "That's where I heard them, Red and Owen, I mean, arguing just before Owen kidnapped Rosie. Red was holding me by the arm, and it kind of hurt. Owen was really mad about how much trouble they had to go through to steal something for somebody he called 'the old guy.' But whatever they'd stolen, they said it had already been opened, and they were afraid that now they weren't going to get paid. That makes me happy."

"I'm glad too, Sarah," Dar said. "I want you to listen very carefully, because this could be important. Did they say what they were stealing for the old man?"

"Maybe, but I couldn't hear that part," Sarah said. "But you should know."

"Me? Why?" Dar asked.

"Because they said you broke the seal on it," Sarah said. "I didn't know what seal they were talking about, but I didn't want to get you in trouble for breaking something. That's why I didn't want to tell Uncle Mike."

The letters! In all the excitement, Dar had totally forgotten about them.

"Thank you, Sarah! You've been a big help. Before you go, do you remember if they said anything at all about who the old man was or how they'd get the money he was paying them?"

"Nope. Can I still come on Saturday?" Sarah asked.

Dar assured her she could. "And I owe you an ice cream cone for being such a big help. Don't let me forget."

"I'll remember that for sure!" Sarah said. "See you Saturday! Bye!"

Dar said goodbye to Sarah, then Jackie as well, after thanking her for encouraging Sarah to call her. She chewed on the stub of a fingernail and thought about what Sarah had overheard between Red and Owen. There wasn't a doubt in her mind that the old man was the same one she'd visited in prison this morning, but she needed proof. It was time she found out why the letters were of such value to Wes. She texted Daniel and asked him to meet her at the guesthouse.

Within minutes, Daniel arrived, out of breath. "What kind of trouble are you in now?" he asked.

Dar quickly filled him in on her conversation with Sarah. "It has to be the letters that they were supposed to get paid to steal. But they're not lost. I hid them at the guesthouse. This time, we're not going anywhere until we finish reading the entire contents of those letters."

"Lead the way," Daniel said, making a gallant gesture with his arm.

Dar led Daniel to a bedroom on the right, where a large dresser remained halfway in front of the closet door, the same spot where Red and Owen had shoved it after she'd tried to prevent them from exiting the tunnel. She went straight to the bed and lifted the mattress. The letters were exactly where she'd hidden them. Pulling them out, she waved the envelopes at Daniel, then slid to the floor, her back braced against the bed. Daniel joined her on the floor. They stared at the two sets of envelopes, each bound by rubber bands.

"This set of letters look like the ones we found in the footrest, but I'm sure this other set wasn't with them. You pick which group to open first," Daniel said.

Dar chose one, then removed the rubber band, allowing two envelopes to slide apart. Each envelope was addressed to Mr. Edward Montgomery but with no return address. She opened the first one and scanned its contents, then passed it on to Daniel. His eyes grew wide as the subject matter all began to make sense.

"Is that what I think it is?" Dar asked.

"It's a provenance," Daniel said, "but no ordinary one. The artist, Julian Hughes, wrote this letter to our biological grandfather, Edward Montgomery, thanking him for purchasing his three paintings, 'Morning Joy,' 'Afternoon Joy,' and 'Evening Joy,' each mounted in frames hand-carved by his father. Julian goes on to also thank Mr. Montgomery for hosting an art show for him at the estate, which proved to be a huge success, not only with the number of paintings sold, but also in making a name for him in the art world. The dates of purchase and the amount paid for each painting are included."

"At least we know their value now," Daniel said. "But it's still not a substantial amount; definitely not worth the risk of stealing." He opened the second letter.

Seeing his mouth fall open, she couldn't wait for him to finish reading. "What?" she asked.

"It appears the artist died a couple years ago," Daniel said. Holding up cut-out articles from an old newspaper, he added, "And these are news clippings, heralding his art." Daniel continued skimming the articles. "They estimate each of Julian Hughes's paintings to be worth close to half a million dollars each, but his earlier paintings may be worth even more."

Dar and Daniel stared at each other, speechless. Then Dar spoke. "Well, I guess we know why they risked stealing the paintings and the letters. Between the personal letters that prove the paintings' provenance signed by the artist, along with the date of the paintings, our three Julian Hughes originals are most likely worth well over one-and-a-half million. Our biological mom must have hidden the news clippings there along with her parents' letters of the art's provenance. It had to have been shortly before she was murdered. Maybe she suspected Wes would try to steal them one day if he ever learned of their value. I guess we'll never really know for sure."

"We should put these letters in a safe," Daniel said. "A real safe; maybe even a safe deposit box."

"You'll get no argument from me," Dar said. She picked up the other banded set of envelopes. "Then what are these? I only remember finding two letters in the secret compartment. You do the honors this time," she said, handing the banded envelopes to Daniel.

Pulling the rubber band off, he held them so Dar could read them as well. Neither recognized the woman's name on the address, but when they read the return address, Daniel commented, "I'm not sure either of us are going to like what's inside."

When Dar read the return address, Indiana State Penitentiary, her initial response was to burn it. But she reconsidered. This could be the evidence she was searching for. "I'm definitely not going to like this," she said, "but open it anyway."

Daniel slipped the letter out of the first envelope. He read a couple paragraphs before commenting. "This letter makes no sense," he said. "It's jibberish, full of incomplete sentences." He handed it to Dar.

"But it must be important if Wes was willing to pay for it," she said. "Try another."

They shuffled through the letters, but each one was the same, making no sense whatsoever. They flipped the letters and envelopes over, but saw nothing revealing.

"What if it's a coded message?" Dar asked.

Daniel looked at one of the letters again. "These are a lot like the coded notes that the drug dealers would give me to pass on to my foster dad when he made me do drug runs for him. He never knew it, but I was able to decode the last couple messages before I ran away."

It was another reminder to Dar how different their childhoods had been following their biological mother's death. Though she'd been raised by two loving adoptive parents, Daniel had been shuffled from one foster home to another, the last one so horrible that he had to run away.

"Okay, genius," Dar said. "Let's take these back to the house so you can try to work your decoding magic. We can get there through the tunnel and pick up the two paintings I hid on our way. Where did you put the painting Knuckles gave you? I hope you put it in a safe place."

"No worries," Daniel said. "It's safe."

Grabbing a flashlight from the bedroom's bedside table, they made their way through the tunnel and picked up the stolen paintings Dar had hidden. Once they were back at the house, Dar put the letters in the office safe, while Daniel added the two paintings to the same secure hiding spot he'd used for the one Knuckles had given him. It would have to do until they could have them reframed in their original frames.

"While you're working on the decoding," Dar told Daniel, "I think I'll drive back to Reed tonight. There are two very important people there who deserve my time and attention. I'm going to take Merlin with me. Wish me luck, and call when you decode the messages."

Daniel raised an eyebrow. "You mean *if*, don't you?"

"Nope. I believe in you," Dar said. "You've got this! See you tomorrow."

She left the estate, wishing she had the same confidence in herself that she had in Daniel. How was it possible that she still didn't have a clue where her conversations with LaVon and Shawn were going to lead? She did know one thing, though; it was past time she had them.

CHAPTER FORTY-SIX

When Dar pulled onto the long lane leading back to The Contented Canine, it felt as though it'd been weeks rather than days since she'd been there. So much had happened in that short period of time.

The minute she walked through the door, LaVon asked her how she was feeling. Dar was pleased she could honestly say that she was improving; her head and throat hurt considerably less. Merlin sat down next to the drawer full of treats, looked at Dar, then gave a soft whine.

"Gotcha, Merlin," Dar said, pulling one from the drawer and tossing it to him. He snatched it mid-air and may or may not have chewed it before swallowing it. His tail wagged in gratitude. He followed Dar back to her desk, then stretched out on the floor next to her.

"How about if we take a couple of our dogs for a walk?" Dar asked LaVon. "I think Merlin is plenty content right now, and you mentioned several times that you wanted to talk. I feel bad that we haven't had a chance to do that because of me. I really do want to hear what's on your mind."

"Great idea," LaVon said. They grabbed leashes off the hooks, then entered the kennel and opened the cages to two adorable shih tzu dogs. Dar and LaVon laughed as they struggled to attach the leashes to the dogs, who seemed to be nonstop energy. Once accomplished, they stepped outside and started for the path that wound through the woods.

The morning was sunny with a nip in the air. Dar found it refreshing. She loved the seasons and all the changes each one brought, both to nature, as well as her life. She pulled the collar of her jacket up around her neck.

As they entered the woods, her mind wandered to the anticipated conversation. She braced herself for it, hoping she could be supportive if LaVon chose to leave the business. It was impossible for her to imagine running The Contented Canine without LaVon though, especially now. If she left, Dar might be forced to sell the business they'd worked so hard to build, and that thought broke her heart.

"Are you okay?" LaVon asked. "You seem upset."

"I'm fine," she lied. "What did you want to talk to me about?"

LaVon gave her a furtive sideways glance. "What would you say if I told you I wanted to buy your portion of the business?"

Dar stopped. This was not what she'd expected.

"Hear me out before you say anything," LaVon said. "I know you've been struggling with starting the equine therapy group, which has been a dream of yours. And I know you well enough to know that someday you'll want to expand the program. You're also volunteering at the hospitals, and have a newfound twin brother who you're trying to get to know better. It's a lot. And most importantly there's Shawn, who you're obviously in love with, but you need time to work some things out—if you can find time." LaVon took a breath. "Darius offered to help finance the buy-out, and be the on-call veterinarian at a deep discount. He's thinking of building a vet clinic on the property next to us. But if you don't want to sell, that's okay. I will totally understand." LaVon looked directly at Dar. "What do you think?"

Dar's mind was trying to absorb the unexpected offer. The business would be in the hands of someone who had helped build it, someone she trusted.

"Say something. Speak!" LaVon said.

Both dogs sat at the command and began barking. Dar and LaVon burst out laughing, then rewarded the well-trained dogs with treats.

Dar turned and hugged her best friend. "It's perfect!" she said. "I know I should probably give it more thought, but all I can say is that I'm so relieved you're not leaving. I've been dreading this conversation, so sure that you were leaving. But this is too good to be true!"

They agreed to work out all the details soon. Dar's phone rang, and she answered, listening intently. When she disconnected, she let out a loud squeal that set the dogs to barking again. It hurt her throat, but she didn't care.

"What is it?" LaVon asked. "Did you win the lottery? If you did, part of the winnings are mine, seeing as how I'm always with you when you buy those tickets; not to mention I help you pick out the numbers."

Dar stared at LaVon in disbelief at her interpretation of the squeal. "Not even close. Something way better! We've got him! We've got Wes!"

She gave LaVon the shortened version of her visit with Wes and her conversation with Sarah. The recovered letters, she saved for last.

"Okay, now that I'm caught up, who called?" LaVon asked. "And what do you mean, you've 'got Wes'?"

"That was Daniel," Dar said. Her face lit up. "He's cracked the coded messages in the letters Wes sent to Red! They include detailed instructions about each crime; everything from the thefts and murders at CCC, to the locations of the paintings and tunnels at the estate. I'm not sure how Wes knew about the letters and their location inside the footrest, but he'd also included details about its secret compartment and how to open it. I'm guessing he either charmed it out of Erin Montgomery before she knew his true nature, or he was spying on the Montgomerys in their own home."

"So why didn't Red and Owen destroy the coded letters?" LaVon asked.

"Just guessing, but I think they kept them for insurance, so Wes wouldn't rat on them if they got caught. Maybe they planned on blackmailing Wes. Having his own scheme used against him would've been satisfying to see.

"Anyway, Daniel made copies and sent them to Mike. Do you know what this means? We have the proof we need to wipe that smug smile off Wes's face for a very long time." Dar threw her hands up to the sky. "Can this day get any better?"

CHAPTER FORTY-SEVEN

The following morning, Dar recognized the car parked in the drive as she pulled up to the Montgomery Farm Estate. Annalise, the master equine therapist she'd hired, had arrived early. She quickly parked next to her, then hurried to the stables where she found Daniel talking to Joe.

"You did it! You broke the code. I knew you would. What did Mike say when you told him?" she asked.

"I think you can guess," Daniel said. "I might have even heard the sound of Mike cracking a smile over the phone."

Dar laughed. "I think you have a vivid imagination," she said. "What about the prosecutor?"

"She said that pretty much cinched her case against all three," Daniel said.

"All thanks to you," Dar said before glancing over her shoulder. "Annalise is here, and the children will be arriving soon, so I've gotta go. Best. Brother. Ever," she said, pointing at him as she backed away to join Annalise.

On her way, Dar collected the basket of apples and carrots. They planned to have them available in case any of the kids felt brave enough to give their horse a treat today. She found Annalise walking the horses around the inside arena, so Dar grabbed a rein and caught up with her. They discussed the day's therapy plan, which included the children watching the horses from a safe distance, but not riding. That would come later. Today the focus would be on having the children get acquainted with the smaller animals. Discussions would focus on the animals' anxiety, and how they might be feeling around all the children whom they'd never met before. By focusing on the animals' feelings, they hoped it would be easier for the children to later talk about their own. At last, Dar and Annalise decided they were ready to greet the kids.

Sarah arrived first with her parents, who shrugged, saying she'd insisted they get there early. Most of the other children were reluctant to leave their parents' sides and required a bit of coaxing. Dar brought out Fluffy, the rabbit, to help facilitate their comfort level.

Soon, all the children were introduced to the rabbit, cat, hamster, lamb, and of course, Merlin. As they became more comfortable around the animals, Dar and Annalise led the discussion on what the animals might be feeling. All the while the horses were within view, but not so close as to frighten the children.

Annalise and Dar were careful not to leave Sarah alone for a single moment. Though she appeared to be enjoying herself, she jumped whenever anyone approached her from behind. At one point, Dar noticed Sarah looking in the direction of the bunkhouse door and holding Fluffy extra tight. Dar reminded her that she was safe, and that her Uncle Mike had made sure the bad man and woman were locked up and would be for a long time. Sarah stayed quiet, running her hands across Fluffy's long ears with gentle strokes.

When group time was over, many of the kids didn't want to leave the animals, and Sarah was no exception. "Can I come back next week?" she asked.

"Of course," Dar said. "Your parents said it would be okay, but that it was up to you. You know, you're very lucky to have parents that love you so much."

"And don't forget Uncle Mike," Sarah added. "He loves me a whole lot, too!" She gave Dar a hug, then ran straight into her parents' arms.

After saying goodbye to the last child, Dar compared notes with Annalise. They were pleased with their first group, and shared ideas on how to best help the two children who struggled the most. A plan was drawn up for their next session, based on those ideas. They would most likely need to split the group for those not ready to move on to the horses. Dar was relieved that she had Annalise to help do exactly that.

No sooner had the parents left with their kids than another group of cars began pulling up in the circular drive. Dar smiled, recognizing each one.

"Party?" Annalise asked.

"You could say that," Dar replied. "You're welcome to join us."

Annalise thanked her but said she had another engagement, and if she didn't hurry, she'd be late. They said their goodbyes, both looking forward to the following week's group.

Dar let out a breath and lowered her shoulders. She hadn't realized how tense she'd been, but now that the first equine therapy session was over, she felt she could relax. For the first time that day, she took in the radiant spring day. Everything from the blooming flowers and fruit trees, to the sparkling water on the pond, reflected her mood. Shawn caught up with her before she reached the house, and her smile broadened.

"Are you ready for this?" Shawn asked her.

"For which part, our friends, or the rest of our lives?" Dar asked. She kissed him as he wrapped her in his arms.

"Forget friends, let's move on to the rest of our lives," Shawn whispered in her ear. "Maybe we should explore the guesthouse."

She knew exactly which room he meant to explore as he brushed her neck with his lips, sending shivers down her spine. She was tempted to take him up on his offer until she saw all the cars parked in the drive.

"Our friends, remember? Do you have it?" she asked. She couldn't stop smiling.

Shawn tapped the pocket of his jeans, then placed an arm around her shoulder as they walked toward the house.

When they entered the house, they were greeted by their friends. Ethel, Shawn's grandmother, rushed up, grabbed his face in her two hands, and kissed him on the cheek. Daniel was grinning like a kid with a special secret. It was obvious to Dar that Shawn had already spoke to them.

Dar couldn't believe the difference one day had made in her life. After leaving LaVon at The Contented Canine, she'd met Shawn at her home in Reed last night. At last, she'd found the courage to be honest with him, pouring out her torn feelings that split her heart between two cities, Reed and Fort Wayne. She'd shared her panic at being unable to arrive at a decision for fear of losing him and disappointing a friend or brother.

LaVon's offer meant she no longer had to fear she'd be letting her friend down if she pursued her dream of expanding the equine therapy program. But she made it clear to Shawn that her dream wouldn't be the same without him.

Shawn had listened intently, giving her a chance to finish before he spoke. It was all he'd been waiting to hear from her; to know she longed for a commitment as much as he did. He didn't care if that meant he stayed in Reed, or if he accepted a position as the head of pediatric cardiology at a hospital in Fort Wayne. That part had surprised her. She couldn't believe he'd already interviewed for the position. For once, she'd found herself at a loss for words, until he'd proposed.

"Congratulations," Daniel whispered to Dar.

"But how did you know?" she asked.

"I may have asked his permission to marry you," Shawn said. Dar saw the twinkle in his eyes, and loved him even more for the gesture that acknowledged the importance of including Daniel as family.

She slugged Daniel in the shoulder.

"Ow! What was that for?" Daniel asked.

"For not telling me you knew." Then she looked at Shawn. "And what would you have done if Daniel had said no?"

"I would have convinced you to elope, then charmed my way back into his good graces." Shawn ran his hand through his hair, but this time he did it with arrogance rather than anxiety.

Soon, all heard the good news of their engagement and surrounded them with congratulations, though no one seemed surprised. After the last person had congratulated them, Shawn spoke.

"Listen up, everybody," he said. "Since our engagement surprised none of you, I think what I'm about to say will. Dar and I would like all of you to attend our wedding—today, that is, if Mike will do us the honor of marrying us."

"If that's what it takes to keep you two out of trouble for a day, then I'm all in," Mike said. Everyone laughed before he added, "Actually, I'm the one who would be honored."

"Thank you," Shawn said. "And Daniel, will you be my best man?"

Daniel agreed heartily and shook Shawn's hand, followed by congratulatory slaps on the back.

Dar stepped in front of them. "Whatever happened to 'ladies first?'" she said. "And LaVon, I would love it if you would be my maid of honor." LaVon nodded and hugged her, too choked up to answer. "I'll take that as a 'yes,'" Dar said, laughing. The two looked at each other and squealed with delight.

Joe set up chairs outside for everyone on the lush green lawn. The impromptu ceremony was simple and perfect. After everyone had taken a seat, Shawn walked Ethel down the aisle to a front-row chair, kissed her on the cheek, then stood next to Mike. Dar stood behind the rows waiting. She wore a cream-colored summer dress that she had brought, and carried a bouquet of daffodils and tulips that LaVon and Rosie had cut from the garden. She laughed when she saw they were held together with a zip tie.

Taking Daniel's arm, he led her down the aisle to Shawn, who took her hand as she stood next to him. LaVon and Daniel framed the couple on either side as they said their wedding vows. Even Merlin and Buddy participated by barking and circling when Mike declared them man and wife.

With Wes, Owen, and Red behind bars for a very long time, Dar felt free to concentrate on dreams rather than nightmares. She loved that she could share those dreams with Shawn, who today had become a permanent part of her heart and her life.

Her thoughts were interrupted by a butterfly that fluttered onto one of the yellow daffodils she carried in her bouquet. It reminded her of the small chrysalis that had hung from a branch of the crabapple tree in her backyard. Like that chrysalis that had survived the harsh winter, she had survived as well. Their lives had both morphed into something unexpected and beautiful, and having stretched their wings, they were ready to fly.

ACKNOWLEDGMENTS

There are many people I would like to thank for their invaluable help in the process of writing this book. First and foremost, I would like to thank my ingenious husband, Tom, who had the brilliant idea of creating the design for the cover photo out of styrofoam, duct tape, a blow torch, and a little paint. Though I was skeptical initially, I couldn't argue with the fantastic results. Thank you for your time, effort, and persistence.

To my copy editor, Parisa Zolfaghari, who worked diligently despite an injury (don't worry, I won't share specifics), yet went above and beyond with her editing services, thank you so much! This is the third Darla Kelly book that she has edited for me, and I highly recommend her to other authors. Her sense of humor throughout the edits made the whole process brighter.

I'd also like to thank my beta readers, Brittany Landreth and Tom Koontz, who didn't hold back with their critiques. Thank you for taking the time to provide your input, both positive and negative. Love you both!

Finally, for a better understanding of an equine therapy program, I reached out to Allison Wheaton, director at Summit Equestrian Center in Fort Wayne, Indiana. She graciously invited me to the stables and shared her personal story of starting the equine therapy program, which now provides services to a wide range of groups. Thank you for your insight.